BROKEN EAGLE

F L A S H P O I N T

★ STAN FLEMMING ★

BROKEN EAGLE

FLASHPOINT

With contributions by
Colonel James Scott Green
Emily D. Ganyo, JD

Archway Publishing books may be ordered through booksellers or by contacting:

Archway Publishing
1663 Liberty Drive
Bloomington, IN 47403
www.archwaypublishing.com
1 (888) 242-5904

ISBN: 978-1-4808-1477-6 (sc)
ISBN: 978-1-4808-1478-3 (hc)
ISBN: 978-1-4808-1479-0 (e)

Library of Congress Control Number: 2015902303

Print information available on the last page.

Archway Publishing rev. date: 3/5/2015

Great leaders are defined not merely by the words they speak but by their deeds. Their greatness comes from how they choose to set their moral compass through the values they embrace and the moral character they develop from within and from those they lead.

—Brigadier General Stan Flemming
United States Army

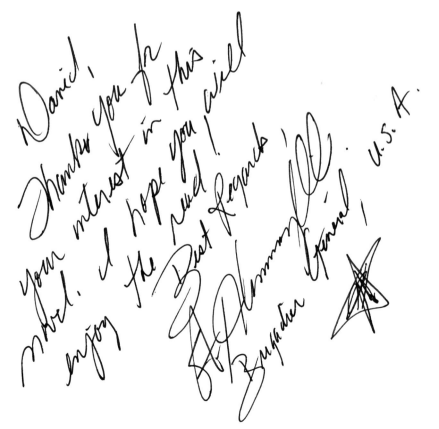

To Major General Tod Carmony, a
teacher, coach, mentor, and friend who
has always led his soldiers with integrity,
conviction, and commitment to doing what
is right even in the face of adversity

Also to Colonel James (Jim) S. Green and
Major James (Jim) Malone, MD, whose
professionalism and tenacity for the
truth has made them truly outstanding
leaders in today's United States Army

May we always remember the men and women who served
or currently serve as citizen soldiers, volunteering selflessly in
defending our great nation and promoting peace globally as
members of the Active Army, US Army Reserve, and Army
National Guard. Together, they are proving the value of the
operational US Army Reserve and Army National Guard force
as true professionals and force multipliers that are integral to
the functionality and success of today's United States Army.

FOREWORD

In the early 1990s, the former Yugoslavian president Slobodan Milosevic made an audacious move to prohibit the autonomy of the Kosovo people living in the central province bearing the same name. As a result, the Albanian-dominated province declared its independence, which was recognized initially by the neighboring country of Albania. Following these actions, tension grew until 1998 when fighting broke out between the Serb military forces and the Albanian-led Kosovo Liberation Army (KLA). Between March and June of 1999, NATO intervened with the strategic bombing of Yugoslavia, forcing Milosevic to withdraw his forces from Kosovo. However, this action failed to cease hostilities. The KLA continued engaging Serbian contingents until international pressure forced Milosevic to accept the foreign-military occupation of Kosovo for the purpose of conducting peacekeeping operations. These foreign military forces included United States Army deployments. Despite the presence of NATO forces, rogue factions continued random killings of innocent civilians. By the end of hostilities, it was estimated that nearly one million Albanians had been forced from Kosovo, another eleven thousand had been killed, and three thousand remained missing.

In the early 2000s, the United States was completing the first year of the war in Iraq and beginning operations in Afghanistan in response to the Global War on Terrorism as a result of the 9/11 attacks in New York and the nation's capital. Despite the expansion of new theaters of operations, the United

States continued deploying rotations of fresh combat forces into the Balkan region, assuming command and control for the Multinational Brigade that protected the American sector. The brigade consisted of infantry, special operations, and aviation battalions from the United States augmented by additional infantry battalions from three other ally nations. In support of the brigade task force the army attached a medical group that provided command and control for the medical task force that consisted of a field hospital unit and several other medical detachments and that oversaw medical operations in the sector.

Broken Eagle: Flash Point is a novel based on a true story of a failed system of leadership, fraud, and deceit and an attempt to cover up facts. In the end two officers who faced overwhelming odds overcame extraordinary pressure and did what was right.

My first night at the American Forward Operating Base in Kosovo, the sky was crystal clear. The faint notes from a bagpipe hung eerily in the cool air and seemed to penetrate the defensive concertina wire gliding beyond the perimeter and into the dark valleys that lay beyond. The smoke and stench of the great blaze still hung in the low spots around the encampment. Surveying the terrain, I had a strange feeling from the unseen threats. The spirits of ancient warriors cried out in warning of what lay ahead, yet I did not know what they were saying.

Some have called us ideologues, and others have argued that to stand up against what was wrong reflected great carelessness with the future of our careers and the welfare of our families; I will argue that we were bound by our moral and ethical compasses as senior leaders to a course that we did not choose but one from which we could not stray.

James S. Green
Colonel, Infantry
United States Army

★ 1 ★

CAMP ATTERBURY, INDIANA

"Colonel," the captain said, pulling up a chair behind the gray, metal, military-style desk. The young psychologist tried to make the colonel feel comfortable, approaching him with a friendly smile, but instead found himself working to feel comfortable with the colonel. "How was your deployment to Kosovo?" As a new clinician to the army, the psychologist was naive to the issues facing soldiers who had been in combat, but he was committed to doing his best to identify and treat those who suffered from the post-traumatic stress disorder that was destroying the lives of so many of America's modern warriors.

"It was fine," the colonel replied. As a physician himself, the colonel knew how to game the young psychologist.

"Sir, did you face any stressful situations that you want to talk about?" the captain asked.

"None." He was brief and direct. "Now, Captain, would you mind signing off on my medical screening so I can get out of here?" He wasn't in the mood to be humored by the psychologist.

"Sir, is there anything you would like to share with me? Anything at all?" the captain pressed.

"No!" Sitting straighter in his chair, the colonel stared down the captain with the weight and authority of his eagle. At six foot, he towered over the shorter captain. He was handsome and fit;

wore frameless glasses; and had neatly combed, black hair, parted on the left, and a matching mustache. His soft, tanned skin was from an unusual blend of East Indian and Native American genes that gave him more of a distinguished, exotic Middle Eastern appearance. Colonel Steve Franklin was a seasoned commander who drew on the strengths of his cultural heritage and his experience as a military leader. He'd come up through the ranks as a mustang, starting his career as an enlisted service member. He was agitated by the captain's persistence but also knew he needed to maintain his cool in order to get the captain's clearance. With the captain's signature on his medical screening form, he would be out of the medical review station and one step closer to putting Kosovo behind him and one step closer to home—one step closer to peace of mind, one step closer to the ones he missed and loved, and one step closer to his beloved Washington State. It was time to move on.

"There you are!" the colonel's Executive Officer, Lieutenant colonel Barry Carlson, said as he appeared in the doorway. He was a short and stout man of solid build, commensurate with his past experience as a firefighter. His receding hairline made him appear older than he was. "Hey, Captain, did the colonel tell you about his ordeal in Kosovo?"

"That's enough, Barry!" the colonel snapped.

The captain had started penning his signature to the form but paused and laid his pen down. "Sir, I think there is something you want to share with me."

"There is nothing to talk about, Captain. While my XO may have thought it was something, it was an uneventful, routine deployment in a combat zone for a seasoned combat vet. However, if you'll promise to sign off on my clearance, I'll share with you what happened. Deal?"

"Deal," the captain replied.

★ 2 ★

WASHINGTON, DC

The rain danced in windblown sheets across the blackened asphalt of the Washington, DC, streets as government employees and tourists scurried about their business in a sea of umbrellas of various colors and shapes. Deployed in a helpless defense against the downpour that swirled between the stately buildings of the nation's capital, the umbrellas were for the most part a futile effort. A few miles away across the Potomac River, military leaders and planners within the maze of Pentagon offices sipped mindlessly on freshly brewed, steaming pots of black coffee as they went about their morning routines of managing the defense of the nation.

Easing his late-model Chrysler into his restricted parking space, lieutenant colonel William Weston slid the shifter into park and shut off the engine. Leaning back in his seat, the gray-haired officer sighed, taking in the view of the concrete fortress. A broad smile broke slowly across his large, grandfatherly face, extending to the corners of his cheeks. He retrieved his identification badge from the console, examined the front and back side, and smiled again as he clipped it purposefully to the outer pocket flap of the light-green, open-collared shirt of his duty uniform. The bold black lettering beneath his picture noted he was a member of the Pentagon staff. Patting it like a badge of honor, he donned his black beret and exited the vehicle, moving purposefully toward the five-sided national military headquarters.

Approaching the security checkpoint, the lieutenant colonel flashed his badge at the guard and continued toward the second screening, slowing just enough for the sentry to check his picture.

"Rent-a-cops," he grumbled beneath his breath. He loathed the fact that the world's most powerful military headquarters lacked any semblance of a professional military presence guarding the symbolic edifice. It seemed indicative of the weakness of a great nation struggling to maintain a facade, much like the great Wizard of Oz. He was bitter toward the successes that those who worked within the Pentagon achieved. Seething with contempt, he viewed the Pentagon as no more than a gathering place for wannabes where half of the staff took their jobs seriously and the other existed as parasitic saprophytes squeezing the system for all they could get out of it. For many, their importance was an indulgence in self-grandeur. It was a military within the military—another world that lacked any connection or understanding to the issues or needs of the real military services. The grand marble-and-stone building served more as a training ground where bandit companies that lined the beltway could cream away talent to further their objectives of securing another government contract and fattening their investors' wallets. In a cartoon sense, the corporations were an obscene orgy of pigs at a trough gobbling up everything they could get their snouts on, squeezing the system for all they could.

"Good morning, Colonel," the sentry said acknowledging the distinguished-looking officer.

"Good morning," he replied politely.

Entering the secure area of the building, the lieutenant colonel flashed his badge at another security guard, activated the turnstile by waving the badge over the sensor, and continued up the broad, impressive staircase, disappearing down the wide hallway lined with historic memorabilia of past military campaigns and leaders.

After a few more turns, the lieutenant colonel stopped before a set of heavy, mahogany-stained doors. Taking a deep breath, he pushed down on the brass handle and entered the outer-office area where a young, attractive female sat busily typing at her computer. As he closed the door softly behind him, the noise of the hollow hallway faded to the silence of the office.

"Good morning, Colonel," the young woman said, breaking into a youthful smile. Her blue eyes sparkled like precious gems, accented by her long, blonde hair that appeared as fresh as her innocence. She looked more like a fashion model in a woman's magazine, sporting a colorful, spring like, v-cut blouse and matching skirt. Her midsize breasts were professionally concealed yet teasing with just a hint of her cleavage. The lieutenant colonel estimated her to be in her mid to late twenties. Unseasoned in her role as a general's secretary, he guessed she could have not been in her position no more than six to eight months. He surmised from the appearance of her skin—pale, milky white—and the lack of a wedding band that the young woman was more into making a successful career at the Pentagon than she was into tanning beds or chiseled boyfriends.

"How may I help you?" she asked in a friendly manner, looking up from her computer.

"Good morning," the lieutenant colonel replied. "Perhaps you might help an old man get out of a little trouble this morning. You see, I was supposed to get this document signed by the general yesterday, but it completely slipped my mind. Now my boss is about to have my head. He's furious and all over a simple piece of paper. Do you think it's possible for me to get just a moment with the general?" He broke into a warm, soft smile.

"The general is getting ready to leave for a morning briefing with the chief of staff. Did you have an appointment?" the young woman asked.

"No, unfortunately I don't. I know it's my fault, and I'm truly sorry. However, if I don't get this signed, my boss will fire me, and that'll be the end of my career. I promise it will only take a minute. I promise ... I won't hold him up." The lieutenant colonel paused, looking helplessly at the young woman. "You know how it is when the brass gets all worked up. Only you can help me now. Please?"

"Okay, let me see what I can do. I know when those guys get mad, everyone pays," the young woman said empathetically. "You shouldn't have to put up with that. I bet if you were a full colonel they wouldn't bother you so much." Getting up from her desk, the young women disappeared through the closed door behind her. Returning shortly, she ushered the lieutenant colonel through the door.

"You have only thirty seconds ... The general said that, not me," she said with a soft giggle.

"Thank you. You are indeed as kind as you are beautiful," the lieutenant colonel whispered as he passed.

"Colonel, what's so important that it can't wait?" the general asked gruffly as he slipped into his two-star jacket. He was a crusty, well-seasoned senior officer who had punched his ticket in the field at various posts but now found the cushiness of the Pentagon life much to his liking. He enjoyed rounding out the final years of his career sitting behind his broad mahogany desk, schmoozing with senior military leadership and politicians and influencing policy for the future.

"Sir, I'm sorry to bother you. I know you're a busy man, but all I need is a quick signature for the J8, and I'll be on my way," the lieutenant colonel said in a respectful tone, holding out the papers. The general took them and scanned each one quickly. "You're sure this can't wait until I get back?"

"I wish it could, sir. It's my fault I got them to you late, but the J8 is chomping at the bit."

The general glanced up, hastily scribbled his signature, and returned the papers to the lieutenant colonel.

"Thank you, sir," the lieutenant colonel said.

"No problem, Colonel. Wish I could give you more time, but I can't keep the chief waiting," the general said, referring the deputy chief of staff for finance. "By the way, how is the J8 doing?"

"Fine, sir. You know, he's always counting the nickels and fighting those bastards in Congress for more money."

"Yeah, I know what you mean. If those flaming liberals in Congress had their way, they'd shut us down and hand the keys of the country to our enemies while kissing their asses," the general said. "You can't live with them, and you can't live without them."

"Yes, sir. I think you're right. Thanks again," the lieutenant colonel replied. He exited the general's office, closing the door behind him. He then made a point to stop one more time at the young secretary's desk. "You're an angel, my dear. You've saved my life and my career," he said with a warm smile. "I owe you, and I promise to make it up to you next time I'm here." Closing the outer door behind him, he reentered the hallway and disappeared into the light crowd of bureaucrats and uniformed service members.

The rain squall that had blanketed the nation's capital earlier in the morning had finally eased, giving way to sunny breaks that accentuated the majestic beauty of the alabaster congressional buildings and the nation's capital with its iconic rotunda jutting upward toward the blue-tinted sky. It was a postcard moment. The last of the storm's rainwater flowed along the streets, gurgling as it passed into storm drains along the road. Clad in his black military raincoat, the lieutenant colonel purposefully strode along the busy street and up the short flight of steps that led to one of three buildings that housed the congressional representatives from the various states. Entering the building, he flashed his Pentagon identification badge, passed through the metal detector, and continued up the marble stairs beyond the screening area. Pausing at the top of the staircase, he scrolled his fingers carefully down the directory, stopping at Armed Services Committee Hearing Room. He moved his fingers laterally, noting the room number. He made his way toward the elevator and pressed the "B" button for the basement floor. Exiting the elevator and proceeded down the hallway, stopping short of entering the hearing room.

He quickly scanned up and down the hallway and then entered the back of the room. It was beautiful—rich and elegant with hand-polished walnut wall paneling and decorative furniture. In the audience sat people wearing business suits, dresses, and different uniforms of varying ranks, each listening with great interest to the individuals parading before the committee to testify on various military topics. The lieutenant colonel slipped quietly into a vacant seat toward the back of the room. He hadn't quite settled in when the chairman gaveled the meeting to a close. That was his cue to move. Like a determined salmon swimming upstream, he made his way through the crowd of exiting attendees to where the chairman stood engaged in small talk with another member of the committee. From his position behind the dais, the chairman was unaware of the officer closing in on him. Pausing momentarily, the lieutenant colonel reached slowly into the breast pocket of his coat retrieving the folded piece of paper.

A seasoned member of Congress, the chairman looked like the stereotypic politician whose physique had given way to too many cocktail parties, state dinners, and age. His hair still sported the John Kennedy look but was graying rapidly with time. Short in stature, his bodily frame did not conceal well his rotund belly that accompanied his developing jowls.

"Excuse me, Mr. Chairman; may I have a minute with you?" the lieutenant colonel asked.

"Sorry, Colonel, I'm late for my next meeting. You can

schedule some time with my staff to address your issue," the chairman said, moving toward the door.

"Sir, it'll only take a minute. I'm here from the Pentagon. The SecDef needs a quick signature from you. He sent me over here to find you … said it was important," the lieutenant colonel pleaded, holding out the paperwork.

"What is it?" the chairman asked, pausing at the door.

"I don't know, sir. I presume it's something between you and him. I'm just the lowly courier," the lieutenant colonel said, breaking into a jovial smile.

Taking the papers, the congressman scanned them quickly, held them up against the wall, and executed a quick scribble across the bottom of the page.

"Okay, here you go, Colonel. Give the SecDef my regards." The chairman turned to leave the room. "And tell him not to wait till the last minute next time! I'll cut his budget!" he yelled over his shoulder as he vanished down the hallway.

The lieutenant colonel folded the papers and tucked them into the breast pocket of his jacket. "I will," he muttered. "I'll be sure to tell him." The lieutenant colonel descended the stairs, exited the building, and disappeared into the crowd on the sidewalk.

★ 3 ★

It was still dark as the lieutenant colonel executed a left turn and drove his Chrysler down the rain-slicked boulevard toward the iconic Walter Reed Army Medical Center, which served as the flagship to the military's medical department, providing major medical services to wounded soldiers, active and retired military service members, and members of Congress.

Executing a second left turn, the lieutenant colonel departed the boulevard and approached the main gate. Examining his identification badge, the civilian security guard waved him on. It was just too easy, the lieutenant colonel thought. No, it was embarrassing. Feeling the challenge had diminished, the lieutenant colonel laughed. Proceeding slowly beyond the main gate, he continued to the left of the hospital and past the row of senior officers' quarters and pulled into an empty parking space alongside the hospital. Entering the building, he found himself in the headquarters of the US Army Reserve unit that provided medical support to the medical center on weekends and during the summer months.

"Good morning, Colonel. How may I help you?" a major inquired. She was much older than the average major in the army. Her long gray hair was neatly tucked in a bun at the back of her head, her facial wrinkles revealing that she was more seasoned and experienced than most army nurses. She'd begun her military career late in life, but her stamina and enthusiasm more than made up for any physical shortcomings she may have had. It was out of patriotism and love for her country that she'd joined the army, not because she expected anything in return. She was there to serve, not be served.

"I'm looking for credentialing," the lieutenant colonel said politely. "I'm new to the unit and need to get my paperwork processed before I deploy."

"I'm Major Habercheck, Barbara Habercheck, Assistant Chief Nurse and chief of credentialing for the professional staff," the major replied, extending her hand in a friendly gesture. "I can help you right here in my office." She motioned the lieutenant colonel through the open door and followed close behind him.

Taking a seat alongside the desk, the lieutenant colonel asked, "What exactly do you need from me?"

"Well, sir, I'll need a copy of your medical degree, license, medical school diploma, documentation of any postgraduate training you have received, your DEA license, state license, and three peer references," she said without taking a breath.

"I thought you might need those things, so I brought all of them here with me, including several peer references and letters of recommendation." The lieutenant colonel passed over a short stack of documents.

"Wow!" the major said with excitement as she pored through the documents. "Your credentials are so very impressive! Harvard … Yale … and George Washington University! Graduate … fellow … and faculty. I'm impressed! And a psychiatrist at that! The army is so fortunate to have someone like you in the ranks."

"They pale against you and your smile," the lieutenant colonel said in a warm tone.

"I wish all the doctors were as put together as you." The major smiled like a kid in a candy store. "You've made my life so much easier."

Standing up to depart, the lieutenant colonel added, "Did I mention that I'm scheduled to deploy very soon? So I'd be indebted to you if you would be so kind to expedite approval of my credentials. My report date to Fort Bliss is imminent and can't be delayed." He appeared sincere. "Soldiers are counting on me, and I cannot let them down; after all, they have sacrificed so much in defending our country."

"I agree," the major replied. Gathering the documents from the desk and shuffling them into a neat stack, she concluded, "Like I said, I wish there were more caring doctors like you. I'll personally take care of these."

The lieutenant colonel shook the major's hand. "I knew I could count on you."

After the lieutenant colonel left, the major returned to her desk and sifted through the stack of documents. It had been missed the first time, but on a second look, the major spotted it. Gathering the papers, she proceeded quickly down the hallway to the conference room where she laid them out on the table. Returning to the hallway, she intercepted several of her nursing colleagues and led them back to the conference room. She asked each one to review the documents and comment on his or her initial take after scanning them.

"Barbara, I don't see anything unusual," one of the nurses said as she scanned the documents. "I'm truly impressed with his credentials. Very unusual for the military to attract someone who is so uniquely qualified."

"Look again," the major insisted. "Look at those letters of recommendation."

"Well, they're all outstanding, but ... I think I see now. Do you think they were written by the same person? But that's simply not possible ... they're signed from people all over the country," a second nurse noted.

"I think we're all reading more into this than there is here," another said. "Did you meet with him?"

"Yes, and he's a verrry nice man," the major said with a small giggle. "Gentle, caring, and ... well, he's the kind of doctor we wish they all were."

CAMP BONDSTEEL FORWARD
OPERATING BASE, KOSOVO

The brilliant Balkan sun glistened sharply against the snow-covered Ljuboten. Known to US military personnel in the region as "Big Duke," the magnificent mountain served as a backdrop for the American forward operating base and home for the US contingent of NATO forces. Having the latest in satellite communications, medical services, and ancillary soldier services such as a theater, Post Exchange, and food services, it was the crème de la crème of forward operating bases in Kosovo. The base, as it was known to all in the region, was located in the US-controlled sector, a short three miles northeast of the small city of Uroševac. The base was named for a Medal of Honor recipient and was heavily fortified with concertina wire and defensive eight-foot-high earthen wall berms. To any would-be attacker, it was a formidable fortress. For the next eight months it would serve as home for the American task force and the newly promoted colonel who would serve as the task force's psychiatrist.

The rain from the previous night had cleansed the otherwise polluted air of the heavy smoke from fires that had burned in the distance several nights before. The sky now sported a brilliant blue hue and a summer-fresh smell. On the far horizon, the clouds hung suspended like an array of cotton balls against the distant mountain peaks that separated Kosovo from the newly renamed country of Macedonia to the south. The camp was for the most part a semi-permanent installation built mainly of wooden South East Asia (SEA) huts. As far as forward operating bases went, it was a moderate to large installation spanning nearly 955 acres of land. To construct the base, two hills had been flattened, filling in a small valley that had existed between the two small peaks. During the early days of the camp, several improvements had been made, including an airfield with helipads to accommodate the transport and gunship helicopters and a state-of-the-art modular hospital. The hospital housed a fully equipped intensive care unit, decontamination unit, two operating rooms, an emergency department, ancillary healthcare services, and a medevac station that provided medical care to NATO soldiers stationed in the area.

It had been a long year for the departing command group and soldiers who had endured attacks and riots propagated by infiltrating Serb units who lined the border region near the camp. The result was a command that was more than eager to go home. As the morning wore on, soldiers of the departing task force worked alongside their incoming comrades, preparing for the Transition of Authority ceremony that would officially signal the end of one and the beginning of a new rotation of fresh troops. At the helm of the incoming task force was a seasoned general assigned from the Army National Guard, Brigadier General Thomas Mathew Moore. The general was a solidly built man in his mid-fifties who stood roughly five foot eleven inches and sported a typical military-style crew cut. Among his peers, he was a standout—a solid strategic thinker, tactically brilliant leader, and an operational genius. His years in varying leadership levels throughout the army had prepared him well for the challenges he faced as a tough, no-nonsense military commander. He was not afraid of being decisive, unlike some officers of the day.

Crossing the small parade field in front of the task force headquarters, the general made his way purposefully toward the large hangar on the perimeter of the airfield that served as the venue for the pending ceremony. Approaching the hangar, the general extended a warm greeting to the commander of the medical task force, then stopped abruptly.

"Colonel ..." the general said.

"Yes, sir," the young colonel replied, rendering a sharp salute. Young for his rank, the colonel had advanced quickly through the ranks as a special operations officer, becoming a colonel only twelve years after receiving his second commission in the army. Unfortunately, this commission also included a demotion from major to captain as a penalty for changing his branch to the Army Medical Corps after completing medical school. Like the general, he too was a no-nonsense leader, setting high standards for himself and his subordinates. As a result, his various commands had always been in the army's top 1 percent of performers. While tough on his leaders, he had gained a solid reputation for the love and admiration he had for his soldiers. He'd also earned himself the nickname "the Cleaner" because he did not hesitate to relieve commanders and staff for incompetence or a lack of caring for their warriors or equipment.

"The next time you forward a letter of recommendation for a soldier from your command for me to sign, I expect to see your endorsement as a cover letter," the general said admonishing the Colonel. His message was clear and direct.

Not knowing what he was referring to, the colonel simply replied, "Yes, sir. I'll look into that."

The ceremony occurred in true military fashion. The foreign civilian and military dignitaries in attendance added to the pomp and circumstance provided by the army band and the colorful flags and battle streamers of the multinational forces in theater that lined the hangar. Standing proudly at the front of his task force, the colonel surveyed the event and felt honored to be a part of the American presence in the region. It was nothing short of spectacular.

Returning to the medical task force headquarters located within the hospital, the colonel summoned his S-1, the primary staff officer responsible for personnel matters. The young captain appeared at his office door. She was short and slightly portly in stature, her uniform doing little to complement her full figure. How she'd managed to stay off of the Army Weight Control Program had always puzzled him, but she met the standards, and no one could debate that. Vanilla in appearance with long, dark hair combed back and secured in a bun at the back of her head, she didn't seem to turn any heads. Although she wasn't the most competent officer to have ever served on his primary staff, she knew just enough to fly below his radar, which seemed to frustrate the noncommissioned officers (NCOs) who served under her, as well as the other officers of the primary staff.

"You requested me, sir?" she asked.

"Yes. The general cornered me at the ceremony this

morning—mentioned something about a letter of recommendation for one of the colonel's in my command that landed on his desk without my endorsement. Do you know anything about that?" the colonel asked, a bit annoyed.

"Sir, we haven't been here long enough for you to have sent any correspondence to the CG, but I'll look into it and get back to you."

It took the captain just a little over an hour to complete her investigation and return to the commander's office. She was thankful that neither she nor her staff had been responsible for the action that had drawn the general's attention.

"Sir, it appears that the colonel in question took the letter over to the general's office himself, bypassing my office."

"Who is this colonel?" he asked.

"He's the chief of psychiatry. I don't know a lot about him, as he is a holdover from the previous task force," the captain replied.

"Track him down, and have him report to me."

"Will do, sir," the captain said, disappearing again from the office.

A short while later, the silver-haired chief of psychiatry entered the medical commander's office as if he were in a theatrical scene. His grandfatherly appearance gave him the presence of a seasoned senior military leader and distinguished physician. Moving smoothly across the small room, he took up a seat on the short sofa against one wall of the office.

"At last, oh my ... I get the privilege of meeting my new boss ... and one who is so young!" the psychiatrist said with a warm smile. "It was nice of you to invite me to your office to join you for tea." His attempt at schmoozing his new commander did not draw much of a response.

"It wasn't for tea," the young colonel said. "I think we need to talk about protocol and how things are done in my command and, more importantly, how they're done in the army.

If you're going to visit the general, I want to know about it. If you're going to seek a letter of recommendation, I want it going through my S-1 first for an endorsement." His tone was direct yet respectful.

"I'm sorry if I got anyone upset," the psychiatrist replied. "The previous general had offered to write a letter of recommendation for me but left before signing it. I didn't want to bother you, since you weren't involved in it before, and I thought the new general wouldn't mind signing it since his predecessor had approved it."

"If that had been the case, you should have mailed it directly to the previous general instead of going to General Moore."

"You're right, sir," the senior colonel said. "You see, I haven't been in the army that long, so I'm still learning the protocol stuff. I was one of those direct commissions based on my credentials. I'm just trying to do the right thing," he said remorsefully.

"I understand," the younger colonel replied. Inwardly, he resented the army's program of directly commissioning officers to the senior ranks based on civilian credentials. Most of the time they failed, not because of a lack of professional competency but because of a lack of military competency. With rank came responsibility and the assumption that the individual holding that rank knew what he or she was doing when it came to performing his or her military duties.

"Please don't let it happen again. If you have questions, then ask one of my staff. They'll help you," the younger colonel said.

"Thank you," the psychiatrist said. Standing, he gave a grandfatherly smile and departed. Pausing briefly outside the commander's office, he grinned again, shook his head, and proceeded down the hospital corridor.

The first week in Kosovo had not been easy for the medical task force. Comprised of active ready-reserve, National Guard, and active-duty soldiers, the task force had been deliberately challenged from the outset by the active-duty contingent of evaluators from the higher medical command. They didn't see their reserve counterparts as equals and instead viewed them as a cluster of misfit soldiers who were less competent than themselves. Validating the competency and effectiveness of medical staff was becoming increasingly frustrating while the friction grew, and the mission became progressively jeopardized with each passing day without any justifiable reason. There was no reason for the validators' actions other than they could, and so they did. It was pure jealousy, and they knew it.

Complicating matters was their unwillingness to acknowledge the composition of the task force. Unlike the outgoing task force of soldiers who had failed to transition from the typical reserve soldiers of the past, the current task force was comprised of a highly professional medical staff and soldiers who were operationally oriented toward the modern US Army Reserve. They came from top-performing units, active practices, and teaching universities back in the States. They were an essential part of the new army—a professional army that was fully integrated, where the expertise and experience of the reserve component equaled or in some instances exceeded that of the active-duty component.

The general was equally under increasing pressure to ensure that his entire task force performed to the standards that had been established for American forces operating in the Balkans. Like the med task force, his army consisted of soldiers from the Active, reserve, and National Guard components. As such, the pressure rolled downhill to the medical task force. In addition to the mounting challenges the medical staff faced, a different tug-of-war was being waged between the commanding general of the regional medical command and the commanding general of the task force as to who ultimately had authority over the medical task force. Suffering at the end of the line was the operational effectiveness of the medical task force itself.

"Colonel, I have growing concerns that your task force will not validate in the next go-round of exercises we have planned for you," the senior evaluator said as he laid out his plans to the younger colonel. "You see, if you fail to validate on a mass-casualty exercise, we may have to bring in another task force to replace you ... probably one from the active component in Europe. In turn, we'll send your task force home."

"I don't think that will be necessary," the colonel replied. "I know my command. It is trained and ready to fulfill this mission, and you know it! Why don't you simply admit that it's the status of the soldiers' component that is bothering you, not their competency?" The colonel was less than patient.

"Let's see how you do in the next forty-eight hours," the senior evaluator concluded in an arrogant tone of voice. "The problem with you reservists is that you all think you're soldiers, unlike us who are the real ones. Why don't you guys just go home and leave the real soldiering to us?"

Closing in on the evaluator's face, the colonel rose to the challenge. "Last time I looked, asshole, we're all in the same army—same standards ... same goals ... same enemies!" He didn't back down.

"Like I said, Colonel ... go home ... back to your cozy little community, your wife's tea parties, and your fancy country clubs. You don't belong in a real war!" the senior evaluator said. Turning, he retreated from the office.

Slamming his fist on the file cabinet, the colonel accepted the hard reality that nothing was going right and that this deployment, unlike those in his past, was going to be extra difficult for him and his command. It was slipping uncontrollably into the abyss, and there was nothing he could do to slow it. He questioned whether or not he was truly the one to be leading this task force. Was it like the validator said?

★

Sitting alone in the dining facility, which soldiers of past eras had once fondly called the "mess hall," the colonel poked at his food, not feeling the urge to consume it.

Without the colonel noticing, a lieutenant colonel stopped short of his table and said, "Excuse me, sir; I'm Lieutenant colonel Smitherman from the post headquarters. There's been an accident involving a contractor. They're requesting a physician in the morgue. I was told it had to be cleared through you to send a doc over there."

Standing up, the colonel muttered, "I wasn't hungry anyway." Following Smitherman, the colonel informed him there was no need to go up to the hospital. "I'll pronounce him dead myself."

Outside of the dining facility, a vehicle waited with its motor running. Entering the opened door of the sedan, the colonel took his place in the right rear seat as the lieutenant colonel took his place behind the driver on the left. The sergeant who stood beside the car closed the door and took his place in the right front seat as they sped off hastily up the hill and to the morgue, which was a short distance away.

Painted a light green, the room was spartan with a Formica countertop along one wall and a refrigerated storage unit for bodies along the other. In the center of the room was a stainless steel table with the naked body of the deceased. Rigor mortis had already set in, causing the body to stiffen. Lying on his back, the deceased's arms and legs extended upward and were bent as if he had been sitting in a chair with his arms on his lap before death, but now the 'chair' was lying on its back. A group of eight men surrounded the corpse and talked among themselves as they stared at their dead colleague. Each had a morbid curiosity as they studied the man's position and facial expression that had now become lifeless.

"What do we have here?" the colonel asked, approaching the body.

As he neared the table, the men slowly backed away, leaving room for the colonel to examine the body more closely. Walking slowly around the table, he examined the dead man with only his eyes at first.

A man dressed in a black field uniform approached from behind the others who were standing to one side. He was tall and fit, in his mid-fifties. His jet-black hair was neatly combed and parted on the left. His tanned skin revealed he had spent much of his time in the outdoors. "He committed suicide by hanging himself. I have completed all the necessary paperwork; all it needs is your signature," the man said, extending his arm with the document.

Without looking at the man in black, the colonel continued to circle the body and asked, "Who made that determination?"

"I did," the man said with an authoritative tone.

"I take it you're the medical examiner or at least a physician?" the colonel asked sarcastically. "If you are, why did you ask for me? Better yet, why don't you just sign it?"

"I've seen enough of these to know when it's a suicide," the man in black replied. "I took him out of the noose myself."

The colonel rolled the victim onto his side. "If that is the case, can you explain to me why there is no rope mark around his neck or why hypostasis has involved only the upper shoulders, neck, and face?" he asked, referring to the pooling of blood that had occurred postmortem. "What did he do, hang himself upside down?" The colonel wasn't being humored.

The man in black was silent.

"When did he die?" the colonel asked

"A little over an hour ago," the man replied.

"Doubtful," the colonel snapped back. "Either it's a miracle, or this man has been dead somewhere between six and twelve hours." The colonel continued probing. "Was he depressed?"

"He had his issues."

"What does that mean?"

"He was dating the daughter of one of the local mob bosses."

"How did you find him?"

"He was hanging from a beam in his home. I went over to check on him when he didn't show up for work."

"Wrong again!" The colonel raised his voice. "From the wrist and ankle marks, I'd guess the man was tied to a chair and turned upside down. Just how he died or why he died is still a mystery. No signs of a struggle … no obvious wounds, abrasions, or bruising." Taking the document from the man, the colonel drew a deliberate, firm line through the statement of suicide as the cause of death and wrote, "Cause of death: suspected homicide." Signing it, he passed it back to the man in black.

"Colonel, this won't be accepted. Now just sign the goddamn record as it's written." The man extended the document back to the colonel.

"Not my problem," the colonel replied. "One thing I do know is the body never lies, and this body is telling me it wasn't a suicide."

"You're making a big mistake by making us take it to Europe where we *will* get the medical examiner there to overrule you," the man argued. "Do you really want to do that? Do you?" He was becoming equally irritated.

"It's not my problem. It's yours, mister! If you want the examiner up there to do your dirty work, then that's a matter between you and the examiner. That's his or her credibility on the line. If you're trying to cover up something, I won't be a part of it. I'm done here, gentlemen."

It had been an uneventful morning. Crossing the camp, the colonel made his way along the makeshift dirt walkway, past the rows of SEA huts and the dining facility, and up the short hill to the hospital. In front of the hospital, the nation's colors hung limply on the flagpole, lacking any forceful breeze to unfurl the flag. As he entered, he set out on his morning routine, walking through the hospital's departments and sections, greeting staff, and assessing the status of the facility. The colonel loved his job, especially the time he could spend with his troops. It not only allowed him be close to those he led and maintain a command presence, but it was also a way of keeping a pulse on his command. As a young enlistee, he had always resented the lack of presence of his officers except during the command inspections or visits by the higher-ups in the chain of command. In the field, officers tended to keep to themselves, rarely interacting with the troops.

Absentee leadership often led to a demoralized and poorly performing unit. As a result, he had learned early on the significance of soldiers being able to not only see their leaders but interact with them as well. An eclectic collection of individuals from eighteen different units and components from throughout the army formed the medical task force in a smooth and professional manner. No one would have guessed that these soldiers had never served together. It was seamless, the way the colonel imagined the army should work, and it made him proud to be serving as their leader.

Outside by the emergency department entrance, two soldiers stood taking in the magnificent morning with a video camera, panning the landscape and adding their own narrative for family and friends to enjoy back home as they recorded the view.

"Holy ... shit!" one exclaimed, lowering the camera just enough to get a glimpse of what he had just witnessed through the lens. In the distance below the hill where the hospital stood, a fuel tanker had pulled alongside of a fuel tank at the refueling station. With one soldier on top of the tanker and another standing next to it, they had begun refueling operations when a gigantic fireball erupted from the tanker. Returning the camera to his eye, the soldier zoomed in on the refueling depot a quarter mile away at the bottom of the hill to capture the evolving disaster. A loud explosion rocked the camp as the thick, orange, mushroom-shaped fireball and bellowing black smoke rose from where the fuel tanker had stood.

"Oh my God, did you just see that?" he exclaimed, continuing to film the developing tragedy.

"Oh shit, we'd better get some help down there!" the other yelled as he sprinted toward the emergency department entrance. Breaking through the door, the panicked soldier grasped the countertop to catch his breath and shouted, "Explosion at the fuel dump—it looks really bad!"

In the distance sirens from the deploying fire trucks whined in a mournful manner as they made their way down the hill to the burning inferno. In response to the soldier's report, the emergency department nurse sounded the alarm in the hospital to standby to receive potential casualties. On cue, the hospital staff sprang into action as the ambulance crew sped away to the developing catastrophe.

As he entered the emergency treatment area, the colonel's

command presence was formidable yet calming. "What do we have?" he asked.

"Not sure just yet, sir," the charge nurse replied as she began organizing the staff and equipment to receive patients. "All we know is there's been an explosion at the fuel dump involving a tanker. Ambulance and fire crews are on the scene. Eyewitness account says at least two, possibly more, casualties."

"Recall the OR team, and have them stand by. Get the surgeon here in the ER, and notify the TOC we have a potential mass casualty. This is not a drill. Recall key hospital staff, and have them stand by, and plus up the ER support staff. Litter teams to the ready!" the colonel ordered without hesitation.

Within a minute, the radio in the emergency department came alive. "Ambulance team 01 Charlie: inbound, two casualties—foreign soldiers, condition critical with extensive burns. ETA 1 Mike!" the medic yelled, indicating they'd be pulling up to the entrance in less than a minute. The siren of the ambulance grew louder as it approached. Executing a sharp turn off of the main road into the driveway, the ambulance came to a screeching halt in front of the emergency room entrance.

"Litter teams … out now!" commanded the NCO standing near the door as the rear doors of the Humvee ambulance flew open. The medics raced to retrieve the victims and rushed them into the ER on gurneys.

As if it had been scripted, the emergency physician barked out orders as he conducted an initial assessment of each victim. "Get me some lines established now—LR, wide open. Type and cross for four units each. Anesthesia, can you secure an airway and put these guys under now?"

The ER staff scurried about, each doing what he or she was trained to do. Burned beyond recognition, the two soldiers lay on the gurneys like guppies out of water, staring wide-eyed toward the ceiling and gasping hard as their seared airways began closing down with the growing edema. Their melted weapons had become one with their flesh as they suffocated in a grotesque manner. The first victim was the least fortunate of the two, having suffered burns approaching 90 percent of his body, while the second one had burns over 50 percent of his body. Neither one of them for the moment had a chance of surviving the calamity.

"We're going to need two ORs stat!" the surgeon arriving on scene ordered.

"Sir, we only have one surgeon available ... that's you," the charge nurse said. Staffing requirements for the hospital had been unilaterally cut without regard to the mission. To the medical staff, saving lives took precedence over any other consideration, but to the bureaucrats, it was more important to save money than lives. Thus, sacrificing the operational needs of the task force was considered a small price to pay for the financial gains that would be achieved.

"I'm not sure what we're going to do. I can only manage one case at a time," the surgeon replied. "I suppose we should try to save the least burned victim and make the second one comfortable. Categorize him as expectant, and give him a good dose of morphine."

"Counter that!" the colonel said from the corner of the room. "Have the OR move the table from OR 2 to OR 1, and set up two surgical teams in OR 1," he directed. "I'm scrubbing in for the second case; the surgeon can do the more serious one and talk me through the second one." Although trained in family medicine, the colonel had also received extensive training in surgery during his residency, which from time to time had proven to be advantageous during his previous stints with the army in the Southeast Asian jungles.

Stabilizing the patients was no easy task, but the team performed flawlessly. Within minutes both victims were anesthetized and in the OR undergoing extensive life-saving debridement of their wounds.

"What are we going to do once we stabilize them?" the surgeon asked. "We're not equipped to manage trauma like this."

"We're going to require a medevac from theater," the colonel said as he continued debriding the crispy, charred skin and performing deep-tissue fasciotomies on one upper extremity with his scalpel. By making longitudinal incisions eight to ten inches long around the upper and lower limbs, he could relieve the growing pressure building up from leaking damaged cells and manage the viable damaged tissue. Without the procedure, the edema within the tissue would strangulate the extremity and force an unnecessary amputation.

"Notify med operations in the TOC," the colonel said.

"Got it," the OR nurse said as the two doctors continued their work, desperately trying to save the lives of the two soldiers.

A few hours later, the procedures were successfully concluded, and both victims were in the intensive care unit awaiting their fate. While stable for the moment, all bets were off regarding the survivability of either soldier. No one with such extensive burns or wounds had ever survived such an ordeal.

Leaving the operatory, the colonel was met by the medical operations major. A young mustang like the colonel, the major had been handpicked to serve on his staff. He was an experienced officer whose knowledge regarding operations and logistics far exceeded any officer of his rank or higher. He was destined for greater levels of responsibility, and the colonel knew it.

"Sir, I've been in contact with the burn center in San Antonio. As luck would have it, they have a trauma burn team and a C-141 bird up in Germany at this time picking up a patient. They say they can divert it to us, but because the soldiers are not US, we're going to need approval from the State Department." The center in San Antonio was a world-renowned trauma burn center. If the soldiers had a prayer of surviving their massive wounds, it would be under the care of those skilled trauma burn teams.

"Okay," the colonel replied, "let's get a call into the State Department."

"Already did. They want us to complete some forms and send a request through official channels. They said they can have an expedited review and then get back to us," the major said.

"How long will that take?"

"It could be a couple of days to possibly a few weeks."

"We don't have that kind of time!" the colonel snapped. "Give me some options."

"Well, sir, we can bypass the bureaucracy and go straight to the secretary of state if you want to risk that."

"Isn't there anyone else we can talk to in the food chain between us and the secretary?"

"No, sir. I'm told only he can do an override of the standing protocol."

"Then do it," the colonel ordered. "Get hold of the sec-state—high priority call—and notify the CG's staff of our action. I'll go over and brief the general myself."

Within a half hour, the secretary of state had been notified and briefed. His orders were short and to the point. "Divert the aircraft to Kosovo, and move the soldiers expeditiously. The paperwork and diplomatic approvals can be worked out later. Saving the lives of soldiers is the priority."

★ 7 ★

It was nightfall when the UH-60 Black Hawk medevac helicopter touched down on the hospital's helipad. Its flashing lights and familiar whine from the turbines made it appear more mystical than it was. As the cargo door drew open, the trauma burn team emerged like a crew heading for the space shuttle. Clad in flight suits, each team member moved purposefully, each carrying a bag of equipment needed to treat and stabilize the burn victims. Greeted by the intensive care unit physician and surgeon, they began their transfer briefing enroute to the unit.

"Great job!" the physician said as he examined the victims. Young for a lieutenant colonel, he was an expert on burns and head of the team. "I doubt we could have done any better ourselves. There's really nothing for us to do other than transport these guys. Thanks for all you've done."

The team escorted their preciously wrapped cargo back to the helicopter. After loading the victims carefully, the burn team boarded the helo and lifted off for Pristina airport where the C-141 Starlifter cargo transport plane stood by awaiting them. Eleven hours later both victims were in the burn center's operating room. It would be another six months of surgery and rehab before the soldiers would return to their homeland. Under any other circumstances the burns each soldier had suffered after their tanker unexplainably exploded during a routine refueling procedure likely would have been fatal, but fortunately for both, they experienced nothing short of a miracle. Due to the initial medical team's quick reaction, the trauma burn team, and the secretary of state's decisiveness, the lives of two soldiers were spared.

Settling back into his desk chair, the colonel sighed deeply following two rather intensive days. He knew his team had performed well. Despite the friction that existed between the validators and the command, the colonel knew his team was not only the best but also the right team at the right place. Contemplating next steps, he began reviewing the schedule for the following day.

Lost in his work, the colonel did not hear the knock on his office door.

"Colonel ..." The senior validator stood in the doorway of the office. "May I have a word with you?"

"Sure. C'mon in," the colonel replied, motioning toward the sofa. "What's up?"

"I observed the hospital staff today during the mass-casualty trauma event. Your staff was flawless in how they executed that crisis," the senior validator said. "I just wanted you to know that ... your command is officially validated."

The colonel wanted to blurt out, "That's all? No apology? No ... 'They were the best I've seen!' *What the fuck?* he thought, but instead he said, "Thanks. I appreciate the feedback." Standing, the two colonels exchanged a professional handshake as the senior validator departed.

With a major crisis behind him, the colonel turned his focus to the new challenges that awaited his attention. The previous medical commander had failed to conduct a proper transfer of knowledge of the command, focusing his efforts instead on leaving the theater. The exchange between the two commanders had lasted all of ten minutes. Before his expedited departure, he had given the new commander a binder of disorganized paperwork containing costly budget overruns in expenditures for hospital supplies, an outdated list of laboratory supplies, useless documents, and another outdated list, this one of key medical leaders in Kosovo, which for the most part was grossly inadequate. Leaning back in his desk chair, the colonel took note that it was going to be a long deployment.

"Good morning, sir," the S-1 said as she entered his office. "I've got two things for you to start your day. First, the general wishes to see you as soon as possible."

"What does he want?"

"I don't know. His secretary didn't say."

"What's the second thing?" the colonel asked, somewhat frustrated.

"The deputy commander for the med task force received orders today. He's leaving in a week for home, but no worries, his replacement has been identified and will be here about the same time."

"Do we have a name for him or where he's coming from or what his background is?"

"Uh … no … no … and no," she said as she departed. Her lack of detail and professionalism reminded him of the need to replace her when the opportunity presented itself.

After crossing the parade field that separated the hospital from the general's headquarters, the colonel made his way through the tight security and up the wooden staircase that led to the general's office on the second floor. Entering the small anteroom, he stopped just outside the general's office in front of the general's aide-de-camp's small wooden desk.

"Good morning, sir," the young female lieutenant said with a pleasant smile. There was a good reason why the general had selected her for the position. She was attractive with short brunette hair. On most women, the haircut would have done nothing, but on her, it appeared seductive. Her looks did not betray her. She was equally smart and professional.

"I understand the general wants to see me," the colonel said.

"Yes, sir, just a minute; let me see if he's ready." She walked into his office and returned quickly to escort the colonel in.

The general sat behind his large mahogany desk working through the stacks of paper that covered the desktop. "Please take a seat, Colonel; I'll be with you in a moment," he said in a soft tone without looking up. Putting his signature to another document, the general glanced over at the colonel. "How are things going, Steve?"

"We have no shortage of challenges these days, but we're working our way through them," the colonel said. "Short of that, I think things are progressing quite well."

"Good. Your folks did a great job handling that emergency. Please let them know I'm proud of them."

"I'll pass your compliments along to the staff," the colonel said. "They're a great team."

"Why I asked you over is to inform you that I'm contemplating relieving you from command," the general said in a more serious tone of voice.

"What is the reason?" The colonel was surprised.

"I've learned you're not the senior-ranking medical officer in theater, and according to army regulations, it's the senior-ranking medical officer who is authorized to command a medical task force," the general said.

"Sir, with all due respect, you're right regarding my seniority. Actually, I'm the most junior colonel here. That being said, what are you talking about?"

The general held out a sheet of paper from his desk. "I had a visit from your chief of the mental health detachment, Colonel Weston. He informed me that he was the senior-ranking medical officer in theater and therefore I must appoint him as the medical task force commander ... by the regulation of course."

Taking the paper from the general, the colonel read it closely. He had been a student of army regulations and was aware of what the regulation said regarding who was authorized to command medical units.

"Sir, would you happen to have the page that precedes this copied page from the regulation?" the colonel asked.

"No, why?"

"You see, sir, you're only reading half of the regulation. What the preceding paragraph says is in the event that there is *no* appointed or assigned medical commander; the senior-ranking medical officer shall assume command. I was appointed to command through an army board. That gives me automatic seniority and authority over Colonel Weston. Besides, my psychiatrist, who, by the way, is *not* the chief of the mental health detachment, was not appointed. He's a staff officer." The colonel paused. "You may verify this with your G-1."

"Interesting ..." the general mused. "I should have suspected something wasn't right. He's quite convincing, you know. I think you'd better watch your back; your colleague may be gunning for you."

"I appreciate the friendly advice, sir. I'll do that," the colonel said before departing the general's office.

Three weeks passed. One could sense that the colonel was feeling more at ease in the command as the routine of the deployment began to normalize. Things were for the most part progressing well—perhaps a bit too well. He could feel some of the pressure he had experienced shortly after his arrival in theater slowly dissipating, a change he welcomed.

"Good afternoon, Colonel." The voice came from a young officer standing in the colonel's doorway.

"What can I do for you?" the colonel asked.

"Sir, I'm your new deputy commander."

Looking over his glasses, the colonel replied, "While I should be impressed, I think there has been some sort of misunderstanding. The deputy commander is a colonel. I see you're a major, so I doubt that you're assigned to that position."

"Sir, here are my orders."

The major was young, almost too young. An emergency medicine physician by training, he was clean-cut, tall, and handsome, reflecting all the stereotypes of an Ivy Leaguer.

"Where are you from?" the colonel asked.

"Stanford, sir."

"Uh-huh," the colonel muttered, "I should have known ... S-1!"

"Yes, sir," the S-1 replied as she entered the office behind the major.

"I think there has been some sort of mistake with the major's assignment. He's informed me he's the new deputy commander," the colonel said. He then glanced at the major. "Nothing personal, Major, but that's not going to work for me. All the chiefs are colonels. Captain, please get hold of DA," he continued, referring to the Department of the Army, "get this corrected ASAP, and assign the major where he belongs."

Within a few hours the captain returned, appearing somewhat gloomy.

"Sir, the army has declined the request to replace the major with a colonel and has directed you to make do with what you have."

Feeling exasperated, the colonel gathered the department chiefs to introduce the new major to key leadership.

"Gentlemen," he said, "we have a dilemma. The army has assigned Major Augustus Pierce to serve as the task force's deputy commander. What that also means is he's technically your supervisor. Now I know, it's awkward at best, but I want to hear from each of you whether or not you can make this work." The room was silent.

"I don't think we have an issue here," the chief of orthopedic surgery said. He was the oldest and most senior colonel of all the department chiefs. An active-duty physician, his gray hair was neatly cut and combed in a Cary Grant style. The fine wrinkles that defined his face and gray eyes gave him a rather elder, statesman-like appearance. "We're out here in no man's land, and it's rather clear that no one really gives a shit about us." He was clearly frustrated. "So if it's okay with the other chiefs, we'll be happy to work with the major and let him do the administrative stuff while you handle our evaluations and other things requiring a colonel."

One by one, the other chiefs weighed in, all agreeing with the chief of orthopedic surgery.

"Good, then we have a resolution. Thanks, guys, for your willingness to get this resolved," the colonel said.

"Not so fast, Colonel," the psychiatrist said from the back of the room. "I don't think that is going to work at all! He's only a major, and I will not take my lead from him."

"Okay," the colonel said, "all the chiefs can work with the major, except for you. You may report directly to me." With the matter settled, everyone moved forward, focusing on the mission.

Returning to the medical task force's headquarters following the afternoon briefings, the colonel made a left turn down the corridor instead of his usual right turn that led to his office. He was known throughout the command for unexpected visits to soldiers and subordinate units, and today he had made a spontaneous decision to drop in on his tactical operations center (TOC). Entering the code on the keypad, he pushed open the secure door and entered the room full of map boards, phones, and secured radio communications equipment. Without speaking he moved to the center of the room where the situation board was maintained and where the battle captain monitored all medical operations occurring both inside and outside the camp and the combat environment outside the forward operating base, in addition to maintaining vigilance in the TOC. The colonel stopped and placed his hand on the battle captain's shoulder. Startled by the presence of the commander, the sergeant first class snapped to attention and called out to the room, "Atten … tion!"

"At ease … carry on!" the colonel ordered. "Gentlemen, this is the TOC, the heart and soul of my command. While I appreciate the military courtesy, there's no need to call the room to attention every time I walk in." He was smiling. "Maybe for the general that might be okay."

Patting the soldier on the back, the colonel turned his attention to another soldier and in a soft yet friendly manner inquired as to how things were going. Here, the colonel was in his element. He loved his command, but more importantly he loved operations and his soldiers; and they loved him. He was unorthodox for a medical commander, which only endeared him more to his soldiers and superiors. He was a consummate leader who had worked his way to the top of the senior field grade ranks as a colonel in the nonmedical community. As a second lieutenant, he'd cut his leadership teeth in an infantry battalion as a platoon leader, becoming an acting company commander only six months later. He was a fast study, and by the time he'd made captain, he'd been the operations officer of a group, a position usually reserved for a senior major or lieutenant colonel. From there, he'd become a special operations officer operating in Southeast Asia and, finally, a battalion commander. In addition to his years at various levels of command in and outside the medical community, he had gone to Fort Rucker in Alabama to learn how to fly Huey helicopters. As quickly as he had risen in rank, so had his responsibilities and assignments. From there, he'd opted for a chance to go to medical school, which career-wise was an opportunity to achieve a dream, though at a cost for his military career. Later as a chief of staff for a two-star command, he'd become the first Medical Corps officer to ever hold such an assignment in the army. Before arriving in Kosovo, the colonel had already completed a combat tour of duty with the First Marine Division as a team leader in a special operations battalion during the ground offensive in the Persian Gulf War, which only added to his credibility as a solid leader. He had managed to accomplish all these achievements before reaching his twentieth year in the army, which gave the colonel great satisfaction; he'd exceeded any expectations he could have ever had for himself. Although he'd never practiced medicine in the army, he was a seasoned leader and competent physician. He set high standards and demanded every soldier in his command to rise up to the challenge of being an army soldier. He lived for the army, and in all that he did, he embodied the warrior ethos.

"Give me a sit-rep," the colonel requested from his battle captain, indicating he wanted a situation report. Standing up, the operations NCO began to give a detailed brief of the current events unfolding outside the base, commonly referred to as "outside the wire." In mid-sentence, the red phone rang in the TOC.

A sergeant answered and then, holding up the receiver, said, "Colonel, it's the general's TOC. General Paxton is requesting to see you ASAP in the general's office."

Lieutenant General William Paxton III was a rising star among the senior generals in the army. A tall, handsome African American man, he was noted for being a tough leader. With a solid pedigree he had received his third star and was destined for even greater roles of senior leadership in the army.

"The general doesn't know me from Adam. Request they reconfirm that message with the CG and get back to me before I go over there and make a total ass of myself," the colonel replied. After relaying the message, the sergeant hung up the phone.

The colonel returned his attention to the battle captain's briefing but was interrupted again by the sergeant still standing by the red phone.

"Excuse me, sir," he said somewhat hesitantly. "I've confirmed the message. General Paxton is in the CG's office demanding you report now."

Ending the operations NCO's presentation abruptly, the colonel hastily went to the CG's office. Perplexed that a three-star would travel to Kosovo and request him by name, the colonel was apprehensive as to what possible reason the general might have. Entering the general's office, General Paxton stood with his back to the door engaged in heavy conversation with General Moore. The colonel stood silently at attention as he waited. Sensing the colonel's presence, General Paxton turned, appearing larger than life.

"Sir, reporting as requested," the colonel said with a salute.

Returning the salute, the general broke into a broad smile. His white teeth glistened as he extended his hand in a friendly gesture.

"Colonel ... as I live and breathe!" he said in warm tone.

"Yes, sir," the colonel said, not knowing what next to say.

"I just had to meet *the* one ... the colonel whom all my staff is talking about." The general was still smiling.

"Excuse me, sir?" the colonel replied, feeling perplexed.

"My whole staff is talking about what a unique medical commander you are. I just had to see for myself." The general was laughing now. "A breath of fresh air I'm told; a real soldier and commander for once in the medical community ... Now that's unique."

"Uh ... thank you, sir ... I think." The colonel was more confused. "Is there anything you need?"

"No. I just wanted to meet you face-to-face. That's all," the general said. "You're dismissed, Colonel. Thanks for coming over on such short notice."

Returning to the medical task force's TOC, the colonel expected to resume his informal conversations with his staff, but he immediately sensed something was not right.

"Three, what do you have?" the colonel demanded.

His S-3, operations officer, had replaced the battle captain and taken control of the TOC. Barking orders, the S-3 turned to the colonel.

"Sir, we have a situation developing just over the border. There has been an accident involving thirty children who are trapped in a steep ravine that cannot be reached from the road. Two rescuers are on the scene. Three confirmed dead; the remainder are listed in serious to critical condition. Their government has sent a flash message with an urgent request for a medical team and our medevac helicopter to assist in the rescue. Situation is critical."

"Has the request been routed through NATO in Pristina?" the colonel asked.

"Yes, sir. They have forwarded it to the G-3-air at the general's TOC."

"And?"

"Sir, I have our J-model Black Hawk on the helipad with crew and rescue medic team loaded. Rotors are turning awaiting clearance to launch. Their ETA can be just under thirty minutes." The major had chosen the J model for the mission for a good reason. It was the newest bird in the medevac detachment, received directly off of the assembly line and well equipped for mountain rescue.

"What's the delay?" the colonel asked impatiently.

"Sir, the G-3-air wants to study the situation for medical necessity."

"Are you fuckin' kidding me?" the colonel yelled. "Is he a doctor?"

"No, sir."

"Get the G-3-air on the phone *now*!"

With the red phone in hand, the colonel regained his composure and began to question the G-3-air. Although the mission was validated by the NATO ops center as critical, the G-3-air and the aviation commander (AVCOM) refused to allow the aircraft to launch until they had studied the situation.

"Look, Major," the colonel said, his voice rising, "I don't have the luxury of time to debate the merits of the mission with you or the aviation commander as to what is or is not medically necessary to launch an aircraft to save a life." His patience was wearing thin.

"Sorry, Colonel. Permission to launch is denied," the G-3-air on the phone said calmly.

"Colonel, their government is on line one and NATO command on line two asking for an ETA of the bird and rescue team," the colonel's S-3 interrupted. "What do I tell them?"

There was now a clear sense of urgency in the S-3's voice as the staff scrambled to track and manage the evolving crisis.

Returning to the G-3 Air Operations Major on the phone the colonel said, "Major Adler ... I need that clearance now!"

"Sorry, Colonel, like I said before, your request is denied. We'll need another two to three hours to study the situation, and we'll get back to you as soon as possible."

"Not acceptable, Major!"

"Too bad, Col—"

"Look, you little shit!" The phone went dead, and the colonel hung it up. "Three, keep me posted! I'm headed to the CG's TOC," the colonel shouted as he departed the TOC.

Crossing the parade field at a double-time trot, the colonel passed quickly through the security checkpoint and closed in on the ops-center. As the colonel entered the room, the G-3-air was sitting calmly with his boots on his desk, leaning back in his chair and twirling a pencil through his fingers. Knocking the major's boots from the desk with his hand, the colonel came face-to-face with the major as his chair spun in response.

"What the fuck do you think you're doing, Major?"

The major recoiled, startled by the colonel's unexpected confrontation.

"Do you realize that there are children dying out there while you sit here on your fat ass twirling your pencil?" The colonel was in no mood for a casual conversation.

"Sir, I'm waiting on the aviation commander's assessment before I can make a determination. Only he has the authority to launch the bird, and at the moment he doesn't see it as a medical emergency."

"Get him on the phone *now*!" the colonel ordered.

Springing to his feet, the major began dialing. His fingers trembling, he misdialed the first time and tried again. Then, from behind the colonel came a calm voice informing him his TOC was on the phone. As he took the phone, the colonel listened quietly and then gently returned the phone receiver to its cradle.

The colonel told the G-3-air, "Cancel the call. The mission has been officially scrubbed." Walking slowly toward the secured door of the ops-center, the colonel paused. "All the kids are dead ... Their government is officially blaming us for their deaths because of our unwillingness to help." Glaring at the major, the colonel demanded, "I want a meeting with the chief of staff ASAP."

Grasping the door handle, he exited the TOC.

★ 9 ★

It was quiet in the command section of the task force headquarters. With most of the staff gone for the day, many of the lights had been turned off to save on energy. At a small desk near the entrance to the facility, a soldier sat alone keeping watch as the staff duty noncommissioned officer (SDNCO). In addition to serving as the voice to field important incoming calls after duty hours, his job was to ensure those who entered that portion of the headquarters were authorized and properly signed in and out. It was, for the most part, a boring yet important assignment. The soldier passed the time reading a paperback novel that he had procured from the community lending library. Flipping the page, the soldier sank deeper into another world; he hadn't noticed the colonel coming through the front door.

"Where's the chief?" the colonel asked, looking down at the young corporal.

The corporal flinched; he hadn't expected to hear a voice towering above him. "Sir, I'm sorry ..." He was at a loss for words. "The, uh, chief ... yes, sir ... the chief is still in his office down the hall." The soldier wrestled to stand and regain his composure.

"Good. At ease," the colonel ordered. "I'm just here to see him."

"Could I please see your ID, and would you mind signing in, Sir?" the corporal asked.

"Sure," the colonel replied, retrieving his Kosovo Forces

(KFOR) yellow ID badge from his pocket. The corporal inspected it while the colonel signed in.

"How's the book?" the colonel asked.

"Great, sir," the soldier replied, attempting a nervous smile. "Tom Clancy. I love his books."

"Me too," the colonel said. "I'm one of his biggest fans."

The colonel made his way down the dimly lit hallway to the chief of staff's office. Colonel Sam Logan was a good man. In his mid-fifties, he portrayed every bit the role of a chief of staff for the task force. An infantryman by specialty, the chief had served a career in the army on active duty and in the Army National Guard. He was a solid leader who ran a tight ship in his headquarters. Leaning against the frame of the door and in the shadow of the desk light that faintly lit the room, the colonel observed the chief hunched over his desk reading through documents. The desk lamp provided only enough illumination to light the desk's surface, but the chief had chosen to work with it as his only source of light instead of the fluorescent overhead lights.

"Working late, Chief?" the colonel asked.

"Yeah. You know how that is." The chief glanced up over his rimless glasses. "You're one to talk. I don't know of anyone who can operate on only three hours of sleep like you." The chief chuckled as he threw down the stack of papers in his hand. Leaning back in his chair, he offered the colonel a seat opposite his desk.

"Is your office light not working?" the colonel asked.

"No, it works fine. I prefer the softer lighting. You know … it's the ambience." They both laughed.

"You know, you'll go blind working that way," the colonel said.

"Ha!" The chief laughed harder. "I thought it was doing something else that made you go blind." The two colonels laughed again. It was for the moment a good release from the pressure they were facing.

"I'd offer you a drink, but you know all I have is this non-alcoholic crap," the chief said.

"Naw, I think I'm trying to quit," the colonel replied sarcastically, waving off the offer.

"Well, I guess you're not here to exchange niceties," the chief noted, easing back again in his chair.

"I wish I were." The colonel leaned forward. "I'm here to talk about how we're going to do business during this deployment. Thirty kids died today because of our incompetence and negligence." The colonel's voice had taken a more serious tone. "They didn't have to, but we allowed it."

"Don't be so hard," the chief quickly replied, leaning forward on his desk. "I'm not sure it was avoidable."

"Sam, who are you kidding?" The colonel was becoming agitated. "NATO had given us the green light. My ops major had a bird and rescue team sitting on the helipad ready to launch ... We could have been on the scene in less than thirty minutes, but no ... those two fuckin' incompetent morons, the G-3-air and the aviation battalion commander needed time to study the medical necessity."

"Look, I don't have all the details, but aren't you being a bit too harsh on these guys?" the chief asked.

"Hell no!" the colonel was quick to answer. "If they'd been in my command, I would have relieved both of their asses on the spot! I thought you guys were more put together than that." The colonel sat back in his chair.

"What do you want?" the chief asked calmly.

"I want the G-3-air and the AVCOM removed from the decision-making process when it comes to launching Dust-off medevac missions," the colonel said, referring to the general's staff officer for aviation and the aviation battalion commander. "I want sole authority to make the determination whether or not the mission is justified and to have launch authority."

"Look ... I know you're upset, but I doubt the CG is going

to approve that request. You see, this is an aviation matter per the directive of the DA," the chief retorted, referring to the Department of the Army.

"You know whoever made that decision is just a wannabe who likes playing doctor and doesn't know shit from Shinola when it comes to medical missions or saving lives." The colonel was unreserved in sharing his thoughts. "The decision to consolidate all the army's aviation's assets under the aviation branch wasn't because of operational efficiency or even improving life-saving efficiencies on the battlefield. It was solely about power and control, a power grab that no one had the horsepower to counter. In reality, the decision has produced the opposite effect. Time on the scene for deploying medevac assets has increased at unnecessary costs to American lives. However, I suppose in the Pentagon, it matters little."

"What do you propose to improve the situation?"

"Okay ... I propose we come up with something different," the colonel said. "How about we put together a model that can work and be better than anything the army has in operational use at the present time. As an aviator myself, I think I have a pretty good perspective on meeting both needs."

"Draft it up and we'll go from there," the chief said. "No promises though."

"That works for me." The colonel stood, and after they exchanged a symbolic handshake for a deal, the colonel left.

Making his way back to his headquarters, the colonel's mind drifted momentarily to life back home. He missed his home, his home state, and, most importantly, his family. Life was simple there compared with the complexity of the situation in Kosovo. Like so many soldiers before him, he was torn between those he loved and his love for his duty to his soldiers, the mission, the army, and his country. Taking a long sigh, he entered the building and moved quickly to his office. Following at a close pace behind him was his new deputy commander.

"Sir, do you have a moment?" the major asked.

"Sure, what's up?" the colonel replied, taking a seat behind his desk.

"Sir, as the deputy commander I decided it was important for me to take a look at the credentials of the medical staff as a way of getting to know who the players are." The major paused to draw a breath.

"Of all the things you need to be focusing on, you chose to waste your time on checking credentials that have already been verified by the credentials analyst up at MEDCOM?" the colonel asked, referring to medical command. He was annoyed that the major had lost focus so soon on his purpose and mission.

Despite the admonishment, the major persevered. "Everyone's checked out, except for Colonel Weston's."

"What do you mean?" The major had the colonel's attention ... at least momentarily.

"Sir, Colonel Weston has a degree from Harvard and faculty credentials from Harvard, Yale, and George Washington." The major paused to catch his breath.

"Look, major," the colonel cut in, "what's wrong with that?"

"Sir, there's this thing among the Ivy League. It's allegiance. Being affiliated with one university is one thing. Even two is okay, but three ... that's a red flag. It's almost unheard of," the major said with some confidence.

"Well, I suppose if I had those credentials, I'd feel pretty lucky," the colonel said. "As I see it, the problem with you Ivy Leaguers is that you all think you're something special. Born with a silver spoon in your mouth, you all think you're entitled to have the world licking your boots, and we should be grateful for the opportunity. Well, I've got news for you ... For the rest of us common folk, we're just grateful to have had the opportunities to go to college, earn a degree, and get a job. When I was eighteen, my daddy gave me the boot from our home. Like my brothers, I had to figure out how to make it on my own. Son, I know what it's like to stand in a welfare and unemployment line just to have some asshole bureaucrat call me a gutter tramp, among other choice names, just so I could get a stamp in my book and have some money to buy some food to eat. I worked four to five jobs, from being a janitor to waiting tables, just to pay for my education and put a roof over my head. On Sundays, I'd stop by my folks' home so I could get the molded food my mother was throwing out from her fridge. I used to scrape the top off of that, toss in some ketchup or steak sauce to hide the musty taste, and eat it." The colonel sounded irritated at the major. "Colonel Weston was credentialed by the army; he has already gone through the scrutiny, and his credentials were prime-source verified and reported as impeccable. Thus, it is rather doubtful that you really have a case here. So before you step off that ledge and impugn the record of a senior army officer, my recommendation would be stop wasting your time and get focused on the more-important issues facing the staff ... like staffing ratios, schedules, supplies, and policies. Is that clear, Major?"

"Yes, sir. But, sir, it's not just that. I know there is something wrong here. I can sense it in my gut," the major continued. "I want your permission to conduct an investigation to prove myself right or wrong."

"Okay, major, apparently you didn't get the message. Gut feelings won't fly here; facts do. However, I'll tell you what I will do," the colonel said, being cautious. "Go ahead and check it out. However, I want you to keep it off the radar and keep me posted as to what you find. When you turn up nothing, I want you to get yourself refocused as to why you're here in the first place ... That would be mission, if you forgot."

★

Two more weeks passed uneventfully, and the colonel liked it. There had already been too much drama, and he welcomed a lull in the action. The colonel entered the general's secured briefing room to attend a top-secret briefing. Making his way to his seat behind and above the general's seat, on a row of elevated desks for the special staff, the colonel was surprised to find his seat already occupied. Colonel Weston sat conversing with another staff officer next to him.

"Do you mind telling me what you are doing here?" the colonel asked the psychiatrist.

"Oh … Colonel, I didn't think you were going to make it, so I thought I would sit in on the briefing on your behalf," the psychiatrist replied smiling.

"Colonel, this is a top-secret briefing!" The colonel was angered. "You don't have that level of clearance. How did you get in here?"

"You know, Colonel … it's all just a small misunderstanding." The psychiatrist attempted to make light of the situation. "I have a clearance; they just couldn't find it tonight. I've attended these briefings at the Pentagon; I'm sure they could confirm I have a clearance," the psychiatrist said in a convincing tone. "Since I'm already here, why don't you pull up a chair, and we can attend the meeting together?"

"Get out of here now!" the colonel ordered, pointing to the door. "Security breach … secure the briefing screens and room!" Taking hold of the psychiatrist by the arm, the colonel pulled him from his seat and escorted him from the room as the staff looked on in dismay.

Approaching the security NCO at the entrance to the room, the colonel asked, "Why did you let this colonel into a TS briefing?"

"Sir, I couldn't verify his credentials, but he's a colonel, and he assured me he had the clearance." The NCO appeared visibly shaken. "Sir, I'm just a sergeant … He was so convincing."

"He's *not* cleared for TS briefs," the colonel said, admonishing the sergeant. "No credentials, no entry ... and that includes me or anyone else you can't verify." The colonel jerked the TS security badge clip from the psychiatrist's pocket and handed it to the sergeant. "Now get him out of here!" he said before returning to the briefing room.

Following the briefing, the general gave his usual final remarks and dismissed the staff. He then summoned the chief of staff and the colonel.

"Colonel, I've reviewed your report and recommendations and have made a decision as to how we'll do medevac business for the remainder of the mission. First, we could have done better with the medevac request for help from our neighbors, but we didn't. That was in part due to the inexperience of the decision makers. Colonel, you have a unique qualification of being both an aviator as well as having a medical background. That's a force multiplier for me." The general's confidence in his medical commander was growing. "As such, your recommended policy will go into effect immediately with the following changes: the Dust-off medevac detachment will be transferred to the operational control, i.e., OPCON to your medical task force."

"I doubt the AVCOM will like hearing that," the chief said.

"It doesn't really matter what he likes," the general said. Recognizing the need to include the AVCOM in aviation matters, the general decided to meet the colonel's request halfway. "The aviation commander will still make the determination of mission necessity. In the event the aviation commander cannot be located within five minutes of a mission request or if you disagree with his determination, the chief of staff will be the next in line of authority to make that determination and give approval. Launch authority will be yours, Colonel." The general was firm. "Chief, anything else you'd like to add?"

"Sir, for the record … I relieved the G-3-air of his duties yesterday," the chief reported. "I'll have a new one assigned by tomorrow; however, he will not be a part of this process."

Returning back to his headquarters, the colonel briefed his S-3 and TOC staff of the new procedure. It didn't take long for the new process to be tested.

★ 10 ★

It had been a long day in the field meeting with local leaders within the various health districts and the frustration of how to synchronize the needs of the region with the commitment by the Albanian and Serb health directors who, because of ethnic differences, refused to cooperate was evident in the colonel's face and feelings as he turned in for the night. However, he was determined to break through the barriers and start the process of rebuilding a health-care delivery system for Kosovo that did not discriminate against the local indigent population.

At two o'clock in the morning the colonel's peaceful silence of sleep was broken by his ringing phone. The colonel fumbled for the receiver in the dark and finally lifted it to his ear.

"Sir, TOC!" the voice bellowed at the other end. "We have a situation. There's been an attack on one of our patrols. One known soldier has been seriously wounded; the unit is requesting Dust-off!"

"Get me the aviation commander *stat!*" the colonel ordered. Now sitting on the edge of his bed, he was fully alert. "And give the medevac crew a stand-by-to-launch order."

"Sir, we've been trying to reach him but no reply yet," the battle captain reported.

"Forget it!" the colonel shouted. "Wait … out!" He hung up and dialed the chief of staff.

"Hey, Chief," the colonel said calmly. "Hate to wake you, but I have a mission request from one of our units, apparently an ambush with an IED. I need mission approval. My TOC can't raise your AVCOM."

"Do what you believe is right. I trust your judgment," the chief replied. "Let me know in the morning how it goes."

Pushing down on the cancellation button on the phone, the colonel waited for a new dial tone and then called his TOC giving the order to launch the medevac. The colonel then donned his uniform and hastily made the short walk up the hill to the TOC. Entering the secured facility, he found the room alive with activity. Moving to the battle board, he ordered the battle captain to give him a sit-rep.

"Sir, the bird is airborne over the site circling. No sign of the unit," the battle captain reported.

"Re-verify the coordinates now with the bird and the company commander," the colonel ordered.

Immediately, the radio operator transmitted the order. In turn the medevac and the company commander re-stated their eight-digit coordinates.

"Is the AO secure?" the colonel asked, referring to the area of operations.

"Yes, sir," the radio operator replied.

"Order the unit to pop smoke now!" the colonel said. "Have Dust-off confirm color."

"Sir, smoke is popped!" the company commander screeched over the radio. "Oh God ... please God ... I need that Dust-off now!" the captain pleaded helplessly. "My soldier is bleeding to death ... I can't stop the bleeding!" There was sheer panic in the captain's voice.

"Where's the company medic?" the colonel asked.

The message was transmitted to the beleaguered soldier.

"I don't have one!" the captain replied.

Grabbing the microphone from the radio operator's hand, the colonel took control.

"Dust-off, can you identify the color of smoke?"

"Negative, 0-6 ... We do not see smoke," the Dust-off pilot reported.

"Captain ... I'm breaking radio etiquette. This is 0-6. Get a hold of yourself. You're no good to your soldier if you're not in control. If you panic, so will your soldier. He needs to know you're in command," the colonel said calmly yet firmly. "Dust-off did not see your smoke. It's clear that there is something wrong with the coordinates. According to what you have given us there should be a small school at your location. Can you verify?" the colonel asked.

"Negative, sir. No school!" the captain yelled. "Sir, my soldier is bleeding badly ... shit ... I think he's dying. What should I do?"

"Describe the wounds to me," the colonel said.

"He's bleeding hard from the right side of his neck, lesser from the chest and arms," the captain responded. "There's blood everywhere ... Can the Dust-off help? How soon will he be here? I need help now!"

"Get someone to apply pressure dressings to the chest and arm. With another pressure dressing, apply firm pressure to the neck, but don't close your hands around his airway!" the colonel directed. "Describe what you see around you, and we'll find you ... I promise."

The S-3 had entered the TOC and began directing the staff while the colonel worked with the captain.

The colonel continued to bark orders. "Three, notify the ER and OR to standby to receive one patient, multiple trauma secondary to an IED. Let them know one wound sounds like a severed carotid. Also, notify the CG, chief, and their TOC of the situation."

"Already done, sir," the major replied. His competence made the colonel proud to have him on his team. The major could anticipate, assess, multitask, and act without oversight. That's what the colonel expected in every leader in his command. His S-3 was the best of them all.

"Sir," the captain said, "I'm near a series of buildings that look like stores. One is two stories, and there's a church across the street … How much longer for the Dust-off?" Panic was creeping back into the captain's voice.

"Stand by." The colonel paused. He ran to the situation map and traced his finger in search of the structures. "Son of a bitch!" he exclaimed slamming his finger on a spot on the map. "I know this region, and I know exactly where he is!" The colonel ran back to the where the radio operator sat and grasped the microphone. Lifting it quickly to his mouth, he paused momentarily. Spinning around, he looked at the S-3. "Recall the Dust-off."

Turning his attention back to the radio operator's console, the colonel pressed the talk button. "Captain, your coordinates are backward … I repeat, your coordinates are backward! The medevac is at the opposite end of the sector circling." The colonel paused again. "Dust-off is not coming … Repeat … Dust-off is—"

"Holy shit, sir! I need that Dust-off now … *now!*" The captain was in a full panic mode now. It wasn't his fault that things were becoming chaotic around him. Unlike the battle-seasoned colonel, it was his first combat experience and the first time he'd ever witnessed a human being blown up. Once the captain had time to decompress, the colonel was confident the young man would be a good leader.

"Captain!" the colonel ordered. "Get a hold of yourself now! I need you to focus, and so does your soldier." Giving the captain time to regain his composure, the colonel continued, "I know exactly where you are located. You are currently just over three miles northwest of the camp."

"Sir, I don't know where I am. I think our map is all fucked up!" the captain cried out.

"No problem, Captain. Load your soldier in your Humvee. I'm going to talk you into the camp. Simply describe what you see as you drive … got it?" the colonel asked.

"Yes, sir!" the captain replied with some relief. "We're inbound now. Sir, he's still bleeding pretty badly!"

"Keep the pressure on the right side of his neck. That will keep him alive," the colonel assured the captain. Turning to his S-3, the colonel said, "Three, take a security team to the main gate to escort that Humvee through. Do not let those guards delay it. If they have a problem, have them contact the CG or chief directly."

"Roger that, sir," the major replied. Grabbing his weapon and flack vest, he disappeared through the TOC's secured door with two of his best soldiers.

In the brief time he'd been in theater, the colonel had developed not only a dislike but distrust for the contracted soldiers, who guarded their camp, served their meals, repaired their vehicles, and even manned some of their communications equipment. Hired mercenaries, these civilian, paramilitary soldiers were paid two to three times the amount of uniformed military service members. While the uniformed soldiers looked on, wanting to do the job they had been trained for, the contract soldiers did their work. For the most part the contract soldiers did as they pleased and answered to no one. They had received the largest Pentagon noncompetitive personnel contract in the entire US military, which was legally bleeding the American taxpayer to death by significantly driving up the costs of the war. But there was nothing anyone was willing to do or could do. For every soldier the army fielded, it was required to have a contract soldier with equal skill sets on board to perform the same work. The contracted soldiers ran almost everything in the camp, while the army had to feed, clothe, and house them with the best of what the camp had to offer, with the army soldiers getting whatever was handed them or left over. At the gates to the camp, the contract soldiers gloated about their ability to intentionally delay anyone entering the camp, not for security reasons but because they had the power to do it and so they did.

Tonight was not going to be one of those nights. The colonel had already determined that. He knew and trusted the major could get the job done no matter what the obstacle was.

As the colonel continued talking the captain through the various turns along the road, the anticipation among the hospital staff grew as they stood by to receive the wounded soldier.

The radio in the TOC came alive suddenly. "TOC … Three," the major said.

"Three … TOC," the radio operator acknowledged.

"Echo-Tango-Alpha … three Mikes," the major reported, indicating he would arrive at the emergency room in three minutes.

"Roger … three Mikes … out," the radio operator replied.

The colonel moved expeditiously to the emergency room in time to witness the arrival of the Humvee and the transfer of the wounded soldier into the hospital. The surgeon was already on the scene taking charge as the soldier was carried through the door.

"Take him directly to the OR … and keep pressure on that carotid!" Turning to the colonel, the surgeon said, "Sir, he's pretty torn up. Looks like some shrapnel from the IED took out the right carotid, messed up the right arm, and did some lesser damage to his right leg and chest. I could use an extra pair of hands tonight if you'd like to scrub in."

"I'd love to, Captain," the colonel replied.

★ 11 ★

The surgery had taken over an hour and half, but the soldier had survived the ordeal and had been transferred to the intensive care unit for post-op care. However, he wasn't out of the woods yet. He'd lost a significant amount of blood as a result of the metal fragments discharged by the improvised exploding device (IED) that had torn through the right carotid artery, shredding it and the surrounding tissue. With the type of wounds he'd sustained, the soldier without a doubt had a guardian angel looking after him.

The intensity of the night had charged the colonel's adrenaline. While he wanted to return to where he'd left off in his sleep, he was too wired to fall asleep again. Sitting at the small desk next to his bed, the colonel switched on his desk lamp and logged onto his e-mail. It was one of those modern advances in technology that helped him pass the time and stay in touch with those back home. Typing in his user ID and password, he began working through the awaiting string of e-mails. One in particular caught his attention. It was from an old friend ... female friend to be specific, one he had not heard from in years. He'd known her in their younger days; she had captured his attention while walking into a room full of people at a social event. She was tall and slender. Her natural beauty, long auburn hair, and curvaceous body, matched by her wit and gregarious disposition, made her a standout in any crowd. Her physical beauty was surpassed only by her genius in business, which had made her all the more amazing and intriguing. While he'd been attracted to her, their lives had taken different turns, leading them in differing directions. While becoming highly successful in her world of buying and selling commodities on the stock exchange, she'd found herself lonely and in search of finding herself and hopefully through that search defining some meaningful purpose for her existence.

The colonel was lonely too but had chosen to concentrate his emotions on his career. While his absences from home due to military duty had strained his relationship with his family, he knew, like most men and women who served in the military, that he was doing what was right for them. Unfortunately, his family saw it differently. His absences from family functions only exacerbated the tenuous situation, and it didn't help that other extended family members fostered the notion that his commitment to family was lacking. The colonel was feeling emotionally and physically vulnerable to this dialogue about his military duty and had already concluded this would be his last deployment. While it had been a difficult decision to leave the job he loved most, he knew that it was best for his kids and his wife ... his family.

Reading and rereading her e-mail, he leaned back in his chair into the shadows of the light, clasping his hands behind his head as he mentally debated the pros and cons of replying to her probing questions. He leaned forward and began typing. Hesitating, he leaned back again and sighed deeply. It was better to avoid the situation than to further engage in it. Closing the screen on his laptop, the colonel switched off his desk lamp, crawled into bed, and drifted off to a place where he could reflect more.

The young major walked with a determined step down the hospital corridor to the commander's office. Glancing periodically down at the pristine floor, he rehearsed his forthcoming conversation with the colonel. He was excited but wanted to ensure he presented all the current information he had gathered on the Weston case clearly and concisely without missing a single piece. He knew the colonel did not tolerate speakers who could not stick to the facts or key points. Lost in his thoughts, he hadn't seen the custodian with his mop in hand and bucket. Colliding with the gentleman, the major was as startled as the custodian. The mucky water in the bucket splashed sloppily across the floor that had just been cleaned.

"I'm so sorry!" the major exclaimed, grabbing to stabilize the man as he stumbled backward.

"No problem, sir," the custodian responded with a heavy Albanian accent, regaining his position. Unlike custodians who cared for hospitals back in the states, the custodians in Kosovo were local hires that were mostly professionals—doctors, dentists, or other health-related specialties—who eagerly sought the positions in the American hospital primarily for the pay. Their $1,100-a-month salary was significantly higher than any amount of money they could make outside working in their respective professions. The team of custodians were dedicated to what they did, cleaning the hospital four to six times a day with rags, brooms, mops, and toothbrushes. It was often said that one could literally eat off of the floor and feel safe.

Regaining his focus, the major made his way to the colonel's office. Knocking on the door, he allowed himself the liberty to enter before the colonel acknowledged him.

"Good morning, sir!" the major said in a cheerful tone. "I've got some follow-up for you on the Weston case that I thought you might find interesting."

Looking up, the colonel replied, "What's that?"

"I have received positive confirmation from all three universities that he was never there," the major said excitedly.

"Those are big institutions," the colonel challenged in a

father-like tone. "Perhaps you didn't speak to the right department or person."

"No, sir. I spoke to department heads and the HR directors for each university. No one—I mean *no one*—has ever heard of this guy."

"Okay ... I think this falls into one of those categories of 'Uh ... Houston ... I think we have a problem.'"

"Yes, sir!" the major eagerly agreed. "There's no way that the army could have prime-source verified this guy's credentials. They're bogus!"

"Well, before we jump off the cliff of maligning a full colonel, we'd better have our ducks in a row," the colonel said cautiously. "We'll need to convert this to a formal investigation and gather more facts before we're ready to confront him. Do you have anything else?" the colonel asked.

"Yes, sir." The major was on a roll. "Based on what I found, I also checked out his letters of recommendation."

"And ...?" the colonel asked, knowing there had to be more to the developing story.

"Each individual I contacted stated that he or she had written a letter at Weston's request."

"At least that's a positive thing," the colonel replied with a sigh of relief.

"Uh, no, sir ..."

"What do you mean?"

"You see, I faxed them all copies of their letters and asked them to verify that they were indeed their letters and signatures," the major said.

"Good job, Major," the colonel said. "I don't think I would have thought of that."

"There's more." The Major added. "Of all the letters I sent out, all the respondents stated that their signatures were correct but not their letters. In other words, the letters are all fakes!"

"Okay," the colonel said. "Give me all the stuff you have on this case. I need to go over and brief the chief and CG ASAP. Unless you hear otherwise, continue digging. Like I said, I think we suddenly have a problem here, but I'm not sure how little or big it is at the moment. Contact his medical school and request written confirmation of his attendance with a photo. Also, start contacting his past assignments and confirm whether or not he actually had such duty assignments. We need to start turning over every stone." Standing, the colonel congratulated the major on the work he'd done.

★ 12 ★

A sergeant made his way down the long hallway of the task force. He turned left, continued down another short segment of hallway, and exited the building, passing the colonel, who was entering the facility.

"Good afternoon, sir," the sergeant said in a respectful manner as he continued on his way.

"Good afternoon," the colonel acknowledged politely passing the sergeant and continued on to the chief's office. Walking in, he took a seat opposite the chief, who was lost in his work behind his desk.

"What's up?" the chief asked, pausing momentarily.

"Sam," the colonel said, "I have a developing situation in my command with one of my colonels that you and the CG need to have visibility on ASAP." After laying out the evidence, the colonel said, "How do you think we should proceed?"

The chief moved from behind his desk and closed the door softly. "I think this is some pretty serious shit, if it's true," he said. "I think you, the CG, and I need to have a little conversation on the matter with the JAG." He was referring to the judge advocate general staff officer, the general's chief legal counsel.

The chief and the colonel made their way toward the general's office. Exiting his wing of the headquarters, the chief turned to a staff NCO seated at a desk. "Get hold of the JAG, and have him meet me in the CG's office now," he directed.

Once all the necessary parties arrived at the general's suite, the chief presented the facts to the general, who listened patiently behind his desk. "How reliable is this information and the major?" the general asked.

"Very reliable, sir," the colonel replied.

"Where do we go from here?" the general asked.

"I recommend we notify our higher command," the JAG said.

"Sir, I would suggest that we also notify medical command and continue our investigation," the colonel added.

"MEDCOM?" the chief challenged.

"Yes, sir," the colonel replied. "They were responsible for credentialing this guy in the first place."

"Shouldn't we suspend this guy from seeing patients?" the chief asked.

"No," the JAG interjected. "While this looks bad on the surface, we don't have enough evidence to make a case. Just keep closer tabs on him for now."

"Well, there is more to this," the colonel said. "I recently removed him from sitting in on a classified top-secret briefing. Apparently he has a history of doing that."

"How did he gain entrance?" the general asked, sounding quite concerned.

"He got in under a bogus pretense of having misplaced his credentials. He challenged the NCO for questioning him, pulling rank on him," the colonel said.

"Again, it sounds bad, but still not enough to take any UCMJ or any other disciplinary action at this time," the JAG said, referring to the military's Uniform Code of Military Justice, the law that governed criminal actions by a service member. "At minimum, the general could give him a letter of reprimand now, if he wanted, but my recommendation in a case like this one is to get enough evidence for him to hang himself."

"Colonel, let's keep it close hold for now. Continue gathering your evidence, and let's all make the proper notifications up the chain of command," the general directed. "Any new developments, I want the chief and JAG read in immediately." The meeting was adjourned.

The colonel returned to his headquarters and found his S-3 and two bodyguards known as the long rifle and short gun, based on the type of weapons each carried, standing by his vehicle. When anyone with rank of colonel or higher left the camp, it was policy for at least two bodyguards to accompany the officer, and the officer had to wear full battle gear. Holding up the colonel's flak vest, Kevlar helmet, and sidearm, the S-3 said, "Hi, sir, ready to go?"

"Where are we going?" the colonel asked.

"We're off to meet with the district health leader northeast of here in the small town of Gnjilane to get a feel for his operational needs and assess the current level of care in that area," the major said with a smile. "It's all on your calendar."

The colonel took his gear from the major, and the bodyguards ushered him to the right rear seat of the Mitsubishi SUV. Stopping just short of the door, the colonel paused. "Why do you have me sitting here?"

"It's for your protection, sir," the corporal with the long rifle said confidently.

"One would think, if you're a sniper, you would always shoot the rider in the right rear seat. So let's do a changeup. I'm riding in the front seat, and you two bodyguards fight for who sits where in the back." Throwing his flak vest on the floor of the front passenger seat, the colonel climbed in the vehicle. "Let's go!" he said with a grin.

Perplexed by the colonel's action, the major asked, "Sir, why aren't you wearing your flak vest?"

"The way I see it, if someone is going to shoot me, this flak vest is pretty worthless. On the other hand, if someone is going to use an IED to blow me up, at least the flak vest will provide a little protection from the shrapnel coming through the floorboard," the colonel said as the major started driving. "For the most part, I find these things more to satisfy the peace of mind of the bureaucrats back in Washington and less for the real protection of the soldiers wearing them out here in the field."

They passed through the main gate of the camp, turned right onto the small country highway, and began the journey toward Gnjilane. The drive through the Kosovo countryside was nothing short of beautiful. The open fields, low-lying hills, and streams would have made it a picturesque scene if the Serbs hadn't brutally scarred and defaced it with scattered single and mass graves and blown-up homes, churches, and stores that served as a lasting reminder to all that the Serbs had once roamed the region murdering women, children, and men indiscriminately, old and young, in a genocide that rivaled Nazi Germany, Cambodia, and other regions of Africa. It was unimaginable how barbaric the Serbs had acted. When asked why they had done it, their response was simple and equally incomprehensible: they had been doing it for nearly 1,300 years.

Approaching the hospital, the S-3 slowed just enough to execute a left turn into the long driveway that led around the facility to the front entrance. Built during the Russian occupation, the hospital was simple and unattractive—a four-story concrete structure that was a dirty gray from the heavy soot that polluted the air from the various sources of wood-burning fires and from the lack of maintenance during the past thirty years. The hospital was void of any modern upgrades, including air-conditioning, as noted by the number of open windows throughout the facility. As they rounded the corner of the driveway, the colonel took note of the helipad that stood opposite the entrance to the emergency department. While considered a standard amenity to hospitals back home, it was a novelty at a hospital in Kosovo.

Rolling to a stop in front of the hospital, the colonel exited the Mitsubishi. The director of the hospital and district said with a thick accent and broad grin, "Velcome to Gnjilane!" Extending his big hand in a friendly gesture to the colonel, he continued, "I am so glad to meet you face-to-face." Standing at a solid five foot ten inches, the director was a heavyset man. His charcoal-black hair and heavy eyebrows made him appear more like a stereotypic Russian bureaucrat than a hospital district director. He looked disheveled in his light-gray suit that stank of poor-grade Kosovo tobacco smoke, a white shirt, and thin black tie, but he wasn't. Dry cleaners and irons were simply nonexistent in the spartan region of Kosovo. Ushering the colonel, major, and two bodyguards into his office, the director took his place behind his worn desk, motioning to the mismatched, empty chairs around the room.

"Colonel, some whiskey to celebrate this moment?" the director asked, holding up a bottle.

"I'm sorry; I don't think so, Director," the colonel replied politely. "We don't drink on duty or during deployments."

"Ah ... I see," the director said, slowly nodding as if he were pondering what the colonel had said. "You're good, Colonel. I forgot: Americans don't mix pleasure ...or should I say alcohol ... with war." The director said carefully returning the bottle to his bottom desk drawer. "It, uh, how do I say ... keeps the mind sharp." The director laughed. Holding out a pack of smokes, he said, "Cigarette?"

"No thank you," the colonel said, holding up his hand.

"Then perhaps you might have some espresso then?"

"That will be fine," the colonel answered with a smile.

Knowing the colonel did not drink espresso, the major interjected, "But, sir, you—"

"I know, Major, but today it will be fine," the colonel cut him off and then looked back to his host who was trying to honor his guests with the warm, hospitable gestures.

"Director," the colonel said, "I'm here to see your facility and gain a better understanding of how you deliver care. I'm also interested in how we might assist you in providing better care to your patients. I want to build an integrated health-care delivery system for all of Kosovo. Last year the minister of health returned over thirty million euros to the EU because he didn't know what to do with the money. That is not acceptable when there is so much need here."

"Colonel, you know your predecessors have done much to help me. They built me a new helipad and gave me new refrigerators to store blood and other perishable items." The director was trying to impress as well as bait the colonel. "You see, your predecessors were very successful. By helping they all became generals, except for one I think." Looking to see if the colonel would bite, he continued. "I think you too might be a general someday."

"The beauty of my job is that I will never be a general. You see, I was once considered, but was passed-over. The army promoted a fellow colonel more senior and more qualified. He deserved the promotion. In our army, you only get one chance to be a general so I'm not worried about achieving that goal. I'm here because it's my duty to be here and I love what I'm doing." The colonel stared directly at the director. "By law, we can't give you equipment or build things for you." The colonel was setting the expectation. He knew the things the director had mentioned had been illegal acts, but it wasn't his place to call out his predecessors. He also knew that by getting those items to his hospital, the director had gained power and prestige among his peers and the local people, but he needed more to maintain that leverage. He was counting on the colonel to deliver that prize, but for the moment it wasn't going his way. On the other hand, though the colonel wasn't interested in boosting the director's popularity, he was smart enough to know that he would need the director to buy into his plan in order to move his redevelopment plan for health care in Kosovo forward.

"I would like to tour your hospital if I may," the colonel

asked, wanting to move beyond the stalling tactic and determine if the director had received more help from the US military than he was reporting. In turn, the director was all too eager to show off his facility; it was better equipped than any other hospital in the region, and he knew it. He likewise hoped he could convince the colonel to change his position but knew it was becoming a delicate dance for both.

The walk through the hospital was enlightening for the colonel. He took note of the shortcomings and asked more and more questions as he went. The informational and directional signage was only in Albanian. The EKG machine in the emergency room was antiquated and nonfunctional. The surgical instruments were rusted, and the sterilizer hadn't been started in some time. The windows in the operating room were open, breaking the sterility of the room. There was no evidence of a pharmacy or sterile bandages anywhere. Patients shared rooms with no distinction made between male and female or children and adult patients. All were comingled.

While on the surface the hospital appeared clean for the most part, there was much more work to be done in order for it to meet the minimum standards for such a facility, but the director and the staff were giving it their best with the limited resources they had.

Returning to the director's office, the colonel took his place back in his seat and said, "Director … you have an impressive facility. You have done much to make your hospital operational, but I likewise see there is much to do."

"Yes, Colonel, there is," the director replied. "I have a list of things I need. I hope you will get for me to make my hospital better."

"Director, as I shared with you earlier, I cannot by law give you any equipment or supplies. However, I can offer you some things that will make your hospital the best in the region." The colonel paused, waiting to see the director's reaction.

"Yes, colonel. What is it?" The director was nibbling as he leaned forward.

"I would be willing to have my biomed technicians examine your nonfunctional equipment to determine what it will take to make them work again. We can work with some volunteer NGOs to help repair that equipment." The colonel was referring to the nongovernmental organizations operating in the Balkans. "I would also invite your doctors, nurses, and nonmedical staff to my hospital to be trained by my staff." The colonel had set the hook and was reeling the director in.

"Excellent!" the director exclaimed. "I velcome all that you offer. How soon can we begin?"

"When your hospital stops discriminating against the Kosovo people," the colonel replied with a firm voice.

"Vhat?" the director said, raising his voice with an astonished look. "I most certainly don't discriminate against anyone!" His bewilderment was transitioning to agitation. "We velcome everyone to our hospital," he said, leaning forward and slamming his hand on his desk.

"Director ..." The colonel was equally unyielding. "Can you tell me what happened to the last Serb patient who came to your emergency room?" the colonel asked, knowing he had been shot to death at the entrance.

"Oh ... that." The director leaned back in his chair feeling disarmed and shrugged his shoulders. "It was just a big misunderstanding," the director responded feebly, trying to minimize the event.

"How many Serbs do you have on staff?" the colonel asked.

"Uh ... I don't know," the director replied naively. "I believe we have a few." Lifting the pack of cigarettes from his desk, he tapped out one and lit it, taking in a deep draw before exhaling. It was evident the colonel had made him uncomfortable.

"Director, you don't have any." The colonel had done his homework. "Why is all the signage in Albanian only?"

"I don't know, Colonel. What would you like?" The director knew he had met his match and was now on the defensive. The colonel was good in the art of negotiations, and the director could feel himself quickly being outmaneuvered.

"I want to see some progress toward integrating your staff. I want to see an effort made on your part to welcome *all* patients to your hospital, and I want to see some progress made to cleaning the facility so it will look like a real hospital." The colonel was now solidly in the position to dictate the terms of the agreement. "I noticed you don't have any bandages and few medicines. What do you do for wounds?"

"Patients bring their own supplies and medicines, or we recycle the bandages if we have them," the director said with resignation.

"We will also help you get both through NGOs back in the states." Standing up, the colonel said, "We'll be back in a month to see what progress you've made, and then we'll go from there, Director. It has been a pleasure meeting you." After exchanging handshakes, the colonel and his team departed.

★ 13 ★

It had been a good show in the camp's gymnasium. Although the band was little known to anyone who attended, it was nice to have entertainers from the states singing their hearts out in appreciation for what the troops were doing on behalf of their country. The guys in the band appeared average, but they were performing before America's warriors, and they tried to make themselves look buffer, cooler, and more Hollywood. However, in the end they looked just like any other guys in a rock band. The girls had the advantage, and they used it. Dressing seductively, they willingly fed the overactive hormones of the young soldiers. They sang and shook their well-endowed breasts and asses in unison in response to the encouragement from the young studs that howled and clapped. The lack of attractive females in the camp only contributed to getting the soldiers' juices flowing even stronger.

Returning to his quarters in the SEA huts, the colonel was intercepted by his chief of the mental health detachment.

"Sir, may I have a word with you?" he asked, closing the gap between the two of them from behind.

"Sure, John. What's up?" the colonel asked.

Lieutenant colonel John Bachmeir was a seasoned officer and a social worker by training; while older than the average lieutenant colonel, he was a solid leader who commanded the respect of the soldiers in his detachment. Stateside, he'd served in the colonel's command as his executive officer and was a trusted colleague. In addition to the colonel's familiarity with the lieutenant colonel, competency and leadership had given the colonel reason to select him for command of the mental health detachment.

"I'm running into some challenges with Colonel Weston," the lieutenant colonel said, catching his breath.

"What sort of challenges?" the colonel asked.

"He continues to countermand and undermine my guidance, directing the soldiers to disregard my orders, claiming he is the actual commander of the detachment."

"John, you tell Weston that if he has an issue with chain of command, he can take it up with me. As far as the soldiers go … you need to reiterate your command authority. If they want to challenge that, they too can take it up with me. For now, you're in charge … so take charge," the colonel said. "Is there any doubt as to where I'm coming from?"

"No, sir," the lieutenant colonel replied, feeling the confidence of the commander.

The sweat ran from the colonel's forehead in a steady stream from the beads that grew into larger dots soaking his face and neck, leaving a wet v impression on the front and back of his exercise T-shirt. Rising early, the colonel had begun his day like any other with his morning run along the perimeter of the camp and a set of sit-ups and push-ups. On even days of the week he added weight training down at the gym. Returning to his quarters, he proceeded to clean up, put on a fresh uniform, grabbed breakfast at the mess hall, and completed his morning walk through his headquarters and hospital. Then he went to his desk to work on the morning stacks of paper and e-mails. It wasn't even eight o'clock yet. Sipping his coffee, he was soon deep into his work, loving the time alone.

"Good morning, sir," the S-1 called out as she entered his office.

"Good morning," he replied. "What d'ya have this morning?"

"Sir, Colonel Weston is due to rotate back to the states at the end of the month. He's requested an extension to remain in theater." She passed the request to the colonel. The colonel perused it in detail. Glancing at the bottom of the form, he took his pen and checked the box Denied, signed it, and returned it to the captain.

"Inform the colonel his request has been denied. He's going home at the end of the month," the colonel said firmly.

"Are you sure you want to do that?" the captain asked, puzzled. "He's the only psychiatrist we have, and I don't see another one in the pipeline."

"I'm sure," the colonel answered. "Let Colonel Bachmeir down at the mental health detachment know he's going to have to pick up the slack for now until the army backfills Colonel Weston's position." The colonel was firm.

"Yes, sir," the captain replied as she retreated from the colonel's office.

The major stood quietly outside the colonel's office observing him. Sensing he was being watched, the colonel asked without looking up, "What can I do for you, Major?"

"Sir, just wanted to update you on the Weston case." The major took the inquiry as an invite to enter the colonel's office. "I just got word from one of his former commanders when he was deployed down range in Bosnia. For some strange reason he disappeared from his duty for two weeks and then mysteriously reappeared in Vienna where he was picked up by the MPs."

"Was he charged with AWOL, or did he receive a letter of reprimand or something?" the colonel asked, expecting a yes.

"No … His commander tried to press charges, but the chain of command wouldn't allow it," the major said.

"That's odd." The colonel appeared perplexed. "How can one go AWOL and no action be taken by the chain of command? Rank may have its privileges, but not under those circumstances."

"I know, but that's not all," the major said. "I've heard back from his commander at Fort Bliss. While assigned there, the colonel made a big stink about not being in charge, so the general there made him the acting OIC of the psychiatry department, but it became a huge disaster. The IG was called in, the major continued; referring to the command's Inspector General, but the colonel mysteriously disappeared before the investigation could be completed. When the packet hit the commanding general's desk, the whole file disappeared." The major's voice rose to a level of pure excitement, like a child who had the winning ticket at the school carnival. "The letter of recommendation we received from there regarding the colonel was, like the rest, bogus!" The major couldn't contain himself.

"What happened next?" The colonel leaned back in his chair, taking in everything the major was reporting.

"Nothing! No follow-up. It's like … nothing … zippo … nada. His boss was as perplexed as anyone else. DA made the whole thing disappear as if it had never happened," the major said.

"Well, that makes one more perplexed individual … me," the colonel said. "I've never heard of anything like this before in the army."

"Oh yeah … one more thing," the major said. "The lieutenant colonel from Fort Bliss asked me to pass something along to you."

"What's that?" the colonel asked.

"Watch your back; they're going to get you if you don't stop this investigation."

"What did he mean by that?" The colonel was intrigued by the cryptic message. "And who is 'they'?"

"Sir, I don't know. He didn't say, but I do know he didn't mean it as a threat. All I know is something bad happened at Fort Bliss, but he wasn't willing to elaborate. Whatever it was, he didn't want it happening to you." The major had taken on a somber appearance. "He was very serious about wanting me to tell you to drop the investigation while we still could."

"We're not going there ... at least for now," the colonel replied quickly. "The general has given us a green light to proceed, so let's stick to the plan."

Following the meeting, the day passed quickly, which in Kosovo was considered a blessing; another day done and another day closer to going home. Settling behind his desk on the tiered level of the briefing room, the colonel reviewed his notes for the evening briefing should the general call on him for comment. The briefing was classified and for the most part routine. The American sector was secure, and the general had made significant headway into rebuilding confidence while earning the respect of both the local Serbs and Albanians. They knew he was fair, reasonable, and fully committed to ensuring the peace between both factions, yet they also knew he was a tough, no-nonsense leader. However, that didn't deter the rogue Serb faction from testing his will from time to time.

A young officer entered the briefing room and moved at a quick pace to where the general sat with his back to him. Not noticing the captain rapidly approaching from his blind side on the left, the general motioned to the briefer for the next slide. Stopping just short of the general, the young man leaned forward and began whispering to him. Holding up his hand, the general signaled the briefer to pause. Pushing back from the table in his chair, he continued his conversation with the chief and his deputy commander. While no one could hear the conversation, it was clear from the worried expression on his face that something was clearly wrong. Looking on, the others gathered in the room waited in suspense while the sidebar conversation continued. Standing, the general turned and faced the staff sitting behind him.

"Gentlemen, this briefing is over. One of our companies is currently under attack and pinned down by a Serb unit that has infiltrated our sector. I want every available aircraft in the air now to give those guys some close air support. I likewise want everyone on standby to reinforce and support as necessary." The general looked up at the tiered level of staff desks. "Doc, have the hospital standby for some potential incoming casualties, and get the Dust-off airborne. Air-Ops will forward you the coordinates where the bird can standby. If they need to get in the fight, I want them close. Ops are sending over the coordinates and OPORD to your folks now," he said, referring to the operations order. Scanning the room, he asked, "Any questions?" Seeing none, he said, "Further details will be forthcoming from the TOC ... Dismissed."

The skirmish had lasted a little more than an hour culminating with the American forces decisively driving the Serb unit back across the border, securing the area. The use of force and firepower had been quick, decisive, and impressive, delivering a clear message to the Serb commander. The general wanted to ensure that his adversary clearly understood the consequence for taking on an American unit within the NATO contingent. Unlike other commands that comprised the NATO forces, the general was in no mood to be politically polite. He was a soldier, not a pussyfoot politician. He wanted to be clear about his resolve to address any matter that occurred within his area of responsibility. Enter the American sector unauthorized, and there would be severe consequences. In other words ... stay out! The task force's quick work had caught the intruders off guard and taken the Serb commander by complete surprise, which in turn precluded any casualties for the Americans. The same could not be said for the Serbs.

It was atypical for American military leaders to respond with such resolve. Most military leaders were perceived by their enemies as weak, softened by their attempts to be more politically correct than true warriors. In general, the army as a whole touted the tough "Hoo ... rah ... warrior first" slogans, but many field commanders were ill prepared for their roles as senior leaders. While the responsibility for their lack of skill rested in part with the officer, it was more a consequence of the modern army's policy to rapidly promote and place officers in positions that in many cases exceeded their experience and competence. Leaders lost sight of their purpose of leading and focused more on how to gain their next promotion or assignment. The net result was an increasing loss in confidence by subordinates in their senior leaders and an evolving officer corps that was indecisive of doing what was right, fearful of being relieved by those who sat thousands of miles away from the battle playing the role of a Monday-morning quarterback while attending lavish parties in Europe and Washington, DC, much like the bourgeoisie of the French prerevolutionary. Returning to the camp, the contingent stood down and regrouped for the next time, should there be one. While exhausted from the intensity of the fight, word had traveled fast among the soldiers about how proud they felt about serving with "their" general.

In the minds of the perpetrators, the event from the previous night was over. They had tested the mettle of the American force and had paid a small price. However, for the general it was just the beginning. He was determined to ensure there would be no repeat of the fight during the remainder of his watch. As dawn broke across the crest of the Balkan mountains, the general lost no time in ordering an in-depth search of the area. He had worked through the night planning his next move, knowing his window of opportunity might be limited. His face reflected the fatigue that battled within him, but he pressed on. His work was rewarded with the discovery of new caches of guns, explosives, and ammunition that had been buried in strategic locations throughout the American sector. At the border crossing, every vehicle was strip-searched down to the frame, the contents and parts strewn about the highway. In addition to tightening up the security within the sector, the general took to the airwaves, reiterating his message to the Serbs: don't mess with the Americans. The communiqué was received, resulting in no further attacks against the American sector. Such could not be said for the other three sectors of the region that continued to experience periodic assaults.

Enraged that the general had taken such matters into his own hands against the Serbs instead of negotiating, the NATO commander demanded the general apologize to the Serb government for his actions. The general refused.

★ 14 ★

The rain fell hard, creating small fields of mud and ribbons of chocolate-colored water that cut their way haphazardly across the camp, following paths of least resistance. The warm weather of a Balkan fall was beginning to turn, producing a cooling trend in preparation for the harsh winter that would ensue. Making his way across the camp, the colonel navigated the mud the best he could, but his efforts were futile as the shine of his black leather winter boots slowly succumbed to the rain-soaked earth. His poncho and hood did little to protect his pants and his glasses. Squinting between the drops of rain hitting his lenses, he strained to see his way. With each step, jump, or skip, he could feel the wetness of the water moving deeper into his boots, soaking his wool socks, and chilling his feet. Glancing skyward, he didn't see any signs of the weather improving, and from the darkened horizon in the distance, it would only continue to worsen as the day wore on.

The weather brought back chilling memories of his former days in the infantry as a platoon leader taking his troops through mud-rutted roads in freezing rains that relentlessly pounded the northwest region of the United States where he was serving his first duty assignment at Fort Lewis. It was the not-so-glorious part of being a soldier, but it taught him much about leadership, soldiering, and caring for his soldiers, and it was why he hadn't wanted to spend his entire career being an infantryman. His love for the institution of the army was immense, and from the time he was a private and eventually a second lieutenant, his superiors saw great potential in him as a leader.

Entering the mess hall, the colonel had to remind himself that the army, like most government organizations, was changing and being politically correct was more important than getting the job done. Dining facility was more appeasing to the female gender of the new army; thus the term *mess hall* was now more of a thing of the past, although many soldiers still referenced the name.

"Good morning, sir. Happy Thanksgiving!" the head-count attendant on duty, another civilian contract employee, said, greeting the colonel with a broad smile. The colonel found it hard to accept that another soldier who normally held that job had been replaced. Where was that soldier now? Probably sitting idly in his barracks wondering why he had been deployed to this wasteland of an outpost to simply do nothing. It wasn't the employee's fault. She was simply trying, like anyone else, to make a living and had found a golden opportunity through the Department of Defense. She was making twice of what she might otherwise make doing the same job back home and was paying no income tax. While a little on the plump side, her white shirt, pants, and food-service hat did much to hide her full figure, making her look more like the home-delivery milkman. Her short blonde hair did little to hide her slightly round face, though it did give her a more youthful appearance. Her demeanor was pleasant as she offered up the sign-in book to the colonel.

Taking it, the colonel returned her smile and said, "Happy Thanksgiving." He signed the book, returned it to her, and continued on his way through the food line, choosing from a selection of freshly prepared meats consisting of the traditional turkey, roast beef, and ham. Farther down the serving line were assorted vegetables, breads, mashed potatoes, cranberry, sauces, and desserts to round out the main entrée. Finding a vacant seat, the colonel sat down to celebrate Thanksgiving alone. Lifting his fork, he took a moment to give thanks for the blessings of the day and reflect on all that he was missing back home. His family was close and had spent the latter part of their summer vacationing along the warm shores of Lake Chelan, basking in the sun by day and partying in the bars by night. His reward was the mini photo album from their trip that he kept in his room on the shelf above his desk. They had sent it to remind him of what he was missing. Thanksgiving was another time for family to gather ... another time to party. Once again, the colonel would not be a part of it. Looking down at his plate, he picked up his fork and began eating.

Lost in his thoughts, the colonel was interrupted by a voice across the table. It belonged to the medical task force's deputy commander, Major Pierce. "Excuse me, sir, may I join you?"

"Of course, Augy," the colonel replied, looking up as he shoved a slice of turkey into his mouth. "How's it going?"

"Quiet today, sir," the major answered respectfully. "If you're asking about the investigation, I can only say it's beginning to get uglier by the day."

"In what way?" the colonel asked, still digging at his meal.

"We're beginning to receive complaints from other physicians and patients regarding the care Colonel Weston is giving."

"Can you be more specific?"

"Still getting the details, but it's reported that patients are getting worse, not better, with their treatment. Rumor also has it he had some issues in Iraq. I've tracked down the med commander there and have her e-mail address if you wish to communicate with her to get the details." The major paused, passing a piece of paper across the table.

Retrieving it, the colonel glanced at the name. Folding it carefully, he stuffed it into his pocket.

"Do you know her?" the major asked.

"Yes. She's a pretty popular commander among the senior leaders," the colonel said. "I'll send her an e-mail later to see if she knows anything about this guy or had any issues with him during his tenure under her command. Do you have anything else?" Looking back at his plate, the colonel gathered another bite of meat on his fork and guided it smoothly into his mouth.

"Just more warnings from MEDCOM strongly suggesting we cease this investigation," the major replied.

The rain showers from the day before had left a fresh smell lingering in the air. From a layman's perspective, it smelled like a spring day. To the nose of a scientist, it was no more than free radicals of O_3 colliding to create an unstable form of ozone. It wasn't harmful, and nature had its own way of getting the particles to break the weak bonds and form more-stable molecules of O_2, oxygen.

Crossing the parade field between the colonel's and the general's headquarters, the colonel was unexpectedly intercepted by the camp's inspector general. The lieutenant colonel was attractive, even in her green-camouflage battle dress uniform; one could tell she was all woman. Her slim figure, dark hair tucked neatly up under her Army Combat Uniform field hat, thin face, and soft eyes gave her all the weapons and advantage she needed to disarm just about anyone she encountered.

Saluting as she approached, she began her subtle assault. "Good morning, sir. May I have a word with you?"

"Of course, Colonel," the colonel said, returning the military courtesy.

"Sir, Colonel Weston has come to me and has filed seven complaints against you regarding your denial of his request to remain in theater for an extended period," the lieutenant colonel said. Launching her first salvo, she looked cautiously for a response of surprise from the colonel, but there was none.

"Really?" The colonel entered the dance. "And on what grounds are his complaints?" The colonel was cool. He looked directly at the lieutenant colonel, giving her a commanding look. He was seasoned in command, and a perceived threat from an inquiring inspector general didn't seem to rock him. She took note. He had learned from past experiences that if one was acting within the law and was on solid ground with authority, one had little to fear from an inspector general's inquiry. Unlike many commanders, the colonel had undergone scrutiny from several inspector general inquiries throughout his career as a commander and chief of staff. Each time he'd been vindicated. Each time he'd learned they were only doing their job, which was to determine the truth with each complaint made to their office.

"Sir, the colonel wishes to remain in theater, and you have no authority to deny that request. I'm suggesting you reverse your decision and permit him to extend his tour here in Kosovo," the lieutenant colonel said.

"Colonel, I don't mean to be impolite, but let's get something clear. As the medical command commander in this sector, I have all the authority I need to deny his request, and I have. If you really believed I don't have the authority, you wouldn't be here talking to me. So unless you have a regulation to cite to get me to reverse my decision, it's final. If the colonel wishes to appeal to the CG, he can. I'll take that chance." The colonel was firm.

The lieutenant colonel had underestimated the colonel both in knowledge of how the army worked and in determination. She had perceived him to be like the typical medical commander who simply wanted to make everyone happy and lacked any real command experience. She was wrong and suddenly knew it. Making presumptions, she had failed to do her homework or to understand the colonel's past. She had played her hand and had nothing left to continue the game with. "Uh, sir … I don't have anything to show you at the moment, but I can get that together for you if you wish." She appeared startled.

"That would be fine. Until then, please advise your client he will be departing the theater as planned."

The colonel turned to continue his walk, but the inspector general stopped him, "But, sir..." the Lieutenant colonel burst out. "I am the inspector general!"

"Yes, you are," the colonel said politely. "Is there more you wish to discuss?"

"Sir, Colonel Weston is a kindhearted old man. He means no harm to anyone and only wants to help you succeed. He's a good resource for you, and you really don't have anyone to replace him with, so it can be a win-win for you. Won't you please reconsider?" the lieutenant colonel pleaded.

"No." The colonel was firm. "I can see he has played you too like the rest." He asked, "Anything more you'd like to add?"

"No, sir," the lieutenant colonel said, defeated. Coming to attention, she saluted the colonel. The colonel returned the salute and continued on his way.

★ 15 ★

The night before the first of a series of winter storms had left a heavy blanket of new snow over the FOB and the surrounding landscape. It reminded the colonel again of his beloved Washington and only made him wish all the more that he was home and with those whom he loved. In addition to creating a pristine view, the snow had the added benefit for Kosovo by concealing the mounds of garbage that lined the rivers and streams, transforming the wasteland of filth and destruction to a pristine winter wonderland. Icicles formed around the tree branches, sparkling like beautiful crystals in the glistening sunlight. It was truly a dreamlike sight. Within the FOB soldiers navigated through the snow about the camp bundled in their winter uniforms. At the airfield across the road from the colonel's headquarters, aircraft maintenance crews worked in the frigid cold prepping the helicopters that stood like ghostly creatures covered with snow and ice.

Entering his TOC, the S3 approached the Colonel. "Hey, sir ... I was just coming to find you."

"What do you need?" the colonel asked.

"Chief's on the line, needs to talk to you."

Taking the red phone from the Major the colonel spoke into the receiver, "What's up, Sam?"

"It's the Macedonians," the chief said. "They are requesting assistance from us. It appears they have a conscript observer who has become seriously ill stuck on a mountain peak. Do you think we can help?"

"I don't see why not. What's the altitude of the camp?" the colonel asked.

"I'm told just over ten thousand feet," the chief answered. "It appears you have the only medevac aircraft that can operate at those altitudes."

"What are the options if we can't fly?" the colonel asked, trying to gather more information.

"I'm afraid there's none," the chief said.

"I'll get the medevac commander to make an assessment of the situation and weather. Can you send over the medevac request with the pertinent information? In the meantime let the Macedonians know we're conducting a quick-and-dirty mission analysis and will have a response within … say ten Mikes. If it's a go, I'll take the mission myself," the colonel replied. The colonel returned the red phone to its cradle. Leaving the TOC he made his way to the office of the Dust-off medevac commander.

The mission analysis took less than ten minutes; the medevac commander determined the mission would be risky but doable. To ensure the mission had the best opportunity for success, the commander selected his most experienced pilot, copilot, crew chief, and medic. Before making their way to the helipad, they all went over the plan. The team had no specific coordinates, just a general vicinity of where the soldier and his comrades might be. Once they found the hut, the helicopter would set down, and the colonel and the medic secure the patient and bring him to the aircraft. Once airborne, they would then deliver the victim to the Macedonian Army Medical Center in Skopje. The TOC back at the FOB would coordinate with the Macedonians to get priority clearance into their airspace. Because of the altitude, ground time would be limited, as neither the crew nor the colonel would be using any supplemental oxygen.

Securing their gear, the crew made their way to the Black

Hawk UH-60 sitting on the helipad. Cleared by the air traffic controller in the tower, the pilot looked back toward the colonel, who was sitting behind the copilot, for the go-ahead. Giving a thumbs-up, the colonel signaled the mission was a go. Dialing in the power on the collective as he pulled it up, the pilot watched the rpms of the engine rise on the tachometer.

"Batteries—green; fuel—check; rpms—coming up and holding steading. Okay … I'm coming up," the pilot said over his intercom to the copilot as he pulled up further on the collective, lifting the helicopter from the pad.

Being an aviator, the colonel glanced through the window on his side and said into the microphone on his headset, "Clear right."

"Clear left," the crew chief added.

The power from the large engine launched the bird skyward with a thrust that pushed its occupants firmly into their seats.

"Hmm … she's got a lot of juice," the copilot said.

"Nice, huh?" the pilot replied. "We'll need it today." Pushing the cyclic forward, the helicopter began moving forward. Climbing rapidly, they left the helipad behind as a small square slab of cement with a large white *H* painted on it.

Setting his course, the pilot skillfully guided the large Black Hawk toward the snowcapped mountains, closing the distance as fast as he could. The flight was smooth and uneventful as the image of the mountain grew in the helo's windshield. Reaching the base of the mountains, the pilot pulled again on the collective, causing the aircraft to ascend. The downdraft coming from the mountaintop struck the rotor blades, buffeting the aircraft as it climbed; however, despite the turbulence, the large and powerful engine had no trouble cutting its way through the downdraft. The higher the aircraft climbed, the thinner the air became, though it wasn't noticeable at first with either the aircraft performance or its occupants.

"Eight thousand and climbing," the copilot read off the

altimeter as the helicopter continued its ascent. "Nine thousand ... ten thousand ... eleven thousand ... twelve thousand, thirteen thousand ... leveling out at thirteen thousand five hundred," the copilot concluded with a sigh. The pilot began circling the spot where the presumed injured soldier was held up.

"Any sign of the hut?" the pilot called out over his headset. "My rough coordinates tell me that we should be very near or right on top of them." The pilot said knowing he was only in the general vicinity, he also knew the coordinates given by inexperienced soldiers, regardless of country of origin, were generally inaccurate.

"Nine o'clock!" the crew chief shouted. "Single hut ... at nine o'clock!"

Looking down, the pilot acknowledged the sighting. "Roger ... nine o'clock ... I have visual."

Maneuvering the helicopter over the hut, the crew struggled to get a sighting on the presence of human life. Slowly, a soldier emerged from the hut. Clad in an olive-drab wool uniform, the soldier looked up and waved his arms wildly as if he were trying to get the helo to set down on top of him.

"I can't land," the pilot said as he struggled to hold the aircraft in position. "No space to put down. Sir, do you have any suggestions, or should we abort?"

"We're not aborting," the colonel replied abruptly. "We've come this far; we might as well figure out how to reach them. There's a ledge about seventy-five to one hundred yards to our south. Can you put down there?"

"Not enough room there either for this bird," the pilot said. "I can possibly get one wheel on the ledge, but the rotors will be coming extremely close to the uphill slope. Risky but doable ..."

"Okay ... give it your best shot, and put her down there," the colonel ordered. "The medic and I will jump from the bird onto the ledge and then hike up to the hut."

"Sir, have you ever tried something like that before?" the pilot asked.

"No, but I guess there's always a first for everything," the colonel said with a small laugh.

"Okay, sir. Here's how we'll do it. I'll put down on one wheel on the ledge. You and the medic will have to move quickly and jump from the bird onto the ledge, but stay there until I lift off," the pilot spoke with a concerned tone. "Lie flat in the snow so the blades will clear you and the rotor wash doesn't blow you off the ledge...copy?" The pilot paused to ensure the colonel understood both the risk and the guidance. "I will continue to circle at a lower altitude, checking periodically until I see you back on the ledge. Once you're there, lie flat again. I'll land again with one wheel, and the crew chief will help get you guys and your patient back on board."

"Copy, Chief ... Let's do it." The colonel said, acknowledging the pilot's instructions.

Approaching the mountain perpendicular to the slope, the pilot struggled against the wind to guide the left wheel of the aircraft onto the ledge. Touching it, the crew chief pushed opened the door, and motioning with his hands, he ordered, "Jump ... now!" The downdraft blowing off of the mountain into the aircraft was biting and destabilized the aircraft, causing the helicopter to pitch slightly. The colonel and medic staggered backward. The pilot was quick on the cyclic to correct the tilt.

The colonel threw his bag of medical equipment out the door and jumped into the fresh snow. The crust on the frozen surface gave way under the colonel's weight, and he broke through like a rock hitting quicksand, sinking quickly up to his chest. Realizing it was too deep for the medic, he raised his hand and yelled to her not to jump, but it was too late. The sound of the loud turbine engine and wind drowned out any sound the colonel could have emitted. Exiting the aircraft, the young medic followed the colonel, hitting the snow and rapidly disappearing into it. The unforeseen depth of the snow startled her, and panic quickly set into her face. Looking out of his side window, the pilot could see the team was free from the helo, and he lifted off of the ledge, pointing the nose of the aircraft downslope to gain speed.

With the wind from the rotor wash, micro shards of frozen snow tore across the colonel's and medic's faces, each piece stinging as it struck their exposed flesh. They struggled to hold their position on the ledge. One wrong move and both of them would be victims to a 1,500-foot fall. As the wind subsided, the colonel looked over at the medic. Only her face was exposed. Reaching out, he grabbed her by her jacket and pulled her hard toward him. "Are you okay?" he asked.

Reaching up with her hands, she grasped the colonel's arms. "I am, but my hands … they're freezing!" the medic replied.

The colonel demanded, "Where are your gloves?"

In the subzero temperature and high altitude, the medic's hands were already turning a purple hue. "I left them in the helo. I thought I'd need my hands free to start an IV," she said, stuttering from the cold.

Removing his gloves, the Colonel passed them quickly to the medic. "Here … put these on now!" he directed with a tone of urgency. It was clear he wasn't humored by the soldier's lapse of common sense. The colonel grabbed the olive-drab medic bag and slung the strap over one shoulder and under the opposite one so that it lay flat against his back. Turning back to the medic, he said, "It's going to take us awhile, but we're going to have to make our way up the mountain to the hut through this snow. I'm hoping it'll get a little easier once we're off this ledge. Grab onto the medic bag, and don't let go!"

Turning back toward the upslope of the mountain, he began trudging through the snow away from the ledge. The colonel appeared optimistic as he began his forward motion, despite it being extremely slow and labored. It didn't take long for him to realize reaching the conscripts was going to be more difficult than he had anticipated. After twenty minutes they had covered less than twenty yards.

His lungs burned from the growing exhaustion and the lack of oxygen. He was lightheaded, and a cold sweat had broken out beneath his clothes that spread over his forehead, turning the dry cold to a damp one and freezing his neatly trimmed mustache. Despite his dress for cold weather, the colonel realized quickly hypothermia and altitude sickness, neither of which he appreciated nor was mentally prepared for, were beginning to set in. However, up the slope about another fifty yards or more was a young man who desperately needed medical attention. His only hope rested with the two Americans who were making their way slowly up the mountain. The colonel crossed his arms and tucked his fists into his armpits, hoping to keep his hands from freezing. The light wind blowing off the mountaintop was biting and did little to help make the short journey tolerable. The ache in his muscles and head continued to grow as he pulled the medic behind him with their medical bag, but he kept pushing forward, one step at a time. Slowly, the cold burning sensation crept from his hands up his arms, causing painful cramps in both.

Closing his eyes, he pondered the wisdom of his decision. Had it been a mistake to take on this mission? Should he have listened to the pilot and aborted the mission? It was too late, but even after thinking through the what-if questions, he concluded he was right and the consequences were his alone to bear. For now, he had to remain focused on the goal of reaching the hut ahead. Alternating his shoulders and knees in a forward motion, he used the weight of his body to create a narrow path as they moved much like an ice-breaking ship forging a path in the polar regions to create a channel for shipping. Dumb as the idea now appeared in rescuing the stranded soldier, he knew quitting was no longer an option. Another twenty minutes passed, another twenty yards covered. The roof of the hut was now visible ... close, yet so very far away. The colonel estimated they still had another twenty or so yards to close. He knew focusing on the end target only prolonged the agony, so looking only to what lay immediately a few feet ahead of him, he set small distance goals that helped him remain positive. He glanced up periodically to ensure he was still moving in the right direction. The hut grew in size as they closed in, and the depth of snow lessened.

The sound of the helicopter circling overhead had faded, leaving behind a serene silence. The pilot had dropped to a lower altitude below the mountain to prevent altitude sickness, avoid the use of oxygen, and limit the amount of fuel being consumed in the thin air. Glancing up, the colonel could see the hut was actually smaller than he had originally thought and was constructed of unpainted, partially rusted corrugated steel. On either side of the single door were two cut-out windows, each covered with corrugated steel panels. Through the pitched roof, a single tube of black stovepipe protruded. A plume of sooty smoke rose lazily from the top of the pointed capped tubing, coming from the oil-burning stove inside that served as the only means of heating or cooking meals for the confined conscripts.

Being assigned to the frozen mountain peaks was not a job by choice but more of a rite of passage for the new recruits in the Macedonian army. Each year in the spring, the army drafted eighteen-year-old men who spent their summer months in basic training learning the rudimentary skills of soldiering. From there, they would be assigned in groups of four in the fall to serve as lookouts along their country's border on isolated mountain peaks that served as a natural, formidable barrier to any would-be attackers. Once the winter snow fell, the soldiers could no longer be reached except by air. Unfortunately, the Macedonian military did not have aircraft capable of flying at those altitudes. The second challenge was the army had not given any consideration to developing helipads near the lookout positions should such a situation necessitate the use of one. Thus, for all intents and purposes the young conscripts were permanently isolated for the duration of the winter until they were relieved in the spring. Their rations were likewise limited; they were given only enough food to last them through the winter. If they consumed too much, the outcome would be starvation, which forced the young, inexperienced soldiers to eat less.

Five yards and closing! the colonel thought to himself. *We can do this.* He was exhausted and sick. The nausea grew steadily in his gut, and he fought hard to suppress the urge to vomit. Despite the distance to the hut being so short, the colonel thought it might easily have been a hundred yards, due to the depth of the snow and thin air. It was disheartening as the throbbing in his head became harder and the burning and cramping in his muscles increased due to the growing accumulation of lactic acid in the tissue. Looking over his shoulder, he said, "We're almost there ... just a few feet more."

The medic shouted back, "I can't go any farther. I can't!" Her lips were a deep blue, her face blanched. Her eyes were sunken and black, and reflected a ghostly expression of defeat.

"We're here!" the colonel shouted back at her, knowing she could not see ahead. He knew he was lying, but he also knew it was their only hope of making it to the hut alive. The final few yards took them just under ten minutes to complete; reaching the front door of the hut, the colonel raised his hand weakly to knock when it suddenly flew open. A young Macedonian soldier clad in the same winter wool uniform that they had seen from the air stood in the doorway staring at the colonel. Behind him, another soldier appeared with a youthful face, looking over his colleague's shoulder. They grasped the colonel and the medic and pulled them into the hut. Placing them in chairs nearest the stove, they stood back waiting for the pair to say something. It took a few minutes for the colonel and medic to regain some of their strength and for the pain that now consumed their bodies to subside to a tolerable level.

Scanning the hut, the colonel made a quick assessment of the room. From the center of the ceiling a single dim lightbulb, the only source of light, dangled haphazardly. Electricity that powered the light and radio that had been used to call for help was provided by a generator that ran only during limited times of the day and night behind the hut. The colonel could hear the muffled hum through the thin walls. In the far corner of the hut behind the colonel was the oil-burning stove. The fire that burned from within emitted a dim orange glow, providing the only source of heat. In the center of the room a young soldier lay on the floor groaning, holding his stomach as if he was experiencing severe cramps. The grimace on his face showed he felt severe pain ... but from what? He stared in silence at the colonel and medic with a hopeful look, as if their presence would suddenly make his pain vanish. His comrades stared at the young female soldier. It had been months since any of them had laid eyes on a female. The fact that one had made her way up the mountain and was now huddled warming up in their hut was more than any of them could have ever imagined.

Catching his breath, the colonel looked up from his bent-over position at the soldiers. "What do we have here?" he gasped.

None of the soldiers spoke or moved. Fixated between the medic and their colleague on the floor, the soldiers appeared more like wax mannequins than they did Macedonian soldiers. Searching for any response, the colonel repeated his question, this time a little slower. Again, there was no response from any of the young men. It didn't take long for the colonel to deduce none of the soldiers spoke or understood English. Kneeling beside the soldier on the floor, he began his cursory examination. With his stethoscope in his ears, he gently placed the diaphragm of the scope over the soldier's chest and listened intently as he moved it from side to side. Pulling up on the soldier's shirt, the colonel continued to auscultate the soldier's abdomen, moving methodically from one quadrant to the next. The soldier winced and instinctively pushed the colonel's hand away as the stethoscope passed slowly over the right lower quadrant. Placing his hand gently back on the same area, the colonel depressed the abdomen gently, then let go rapidly, looking at the soldier's face for a response. The soldier let out an uncontrollable, horrific scream as he attempted to curl into a fetal position; however, the intensity of the pain forced the soldier to remain rigid.

"He's got a ruptured appendix, I guess," the colonel said as he folded up his stethoscope and returned it to the medic bag. Glancing over at the medic, the colonel asked, "Are you okay?"

"Yes, sir. I'm fine now," the medic replied. "I'm getting my feeling back."

"We've got to get him back to the ledge," the colonel said. "Once we're back on board the helo, I'll need you to start an IV and push some Demerol for starters. For now, there's nothing we can do here." Looking up at the other soldiers, the colonel motioned like a contestant in a game of charades and said, "We've got to get your comrade back to the ledge, but we're not going to carry him down there. I need two of you to help us."

The soldiers slid their injured friend onto a sheet of canvas that had been stashed in the corner. The soldier cried out from the excruciating pain. Grabbing the corners, the soldiers began dragging their sick comrade from the hut, down the mountain, and back to the ledge, following the path that the colonel and the medic had created. Over each bump, the soldier let out bloodcurdling screams that echoed into the hollowed air, reaffirming the pain he was suffering. It took less time for the small group to return to the ledge than it had to reach the hut. Far below, the helicopter continued flying a circular pattern as if it were oblivious to what was occurring on the ledge above. Then, as if on cue, the pilot broke from his pattern, guiding the aircraft back toward the spot where he had dropped the colonel and medic earlier. He hovered above the cluster lying on the ledge and then lowered the helicopter skillfully back onto the protruding ledge with one wheel as the crew chief threw open the side door. There was no doubt that the skilled pilots and crews of the medevac company were among the very best the Army National Guard had to offer to soldiers in the field. The wind from the main rotor beat down hard on the team as they struggled to lift the soldier onto the aircraft. With a strong heave, the soldiers tossed their comrade like a sack of potatoes onto the floor of the helo. The colonel and medic climbed on board alongside the patient. With the team safely on-board, the pilot leaned the helo to the right, slipping the aircraft off of the ledge. Pointing the nose of the aircraft down, the helicopter gained speed as the crew chief slammed the door shut.

The aircraft had no sooner achieved a level flight than the medic had completed establishing an IV access line and started running a saline solution with Demerol into the soldier's arm. Instantly, the soldier relaxed as the potent pain medication coursed its way into his body, creating a euphoric effect on his demeanor.

Ten minutes later the pilot was in communication with the Macedonian air traffic controller. "Skopje Center, this is US Medevac Zero-Charlie-Zero-Three entering Macedonian airspace."

"US Medevac Zero-Charlie-Zero-Three … Skopje Center … you have priority one route one to Macedonian Army Medical Center. VFR is in effect," the Skopje tower replied, referring to visual flight rules.

"Roger, Skopje Center … priority one route one to Macedonian Army Medical Center. VFR is in effect," the pilot confirmed. "Please advise the medical center our Echo-Tango-Alpha is one-zero Mikes," the pilot said, noting he was ten minutes out from the hospital.

"Roger, Zero-Charlie-Zero-Three. Will advise medical center Echo-Tango-Alpha is one-zero Mikes. Have a good day."

The flight continued to be uneventful as the pilot began his gradual descent. Having administered an antinausea medication to the patient, the colonel glanced out of the side window and scanned the landscape below, pondering next steps with his patient. The colonel's headache had diminished, but the nausea in the pit of his stomach continued to press against his gag reflex, partially driven by his prolonged exposure to the high altitude and the remainder by the stench that filled the cabin from the vomit the medic had produced into a paper bag. The crew chief attempted to alleviate the latter by pulling the side door ajar to vent the cabin, but the effect was minimal.

Approaching the medical center, the pilot slowed the speed of the helicopter and circled the facility to determine where the helipad was located. The medical center wasn't simply large; it was massive. Built in a square, like a fortress around an open-air plaza, it was a typical dreary-looking Soviet-built structure that bore no resemblance to a hospital. Coming to a hover, the pilot informed the colonel, "Sir, I have the helipad below and setting down, but I don't see any medical staff."

"Roger ... thanks," the colonel replied over his headset. "Let's see if they hear us and come out."

Lowering the collective, the pilot set the helo down on the pad and throttled down the engine to an idle. Five minutes passed, and still no one from the medical center had come out to receive the patient, who was now resting comfortably.

"Hey, sir, what do you want to do?" the pilot asked. "I don't think they're coming to us."

"I agree," the colonel replied. "Let's get our patient on the litter, and the medic and I can take him to their ER."

"Sir, I think the ER is on the opposite side of the hospital. At least that is where the action was when we flew over," the pilot warned.

"Hmm … why would they put the helipad on the opposite side of the building away from the ER?" the colonel asked.

"It was built by the Russians. What would you expect?" the pilot said jokingly.

Sliding open the door, the colonel and medic leaped from the helicopter. Taking hold of either end of the stretcher, they carefully lifted the soldier from the aircraft and began their arduous journey along the mammoth building. The weight of the soldier made it difficult for the medic, who was short in stature to carry, but with several brief stops to regain her grip on the handles, the team finally arrived on the far side of the building and the entrance to the emergency department. Pushing their way through the aluminum-framed glass door, they delivered their patient to the medical staff at the Macedonian Army Medical Center.

"Velcome," the Macedonian army officer said, extending her hand in greeting. "I am Lieutenant colonel Patrovsky, physician in charge." Her appearance was feminine and attractive, but her mannerisms were rigid, cold, and uncaring.

Sitting the patient down on the floor, the colonel returned the handshake and introduced himself.

"Vat do ve have?" the Macedonian physician asked, looking down at the young soldier.

"He's got a rigid abdomen with a positive McBurney's sign," the colonel replied. "I believe he has a ruptured appendix."

Bending over the patient, the Macedonian physician pressed firmly on his right lower quadrant. When she released her hand, the soldier let out a wail that silenced all other activity in the room.

"Yes, you are right, Colonel," she said without emotions. Turning to an orderly standing by, she directed, "Take him to the surgery suite." Without any further dialogue, the doctor left the room to continue work.

Returning to the helicopter, the colonel pondered the dialogue that had just transpired between him and the Macedonian physician. It had been formal, brief, and noncollegial and ended abruptly. Perplexed, he shook his head, boarded the UH-60, and departed for the forward operating base.

★ 16 ★

The chief was sitting behind his desk engaged in small talk with the JAG of the command and the inspector general as the colonel entered. "Hey, Sam, what's up?" the colonel asked as he took his place in the empty seat next to the JAG.

The chief said, "Don't shoot the messenger, but the IG is here from our higher headquarters to deliver another message requesting this investigation you're conducting to stand down for the good of the army. Apparently, the powers up the food chain are putting some pressure on the CG up in Europe and he doesn't like it."

Facing the IG, the colonel asked, "Can you tell me what 'good of the army' you are referring to, or is this now more of a cover-your-ass good-of-the-army request?"

"Now wait a minute, sir!" the lieutenant colonel IG retorted.

Sensing the conversation was escalating rapidly in the wrong direction, the JAG quickly weighed in to defuse the situation. "What the colonel meant was can you explain why the army would not want to support this investigation?"

"It's a matter of national security," the IG replied. "You know, it's more of a need-to-know basis, and none of you have that need to know."

"I have a fraudulent colonel in my command!" The IG's stonewalling irritated the colonel. "I can't prove he's a colonel. I can't verify his credentials. I can't prove he ever went to medical school let alone ever became a physician. Damn it … the patients he's treating are getting worse, not better! I've requested a peer review and can't even get the army to do that, you son of a bitch!" The colonel was on a roll. "We just caught him sitting in on a top-secret briefing without a security clearance only to learn he has a track of record of doing that stateside, and nothing we're getting back from his previous commands is adding up. He's been investigated by two previous commands, the records of which have mysteriously disappeared when the files landed on their commanding generals' desks. Doesn't that mean *anything* to the army? Just what in the hell are you covering up and why?" The colonel was clearly angry as he leaned into the IG.

Leaning back in his seat as if he were expecting to receive a blow from the colonel, the IG raised his hands as if he was giving up and said, "Hey, sir ... I'm just the messenger. What you don't seem to realize is that you're all in way over your heads. This is well beyond you or your boss's pay grades, so I would strongly suggest you drop this matter, destroy whatever records you have, and forget this whole thing ever happened."

"We can't do that," the chief said in a calm tone. "The colonel's right. We have an issue here that is of great concern to this command and ... I suppose as you said, national security. It's our responsibility to get to the bottom of it."

Turning to the JAG officer, the IG asked, "Counselor, don't you think you owe it to your boss to advise him to cease these proceedings, especially if it will affect his future in the army?"

The JAG replied matter-of-factly, "I owe it to my boss to advise him on matters that may adversely affect the command. Those in turn would naturally affect his future. Should we fail to fulfill our duties and responsibilities as a part of this army and, in the process, fail to accomplish this mission, then that too would adversely affect the command ... I'm doing that."

"Are you?" The IG let the question hang. "I see there is nothing more to discuss. I'll relay your position to my boss. I'm not sure he will appreciate your response as you really don't understand the seriousness or consequence of your continued pursuit of this investigation. The command has offered you an olive branch—a way out if you will—but you all appear, with all due respect, too dumb to realize that. You have been duly warned." Standing, the IG concluded, "Good luck, gentlemen." He left the headquarters and returned to Pristina to board his flight. *They're as good as dead,* he thought.

Turning to the colonel, the chief said, "Gentlemen, it appears we're on our own. Let's pray we're doing the right thing and hope we have a rock-solid battle plan with our ducks in a row."

"I guess it's time to button down the hatches," the JAG added. "I think things are going to get a lot rougher from here on out. Keep me posted on everything."

The colonel got up to leave, and the chief intercepted him at the door. "How are you doing?" he asked.

"I'm fine," the colonel said. "I'm fine … Thanks for asking."

Taking a firm hold on the colonel's arm, the chief asked again, "Really … how are you doing?"

Looking down at the chief's hand on his arm, the colonel replied, "I'm fine. We're soldiers and … leaders … right?"

Removing his hand, the chief said, "I'm here for you if you need anything or just want to talk."

"I know," the colonel said. "Thanks … that means a lot."

"The CG wants to have a quick word with you. Would you mind stopping by his office?"

"No. I'll head up there now."

When the colonel walked into the general's office, the general was behind his desk, lost in conversation on the phone. The expression on his face implied the topic was serious, requiring his undivided attention. Without a pause, the general motioned the colonel in to take a seat in front of his desk. Hanging up the phone, the general walked to the door and closed it softly.

Taking up a seat next to the colonel, the general sighed as if he was relieved from the pressure he was feeling.

"How are you doing?" the general asked in a caring tone.

"It could be better, but it all goes with the territory," the colonel replied respectfully.

"Thanks for rescuing that Macedonian soldier. I got a call from their high command. They were grateful for what you and your team had to do to get there. No easy task I hear."

"I think he'll be okay, despite the type of medicine they practice in that dinosaur of a hospital," the colonel said.

"I'm getting more pressure from further up the food chain to stop this investigation you're doing."

"I'm sorry to hear that," the colonel said. "I don't want to cause you any trouble, and I don't know why they want us to stop. There is something here that none of us seems to know much about."

"Let me ask you this," the general said after a short pause. "Have you had a good career?"

"Until now, I'd say I've had a pretty good career. I got further in my career than I ever thought was possible," the colonel replied. "When I was a kid, I always wanted to be like my father. Unfortunately, he began his army career as a private during World War II working as an airplane mechanic on P-38s. Because he was a Native American, he was discriminated against by his superior officers. Despite those challenges, he went on to medical school, became a doctor, and rose up in rank to be a lieutenant colonel. He got passed over for colonel because he spoke out against a drunken general one day. It ended his career." The colonel softened his tone. "I thought if I could make it to lieutenant colonel, I would consider my career a success, so here I am … a colonel."

"Do you think you'll ever be a general?"

"No. I had that opportunity once but didn't get selected. So I decided I needed to get refocused on being the best colonel and commander I can be, taking care of my soldiers, and getting the mission done. So often, officers get caught up thinking of their next promotion that they lose sight of what we're really charged with. I was one of those," the colonel said philosophically. "It was good thing in retrospect that I didn't get promoted. The person who got the star deserved it, and the army was right in promoting him over me. I'm thinking of retiring when this deployment is done. I don't think there will be any other opportunity for command beyond where I am at this point in my career. Besides, I think my family would be thrilled."

"Sounds like you have a good perspective on who and where you are. You see, I too have had a good career," the general said, leaning back in his chair. "I didn't think I'd be a general, but here I am. I don't think I'm going anywhere from here too, so now I'm faced with a decision. Either we go forward with this investigation, or we don't." The general was getting serious. "What do you think we should do?"

"Well, sir," the colonel said, "I've always been of the belief that, as officers, we are held to a higher standard. We always do what is right, even when challenged to take an easy way out. Maybe that standard has changed, our morals modified, and I'm perhaps a bit too idealistic, but I do believe in it." The colonel looked for a reaction from the general; he had the general's attention. "If we espouse our values as an army and officer corps, then we need to have the moral courage to stand firm in what we're doing … only if we believe we are doing the right thing."

"Do you believe we're doing the right thing?"

"Yes, sir. With evidence we have gathered to date, I do believe we're doing the right thing, but I don't know why the army wants us to do otherwise."

"I don't think it's the army as much as it might be just a few colleagues who are acting on their own." The general was pensive. "You see, this is our moment. We have arrived at this point in our history and this place in time for a reason. This may very well be our Alamo. If we continue this investigation, they're going to take us down ... and hard. Do you realize that?"

"I know," the colonel said. "I've thought a lot about that. I see this more like Julius Caesar during his time as a Roman general. In 39 BC he too was faced with a dilemma when his superiors ordered him not to cross the Rubicon River. Instead he did it, stating, 'The die is now cast.' I never dreamed in my wildest imagination that I would go through an entire career only to end up in such a situation. This is something that one reads about but never actually experiences. The pressure is equal to a combat situation. It's literally giving me ulcers, and my sleep stinks, but ... why? Why *our* government? What are they trying to hide?"

"I know how you're feeling. I think we're both suffering from the same disease," the general said with a laugh, trying to add some levity to the conversation. "I think we need to continue."

"Sir, if I'm going to swing from the gallows, I don't want to swing alone. If that's the idea, I'd rather stop now. However, if you're willing to hang with me, then I'm in all the way, but I'd like a little insurance to cover me."

"What sort of insurance are you looking for?" the general asked.

"I'd like to request you make it an order in writing."

"You'll have your orders by tomorrow. We're all in this together, regardless of the outcome."

★ 17 ★

The conference room in the medical task force's headquarters had been abuzz for some time with the preparation for the medical team's pending trip to one of the local villages to conduct a medical civic action operation. The major leaned on the podium as he tapped it in an attempt to gain the team's attention. "Good afternoon, ladies and gentlemen. If I may get your attention for the moment, we have some work to do here." The major paused momentarily to see if anyone had responded to his opening salvo of remarks. "For those of you who may not remember who I am, I am Major Tom Meyer, the task force med's operations officer. Tomorrow we will deploy a small contingent forward to the town of Kamenica to conduct a medical civic action operation program, a.k.a. MEDCAP, a.k.a. provide basic health care to those who need it in the village. Our mission is to build goodwill and win the hearts and minds of the people for their government and the US, of course. For those of you who are history buffs, you may know that this is a historic village, as it was once the home to Anjezë Gonxhe Bojaxhiu, a.k.a. Mother Teresa. This is an Albanian-held town, so we are anticipating the threat level to be moderate to low. Having said that, situational awareness and security of our area of operation during our time in the village will remain paramount to ensure that we have a successful exercise and everyone gets home safe. The logistics folks have loaded the equipment you will need. Captain Aiken will be the team OIC and will have some comments when

I'm done. One squad from one of the infantry companies has been detailed to provide security. If you're wondering about the CO, he'll be joining you for a brief time. If you need anything else, let me know."

Following the series of briefings, the team completed their pre-movement checks and climbed aboard their vehicles for the journey to the historic village. Departing the forward operating base, the convoy passed through the main security checkpoint and into the unprotected zone of Kosovo outside the camp. Comprised of the security detail and the medical team of physicians, dentists, nurses, and corpsmen, the small group made its way undetected along the narrow two-lane country road. The cool breeze of the early morning felt refreshing as it blew gently through the truck. The breaking sun crested the surrounding hilltops when the convoy made the outer limits of the town. Entering the village, the convoy passed along old homes, some well-kept, others crumbling from age, and continued along a riverbank that meandered through the center of the town, where the convoy came to a halt at a small open area alongside the river. After dismounting the vehicles, the teams went about their business creating a makeshift open-air treatment site as the lieutenant from the infantry directed his soldiers to establish a security perimeter.

Scoping out the town, the colonel took note of the history that encapsulated this simple place. The Catholic Church Mother Teresa had attended occupied a prominent place in the center of town. Standing along the riverbank, the colonel observed his soldiers preparing for villagers who might seek their assistance. He was proud of his soldiers, and their work reminded him of his earlier years in the army when he had conducted special and medical operations in remote areas of Southeast Asia. Giving rebirth to a concept adopted during World War II and lost to history, the colonel had become the modern-day father of the highly successful medical civic action programs that the military services had now fully adopted and deployed globally to build goodwill among the indigent populations.

It was still early as the contingent put the final touches on their treatment site. A few people and a handful of chickens moved about the town's center oblivious to the soldiers clad in camouflage battle dress uniforms who were completing the makeshift medical clinic. Across the road from the MEDCAP site, a small dirt path led up a hill past the rows of old cinder-block homes. Beyond the homes were the town's limits and beyond that, the open countryside.

Bent over from age and wear on his bony frame, an elderly man made his way precariously down the path toward the town center. Clad in dark trousers and a straw-colored shirt with a matching cap somewhat off kilter atop his head, he looked like a peasant from one of the master's paintings from the sixteenth century. His white hair was contiguous with his beard that terminated mid-chest at a point. Holding a makeshift walking stick in his right hand to steady his gait, the man continued cautiously down the path unaware of his assailants who crouched in waiting in the shadows of a side alley. The element of surprise caught the old man off guard. Without warning, like lions springing upon their prey, the four young men lunged savagely at the unsuspecting man, striking him relentlessly with bricks about his head and body. The unprovoked attack sent the elderly man hurtling toward the ground. Helpless to stop the onslaught of repeated blows, the man raised his hands in a feeble attempt to cover his head and fend off the would-be attackers. His efforts were futile as a spray of bright red blood exploded from his head.

"Security!" the colonel shouted, pointing to the path. "Secure that man and his attackers." Spinning around, the security team was equally surprised. Double-timing up the path, three members of the security team ran shouting at the attackers. They took aim while on the move, prepared to fire if necessary.

As the security team closed the distance rapidly, the attackers realized quickly they were no match for the approaching soldiers. Dropping the bricks they held tightly in their hands, they retreated toward the alley they had emerged from. The elderly man lay motionless on the ground in a pool of fresh blood that slowly meandered in streams down the path away from his crumpled body.

"Halt!" shouted one of the soldiers again, pausing this time to put one of the attackers in his sights. His pause was just enough to allow the attacker time to slip away. One soldier bent forward to examine the elderly man for any signs of life while his two fellow soldiers set up a protective perimeter in anticipation of the attackers returning. Blood continued to flow from the man's wounds as he lay motionless. His right eye dangled freely from its socket, attached only by its optic nerve. As the soldier applied a pressure dressing to the man's head, the old man groaned from his semiconscious state.

"Medic!" the soldier yelled, waving his hand. "I need a stretcher! He's still alive!"

Grabbing a stretcher, two corpsmen and a physician made their way rapidly up the path to where the team huddled tending to the old man. Cognizant of the dangers associated with remaining exposed to the attackers and sensing the urgency to tend to the wounds, the team rapidly placed their victim on the stretcher and retreated hastily down the path to where the remainder of the medical team waited to start treatment while the security team remained fully deployed and alert.

"Whatcha got?" the colonel asked as the medical team arrived.

"A crushing head wound, enucleated eye, and multiple lacerations," Captain Aiken replied. "I can't save the eye, but we can wrap it for now in a saline wrap and medevac him out. They can remove it back at the hospital. I'm not sure he'll make it. He's lost a lot of blood. However, for now we can only try to stabilize him and get him out of here."

"Get the ambulance up here," the colonel ordered. "Radio back to the hospital, and let the EOC know we have one inbound civilian in critical condition. We'll need the trauma team in the ER to receive him."

"Got it, sir!" the young lieutenant of the security team said, still somewhat surprised what had occurred in just a few minutes.

Returning his attention to the old man, the colonel asked if he was still conscious.

"He's coming around," the captain said.

"Ask him what happened," the colonel said, speaking to the interpreter they had with them.

"He's Serb," the interpreter replied after speaking to the old man.

"What do you mean by that?" the colonel asked, somewhat irritated with the response.

"His attackers were Albanian. He's Serb," the interpreter repeated. "The only crime is that the old man was a Serb. Here, we kill people just because they are of one ethnicity or another."

"That's insane!" the colonel growled. "Why?"

"For thirteen hundred years we've been doing that. Why? We no longer know why. It's just a way of life." The interpreter sounded sincere.

"That has to stop. If you kill each other off, there will never be a Kosovo." The colonel was stunned.

"That is why you are here," the interpreter said matter-of-factly. "You, the United States, must stop this insanity. The only way is to occupy us for at least two generations, so the old ways will die off and the new ways of democracy will take hold and grow. There is no other way for peace here in Kosovo or anywhere."

The team worked with a sense of urgency to stabilize the old man and prepare him for transport. Realizing there was nothing more they could offer him with their limited supplies, they lifted him into the ambulance. Slamming the doors, the captain gave the door a firm slap like a quarterback's pat on the butt of his center, signaling the driver they were ready to go. The ambulance sped off, carrying the critically injured man to the American hospital where he would not only be safe but would also receive state-of-the-art medical care and possibly have his life saved.

★ 18 ★

The evening command brief was as routine as one could hope for. Death by PowerPoint was taking its toll on those who were not briefing, and their heads bobbed from nodding off from the sheer boredom. With the CG's concluding remarks and guidance, the colonel made his way down the stairs from his briefing desk, working his way through the sea of staffers toward the door. It had been a long day, and he was eager to return to his headquarters to wrap up some reports before heading down to his quarters for the evening to relax with a cold nonalcoholic beer. Approaching the exit, he felt a firm grasp of his arm. Looking back, he saw the chief. "Got a moment?" the chief asked as the two officers made their way from the mainstream of bodies to a quieter spot against one of the walls.

"What's up?" the colonel asked.

"We're putting together a cadre of commanders and staff who are heading out to Fort Lewis to start training up the next task force who'll be replacing us in the spring," the chief said, looking for a reaction from the colonel.

"Sam … that's my home! How can I get on that team?" The colonel was excited thinking of the possibility of actually making it home, albeit briefly, to train his successor but, more importantly, to see his family. "I think it's only fair that if the maneuver group is going to have a representative at the table, the med folks get the same consideration." The colonel was working the equity-for-all angle in hopes of convincing the chief that he needed to be part of that team.

"Steve, the CG and I both thought the same thing. You don't have to convince us. You're on the team," the chief said, breaking into a broad grin. "They're leaving in a week. You'll need to be ready."

"I'm ready now!" the colonel replied enthusiastically, matching the chief's grin. Returning to his headquarters, the colonel developed a happy step in his gait as he crossed the parade field to make preparations for the journey. It was the best Christmas gift he could have hoped for, recognizing that the operative word was *briefly*. Within a week of arriving at Fort Lewis, he would again be enroute back to Kosovo, departing two days before Christmas. Despite the brevity of the visit, the colonel knew it was still worth the trip.

The snow fell lightly as the two helicopters lifted off from the forward operating base with the transition team on board. The team stopped briefly at the Pristina International Airport and boarded a civilian flight bound for Europe and then on to Seattle. As the giant jumbo jet lifted off from the Frankfurt runway, the colonel leaned back in his seat and drifted off to sleep, dreaming of family, friends, and the one he was so in love with half a world away.

Despite the long flight, it felt like only a few hours since the giant Boeing 747 had taken off. The thud of the wheels touching down on the runway made the experiences of Kosovo seem so very distant and jerked the colonel back into the reality of the moment. For now, the colonel was home—no stress, just peace. He glanced out the window. He was at last again in his beloved great Pacific Northwest and, most notably, his home state of Washington. The overcast sky and light drizzle was indeed the signature mark of the gloomy winter days so unique to this region. After guiding the heavy jumbo jet to the Jetway of the terminal, the captain shut down the four powerful Pratt & Whitney engines and concluded with a short message from his cockpit. "Welcome to Seattle. I hope you enjoy your stay or wherever your final destination may be."

Debarking the aircraft and clearing customs took less time than the team had anticipated. Boarding the awaiting vans, they began their journey to Fort Lewis, the largest army installation west of the Mississippi, which was about thirty-five miles south of the airport. An hour later, the team arrived at their temporary home on the base. Consisting of stick-framed construction, the white-painted wood buildings were built in a series of rows. Originally constructed as temporary structures for transient soldiers passing through the post during World War II bound for the war in the Pacific, the buildings had long outlived their lifespan. Yet they had continued to provide headquarters and billeting to soldiers and their units for the past sixty years. Outside the billets, the colonel's wife waited with anticipation. She could not contain herself and embraced him, giving him a long overdue smile and welcome-home kiss as he stepped from the van. Picking up his duffle bag from the back of the van, the colonel tossed it in the backseat of the car and departed for home. At last, he would have the chance to sleep for the first time in ten months in his own bed and enjoy the creature comforts of home.

The next day the colonel made his way toward his counterpart, eager to meet his soon-to-be replacement for the first time and begin the process of putting behind him many of the ugly challenges he had encountered during the deployment. Over the next several days, the team would work diligently with their counterparts exchanging facts, contacts, and information that would be of significance to the incoming task force. It was critical that when the time came, the transition from one task force to the next would be seamless to the operation and transparent to the Kosovars.

"Hi, welcome to the task force!" the colonel said, extending his hand with a warm greeting and friendly smile. "Steve Franklin."

"Hi ... Mike Adams, the medical task force commander, well ... soon to be the medical task force commander," the new incoming commander said with a jovial laugh, shaking the colonel's hand. "I've heard a lot about you and look forward to learning what you have for me," the new colonel said. Turning to a female lieutenant colonel, he raised his hand as if he was holding a cup and said in a condescending tone, "Hey, sweetie, would you mind grabbing me a cup of coffee?"

Glancing at Colonel Franklin and then at her boss, she replied, "Yes, sir," in a less-than-enthusiastic voice.

"She's my chief nurse, Lieutenant Colonel Sarah Martin," the incoming colonel said. "Kinda cute, huh?" He laughed again.

With a concerned look the colonel asked, "You mind telling me what that was all about?" He was clearly not impressed by what he had just witnessed.

"Oh that?" the colonel said, brushing off the seriousness of the situation. "It's nothing. You know, it's all about keeping the boss happy."

"No, I don't know. I don't know much about you or your command, but if you're hoping to achieve success in Kosovo, you're going to have to change that attitude and what you're doing," the colonel replied. "Perceptions can become realities if you're not careful. Keep that up and you'll find yourself relieved from command before you get started." The colonel was firm. "We've got a lot to do and little time to get it done." Time was passing quicker than the colonel would have liked, and he had so much to pass along from basic support operations to NATO operations to local support to the health districts to ... taking care of his soldiers. He was less than impressed with the first encounter with his successor and felt things were not getting off to a good start. There was much to be done in preparation for the arrival of the new task force.

★

Stuffing the last uniform into his duffle, the colonel turned to his wife and sighed, "It's time. I've gotta go." He was solemn.

"It's two days before Christmas. Do you really have to go?" she asked.

"I'm a soldier. I have my orders. In Kosovo … I have my soldiers. I didn't send them home to be with their families on Christmas, so it's only right that I don't take advantage of the situation. I need to be with my soldiers on Christmas," the colonel said softly yet firmly. "You know, it's that 'do as I do, not as I say' sort of thing. A good leader sets the standards and expectations and then lives and leads by example." He wasn't looking for a reply.

"You are a soldier … a good soldier, and no, I don't know," his wife said. "But what I do know is that you also have a family. Your kids are growing up without you every time the army calls you away. The rest of the family often questions where your loyalty lies. They're angry because you can't be with them at their birthdays, holidays, and family vacations because you're taking care of your damn soldiers. Like your soldiers, they need you. I need you … We all need you. Doesn't that matter, or is it that you just don't care?" Her frustration was clear. "You're a colonel, and you do have a choice. One or two days will not make a difference. I'm simply sick and tired of all the reasons why the army has to come first! You need to get your priorities straight, and trucking back to Kosovo on Christmas is not cutting it!"

"It's not that easy," the colonel protested. "It's not the colonel thing that matters here. It's not about what I'd like to do but rather about what I have to do. One or two days does make a difference between doing what's right and what's not." The colonel was not happy with how the dialogue was going, but somehow conversations with his wife always seemed to go the wrong way when it came to doing what was required for the army and what was needed to maintain a balance with family. Neither was truly compatible with one another, but at times like this it didn't seem to really matter. Leaving family was always difficult for one reason or another and served as a constant reminder to how really lonely he felt inside.

Lifting his duffle to his shoulder, he gently kissed his wife. "Merry Christmas ... Please give the kids a hug. I do miss them and the rest of the family ... perhaps more than they will ever know."

"Why don't you tell them yourself?" she protested. "You need to get your priorities straight, because you clearly have them screwed up!"

"You know why." The colonel paused, choosing to ignore the second half of her comments. "The team is waiting." He wasn't good at good-byes, let alone ones that always seemed to end in an argument. "I'll call or write when I get back in theater." Closing the door behind him, he walked the short distance to the awaiting van. Pausing at the van, the colonel pondered momentarily the rhetorical question of why. Why did he love the army life and his soldiers so much? Why could his wife or family not see where his passion was and what he was trying to do for his family? Why could she not be supportive of him? As a kid he had grown up knowing his father felt no ob- ligation to help his sons succeed in life other than raising them until they reached the age of eighteen. After that, they had been on their own. The colonel was of a different belief. His role as a parent was to equip his kids for life. By creating pathways for success for them, they would have the opportunities to achieve a greater level of accomplishment than he ever hoped he could. It was the parents' responsibility to set their children up for that next level of success and then be there to hold them up should they need it. Joining the other members of the team in the van, his stomach ached as he fought back the tears for having to leave his family and home once more.

The return trip took them through all the same airports as the first trip. It was midafternoon when the jumbo jet touched down in Frankfurt and taxied to its assigned gate. Alike any other international arrival, passengers were politely ushered off the aircraft as cleaning crews raced aboard preparing it for the next set of travelers who would occupy it shortly. The terminal was bustling with travelers from all points of the world, some casually walking and others scurrying to make their flights to their next destination. It was an apiary of activity with passengers, vendors, and security, reminding the colonel of an ant colony with every ant going in a different direction yet all with a specific purpose in mind. Dressed in civilian attire, the team blended neatly with the civilians in the terminal and made their way undetected to their next departure gate. The Lufthansa gate agent was pleasant, offering a warm smile as she checked in the men and gave them their seat assignments.

"The flight is delayed," she said, returning their boarding passes to them. "It appears that Pristina is fogged in, but weather reports indicate it should be clearing shortly."

The news didn't surprise the colonel. The city of Pristina sat in a natural bowl surrounded by low-lying hills. The airport itself was a remnant of an abandoned Soviet airfield that had been constructed during their occupation of Kosovo. What made the airfield unique and a standout was one of the runways had been disguised as a road that led to the base of a nearby mountain. Within the mountain, the Soviets had blasted out the rock and constructed a labyrinth of tunnels that led to rooms, anterooms, hangars, and maintenance bays that concealed the squadron of jet fighters stationed there. On a moment's notice, the fighters could taxi from their concealed areas and directly onto an active runway and be airborne within seconds. When the Soviets left, they had stripped the airport of everything that wasn't bolted down, including the tower, weather-monitoring equipment, and radar. When the NATO forces had arrived to secure the region from further bloodshed between the Albanians and Serbs, they had established a makeshift tower adjacent to the original one, but approaches into the airfield were only allowed using visual flight rules (VFR).

"How long of a delay are we looking at?" one of the team members asked.

"About an hour," the gate agent replied.

Taking their seats in the departure lounge, the team waited to board the aircraft. The hour passed quickly, and soon the passengers boarded for their final destination. It had been a long return trip, and the colonel was beginning to feel the effects of jet lag. It was good to be on board and settled in for the final leg of his journey. He was already looking ahead to how he would celebrate Christmas morning with his soldiers and was hoping for a good enough connection to make a call to home.

The Boeing 737 pushed back from the gate and seemed to taxi forever, making its way from one taxiway to another, meandering about the airfield until it came to a stop at the end of the active runway.

"Good afternoon, ladies and gentlemen," the captain said over the public-address system from the cockpit. "We're number one for takeoff. Please sit back and enjoy our short flight to Pristina, Kosovo." Pushing the throttles forward, the twin CFM International 56-3 engines powered up as the captain guided the midrange jet down the center-line of the wide runway. Without pausing, he continued his roll, pushing further forward on the throttles as the jet roared further down the runway and lifted gracefully skyward. The late-afternoon sun hung low in the distance, casting magnificent red and orange rays over the scattered billowing clouds and atmosphere. It was an amazing display of God's hand in nature, painting a brilliant tapestry as the jet continued its climb out over the lush green German countryside.

Flying south, the jetliner followed a course over Austria, the Adriatic Sea, the Czech Republic, and Montenegro. It was dark when the aircraft finally entered the Kosovar airspace and began a gradual descent for Pristina International Airport. Clearing the mountainous Balkan peaks, the pilot circled over Pristina as he requested clearance for landing. Anticipating further dissipation of the fog if given a little more time, the air traffic controller denied his request, noting that he would have his clearance momentarily. It never came.

After more than an hour of circling the airfield, the pilot grew weary of his continued requests and repeated delays. More important was his growing concern for his fuel consumption. Glancing periodically at the gauges in the cockpit, he knew he was rapidly reaching a critical decision point. Aborting the landing at Pristina and returning to Germany was no longer an option as he calculated the diminishing distance his plane could fly. The pilot requested a change of flight plan to continue on to the Skopje airport. The airfield was a short twenty minutes by air to the south, which gave him the comfort zone he was looking for; he believed he would have plenty enough fuel to make it there and land. Two hours by car would pose a minor inconvenience to the passengers, but it was a safety net for the pilot.

The air traffic controller cleared the airliner to continue on to Skopje with a warning to the pilot. "Be advised, Skopje is likewise reporting intermittent fog, contact their tower on 292.2. VFR is in effect."

Acknowledging the tower's directive, the pilot broke from his pattern and continued south to Skopje. The pilot informed the passengers of the change in plans, and it came as no surprise to him that his passengers were tired and less than enthusiastic about the news. While most of them had been eager to deplane in Pristina, all of them knew landing in the fog at the airfield amid the surrounding hills and mountains was perilous at best.

Contacting Skopje tower, the pilot informed the air traffic controller he was inbound. Following air traffic protocol, he requested permission to land. The tower was quick to respond that landing was not an option for the jetliner. The airport had just closed due to fog, and landing was less than one-mile visibility at one hundred feet or, in pilot lingo, the 1:1 required minimum.

Recognizing his situation was quickly becoming more serious by the minute, the pilot began an urgent search for alternative airfields. Although the captain was a seasoned and skilled pilot, he had underestimated the landing conditions and availability of airfields within the Balkan's region that could accommodate his jetliner. Studying his map, he noted farther to the south was Thessalonica in Greece and to the west, Sofia in Bulgaria. Aware his fuel situation had now become a critical factor, the pilot knew remaining calm was his only ally at the moment, and he worked hard to fight back the anxiety that was building within him. Returning his attention to the map, the pilot realized he no longer had the fuel to make either of them safely.

In Pristina, the military buses and escorts stood by at the terminal awaiting the arrival of their team. The flight was now two hours overdue, and concern was growing in the mind of the officer in charge who had come to the airport to pick up the team. Approaching the ticket counter, he politely asked the gate agent working at the counter, "Excuse me, sir. Can you tell me what the status of the flight from Frankfurt is please?"

"Let me check," the young man said in an equally polite tone. "Hmm ... Frankfurt reports the aircraft has arrived in

Pristina, but we both know that cannot be correct," he said nervously, feeling somewhat perplexed.

"What do they mean by that?" the young officer asked, feeling equally confused.

"Let me make a call. Just a minute please," the gate agent said. Lifting the receiver of the phone, he dialed a series of numbers. He paused and listened as the phone rang. He paused again. This time there was a voice on the other end of the line, and he said, "*Hallo. Dies ist Hans. Ich bin das Tor-Anbieters in Pristina. Ihr Bericht sagt der Flug ist angekommen, aber es hat nicht. Können Sie mir sagen, wo das Flugzeug ist bitte? Uh-huh ... Ich verstehe. Vielen Dank. Gute Nacht.*" Hanging-up the phone, the gate agent appeared more confused and concerned. "Uh, sir, I don't know what to say."

"What do you mean by that?" the captain asked.

"Well, um, you see ... they have lost radar contact and communication with the plane." The gate agent was serious. "They are checking again to be certain." Observing the sudden change of expression in the captain's face, the gate agent said, "Let's not get excited yet." The worry on the agent's face was not convincing.

Realizing the situation had changed suddenly from routine to serious, the captain pulled his cell phone from his pocket and dialed the command tactical operations center.

"Sir, this is Captain Sanchez at the Pristina airport. Please notify the chief I have a potential serious incident report to file." The captain hesitated. "The flight from Frankfurt is seriously overdue ... by three hours now. The airline lost radar contact and comms with it shortly after it entered the Kosovo airspace. They're trying to raise the pilot on the radio as we speak. No further info at this time." The captain waited. "Did you copy that?" he asked. Waiting for a reply, the young officer listened intently. "Roger that!" he concluded and returned the cell phone to his pocket.

★

Eighty miles to the south in the skies above the Macedonian capital city of Skopje a different set of crises was evolving as the pilot of the Lufthansa airliner desperately searched for alternative places where he could safely land. He was running low on fuel, and as the minutes ticked by, so did his options. As if by divine intervention, the pilot scanned his map of Macedonia once more praying he might find someplace ... anyplace. Suddenly he noted something he had missed earlier. To the southwest about 106 miles along Lake Ohrid was an airport. It was off the grid for commercial pilots and was not typically serviced by international airlines; thus its tower was closed for the night. But he saw something more important; the runway was five thousand feet long ... long enough to accommodate a 737 jetliner.

Checking his fuel gauge, the pilot did a quick calculation and exclaimed, "Yes!" He had made a command decision.

With a sigh of relief he informed his copilot, "We're going to Ohrid."

"We're going where?" the copilot replied, somewhat surprised.

Tapping the map, he restated his decision. "Ohrid ... we're going to Ohrid! It has a runway that will accommodate our plane. We have no other choice. There is no other option. Ohrid ... we'll just make it by my calculation."

Contacting the Skopje tower, the pilot informed them of his plans. "Please notify the airport I am coming to Ohrid ... I am low on fuel ... Please stand by." Turning the yoke, the pilot guided his Boeing 737 to a new course ... the city of Ohrid.

★ 19 ★

It had been four hours since the airline had lost contact with its passenger jet on a routine flight to Kosovo. Back at the base camp, the TOC had been brought to full alert. The general and chief sat impatiently at their desks in the center, expecting momentarily to receive bad news. Glancing at his watch, the general tried hard not to focus on the worst-case scenario or when he might be forced to notify his higher command headquarters. On board the aircraft were key members of his command and staff, including his operations cell, maneuver commander, and his medical task force commander. In the meantime, the airline's flight operations staff worked frantically to locate the missing jetliner with 125 passengers and their crew. They had confirmed with the air traffic controller in Pristina that the pilot had been in contact with them and had proceeded to Skopje when he could not land due to the fog and the plane was running low on fuel. Based on the most recent information, the airline company was scrambling to form a search area for the missing airliner in the Skopje vicinity presuming it had gone down in that vicinity.

In the meantime, there had been a shift change in the tower with the air traffic controllers at Skopje. Like Pristina, it was another airfield being operated with NATO controllers; the language barrier and poor operating procedures at times contributed to inconsistencies with the quality of entries in their logs. The fact that the Lufthansa jetliner had been in communication with the Skopje tower had somehow been lost in translation.

Committed to making the Ohrid airport, the pilot set a course that would allow no room for errors. He anticipated a straight-in approach with no opportunity for a second chance should he miss the first time. Having never landed in Ohrid, the pilot knew he'd be relying solely on his skills and experience, which for the moment was all he had going in his favor. Checking his flight instruments, he also realized he would be cutting it very close. Banking on instinct, weather conditions, and prayer, the pilot believed he had barely enough fuel to make the runway. Checking and rechecking his calculations, the pilot noted that his numbers did not allow for a fudge factor. His head told him he'd run out of fuel before reaching the runway, but his gut told him otherwise. Throttling back on the engines, he began his descent and requested the flight attendants secure everything in the aircraft in anticipation of a hard landing. Once done with their duties, he instructed them to take their seats and strap in tight. Hoping the Skopje tower had been successful in reaching someone at the Ohrid airport, the pilot was counting on the runway being lit. If not, he knew his chances for a safe landing would diminish significantly or, worse yet, vanish completely. Fear grew increasingly in the pit of his stomach as the odds of him making it safely continued to stack against him.

Breaking through the cloud cover, the copilot strained to see the lights of the runway. He didn't see them. "Damn it!" he said in frustration. "They didn't get our message!" The copilot was exasperated. "What do we do? We can't land without the runway lights! It will be suicide for us to try!"

"Keep looking," the pilot said coolly. "Keep looking." The pilot knew it was now his only hope.

In the distance, the city lights of Ohrid twinkled in the night, serving as a rough ground reference for the pilot, but he needed more. He needed a straight-in approach, no circling this time, knowing there was not enough fuel on board.

The silence in the cockpit was deafening as the two pilots strained to find the airfield.

"There, Captain!" the copilot suddenly cried out. "At one o'clock! I have visibility on the airport!" The excitement and relief in the first officer's voice was enough for the pilot to give a small prayer of thanks. The rotating international green-and-white beacon emanating from atop of the tower was the most welcomed sight the pilot could have ever hoped for, and he was overcome for the moment like a new mother who'd just given birth to her child. Looking short of the beacon, the pilot nervously strained his eyes to make out the clear white lights of the active runway. Ohrid had received the message and was signaling it was there for the troubled airliner.

Checking his gauges again, the pilot reviewed his airspeed, altitude, descent rate, and fuel. The fuel gauge hovered just a hair above empty. It was going to be close ... very close. The pilot was now relying solely on his faith. *Please, God ... we can make this ... please!* he thought.

The automated voice warning alarms called out to the pilot, "Flaps ... flaps ... flaps." The pilot fought hard not to react too soon, pushing the silence button on the alarm. As the jet continued its descent, the copilot continued to call out airspeed, altitude, and distance to the runway for the captain. Aligning the jetliner for a straight-in approach to the runway, the pilot knew he needed to conserve every ounce of fuel he had. Watching his airspeed carefully and altitude of the aircraft, the pilot waited to the very last moment to apply his flaps.

On the ground, a lone fire engine and crew sat idly smoking their cigarettes at the end of the Ohrid runway, awaiting the arrival of the distressed airliner. Expecting the worst, the firemen knew there would be little they could do should a disaster unfold before them. They were ill prepared to fight a fire from a large airliner, and they knew it. It was more for show than for action. The crash tender was antiquated and not equipped to fight a modern-day airplane fire, especially one created by a 737 jetliner. Scanning the heaven, the firemen looked for any signs of the plane.

"There!" exclaimed one of the firemen. "There ..." Making out the landing lights of the incoming aircraft, he pointed to the horizon at the end of the runway.

"Quick! To your stations!" the lead fireman yelled as he took a final drag and flicked his cigarette to the ground. Stepping on the smoldering tip and grinding it with the toe of his boot, he and his crew donned their firefighting hats, mounted their crash tender, and stood by as the landing lights of the jet grew brighter as it approached.

Word had traveled fast throughout the city like a wildfire in a tinder forest. Although it was now late into the night, spectators had crowded the small terminal and along the fence line of the airfield, eager to get a glimpse of the unusually large airliner trying desperately to land at their airport. Hoping for the best, the crowd expected the worst and wanted to be there to witness it as it unfolded before them.

"Three miles!" the copilot said. "Flaps, Captain? We're coming in too fast!" The copilot was anxious. Less experienced than the captain, the first officer was used to taking directions from the aircraft's computer, not giving them or overriding the system when it was necessary.

"Yes, now ... flaps—thirty!" the pilot ordered without changing his airspeed to compensate.

"Stall ... stall ... stall," the voice alarm sounded as the yoke vibrated in the pilot's hand warning him of an impending disaster.

The first officer glanced at the captain, who was unusually

calm amid the chaos that was evolving in the cockpit. Reaching for the throttles, the pilot increased the power to the engines to compensate for his flaps as the aircraft continued its descent.

"Two miles, Captain!" the copilot sounded as the low fuel light illuminated and the voice alarm sounded. The copilot stared again at the master at the controls. Although quiet, a small bead of sweat had broken out on his forehead, revealing the captain's stress as he continued to guide his airliner toward the runway.

"Flaps—forty!" the pilot called out as his plane continued to descend toward the runway lights.

Outside the cockpit windshield, the lights of the runway continued to grow in size and brilliance. The captain was fixated on the glide path, slope, and altitude of his aircraft, relying on his copilot to manage the ancillary duties. The prelanding checklist was no longer prescriptive to the pilot but a guide to ensure he was not forgetting anything of significance. As the aircraft continued its descent, the pilot ordered, "Flaps—sixty!" as he pushed the throttles further forward. The twin CFM International 56-3 engines roared in response, decreasing the rate of descent.

"Captain, the landing gear. Should I put the landing gear down?" the first officer asked.

"Not yet!" the captain replied, pushing the silence button again as the voice alarm for the landing gear sounded.

"One mile!" the copilot announced. "Airspeed is now one hundred and twenty-five knots … Landing gear, Captain?" The first officer was anxious.

"No!" the captain shouted. Tension had reached a crescendo in the cockpit in the final moments of the flight as the jet continued to descend toward the airfield.

"One-half mile, Captain! Landing gear … I need to put the landing gear down!"

"Yes … landing gear now," the captain said in a calm voice,

knowing that by decreasing the drag on his plane, he could squeeze more fuel out of the engines. *God ... I am so close ... so very close. Help me make that runway,* the captain pleaded internally.

Leaning forward, the first officer pulled down on the lever on the dashboard in the cockpit that engaged the lowering of the landing gear. From the underbelly of the aircraft, the heavy nose and rear gear of the aircraft opened and locked into place with a gentle thud.

In the tactical operations center, the general's patience was growing thin. Pacing the floor, he knew that no news was not in this case good news. As a general, he was used to being in control, in charge, and getting the job done. He was now faced with a situation that directly involved his command, yet he was totally helpless to do anything. Walking to the chief's desk, the general asked, "What do you have, Chief?"

"Nothing new to report," the chief replied. "The airline is continuing to track down leads but nothing with the plane yet. I wouldn't get too excited for the moment until we hear more."

"One-quarter mile and closing!" the first officer said. Grasping his seat, the copilot braced himself and prayed, expecting the engines to shut down any moment with the aircraft plummeting earthward.

"We're going to make it," the captain muttered under his breath. "We have to make it."

The copilot was not convinced. At the end of the runway, the pilot could now make out the dim, rotating red light of the lone fire truck and prayed again he would not have need of it tonight.

On the ground, the chatter among the crowd grew as several

pointed to the big event of the night, the airliner closing on the airport.

Clearing the outer fence of the runway, the jet glided earthward. "We did it!" the first officer shouted joyfully as the rear wheels of the jetliner gently kissed the concrete of the runway. "Captain ... we did it!"

Engaging the thrust reverse on the engines, the captain applied the brakes to slow the jetliner as it roared down the runway. Coming to a brief halt at the end of the runway, he sighed a deep breath of relief. He looked to his first officer and for the first time smiled. "Yes ... indeed *we* made it." Executing a sharp turn, the pilot applied power to the engines, guiding the jet from the active runway onto the taxiway and toward the terminal. As the plane came to a halt, the throngs of people cheered wildly, waving their hands, hats, and anything else they had in their hands. Shutting down the twin engines, the pilot whispered to himself, "Thank you, God. You *are* truly great."

Lacking any equipment to support a Boeing 737, the jet sat idle and out of place at the small airport terminal as the flight crew reverted to using its own staircase embedded in the aircraft belly to deplane the passengers. At the bottom of the ramp local police met the passengers and escorted them into a small room in the terminal. It was unusual having foreign travelers arriving at their airport; not knowing what to do with them, the police detained the passengers with their luggage while they awaited further instructions from their superiors.

In the cockpit, the pilot and copilot went through their post-landing checks. "Thank you, Captain," the first officer said to his boss. "You were amazing. I have learned much tonight of what it means to be a true captain."

★ 20 ★

The night of Christmas Eve had slipped away with the passengers of the Lufthansa jetliner stranded in a strange town and ill prepared to manage their situation. It was now twelve thirty in the morning—Christmas morning—and still there was no word on what to do with the passengers who were now uncomfortably crammed in the small room. Standing in the doorway at the front of the terminal, two uniformed local police officers kept a vigilant watch over the passengers. Another officer was lost in deep conversation on the phone with someone who clearly had more authority. The officer on the phone shook his head, and one could tell from a distance that he was not pleased with how the conversation was progressing, but he was not ready to yield his position in the discussion. Motioning to his fellow police officers, the officer finally hung up the phone and gave instructions to the others.

An officer turned to the passengers and said in broken English with a Macedonian accent, "Good evening, ladies and gentlemen. Thank you for your patience. We have no customs people here. We do not expect to have international airlines land here. We do not wish to keep you here." The officer was polite and calm. "If you are a Macedonian, please form line here with your passport. You may leave when you have been cleared by a police officer. Everyone else, please form line on the other side of the room. Please have your passport; we need your information."

Approaching the officer, one of the team members said, "We are from the United States Army. We need to get to Kosovo. Can you tell us how we might do that?"

"I don't know," the officer replied courteously. Pointing to a bus in the parking lot, the officer said, "There is a bus leaving for Skopje in a few minutes. Perhaps you can take that. It can get you that far if you like."

After the group passed through the police inspection line, the team leader of the US contingent gathered the team together to discuss their options, of which there was only one. It didn't take long for them to reach the decision to take the only means of transportation available for the night. From Skopje the team could coordinate transportation to the FOB in the morning and hopefully get there before Christmas day was over.

Reaching into his duffle, the colonel retrieved his cellular phone and turned it on, hopeful that he could get a cell signal. He dialed the number of his operations center, and a young sergeant answered.

"This is the CO, get me the battle captain," the colonel directed.

After a brief silence the battle captain said, "Good morning, sir." He was excited and relieved to hear the colonel's voice. "The main TOC has been fully activated by the general and is expecting to hear the worst. Last report, your flight was overdue, missing, and presumed down somewhere near Skopje. Everyone is frantic at the moment."

"Call the TOC and advise the CG and chief that we have landed in Ohrid, Macedonia." The colonel was equally relieved that he was at last in communication with his TOC. "Let the XO and S-3 know everyone is safe and we're taking a bus to Skopje tonight. We will need transportation from there to the FOB in the morning. We'll contact you again when we arrive there." The colonel paused and added, "Copy?"

"Yes, sir. I copy and will transmit your message to the CG ASAP," the captain said.

"Out here," the colonel said, pushing the end button on his phone. He then turned it off, hoping to conserve what battery life he had left, and returned it to his pants pocket.

The team tossed their duffles in the undercarriage stowage of the bus, boarded, took their seats, and waited for departure. It had been a long night, and they were simply thankful to be once again on their way back home to the FOB and back to their fellow soldiers. Looking out the window, none of them had any idea of what lay ahead next. Pulling away from the curb at the terminal, the bus driver rambled incoherently in his native tongue. For those who could understand, it didn't take long to comprehend the trouble they were about to face in the mountain pass. The driver was drunk. Operating the massive vehicle on the narrow, crowded streets of Ohrid was like handing a mini rocket to a child to launch and guide. Merging into traffic, the bus willfully forced its way onto the road, causing other vehicles to narrowly miss the side of an oncoming car. Weaving his way from side to side as if he were the only vehicle on the road, the driver propelled his bus down the highway that led to the historic Macedonian capital of Skopje, challenging any car in his path. Accelerating purposefully, the driver pushed his bus on the other drivers' bumpers, intimidating them with the sheer mass of his bus and the intensity of his screaming horn. He was a force to be reckoned with, and he knew it, daring anyone to get in his way.

Executing a quick turn onto another road less traveled, the driver soon left the busy city streets and climbed rapidly along the narrow country road leading up into the passes of the jagged Macedonian mountains. The higher the bus climbed, the narrower the road became and the more treacherous the switchbacks were. The driver careened from one curve to the next, always turning just seconds later than he should have. Each time, the tires of the bus dug hard into the gravel rock or asphalt, jerking passengers from one side to the next. As the bus approached the first summit, the passengers caught glimpses of snow alongside the road in the headlights. Where there was snow, there was ice. The colonel watched with concern as the driver weaved along, each time inching closer to the edge. The colonel noted there was no guardrail to prevent them from plummeting down the steep embankment into the ravine that terminated at a sleepy river wandering below. Periodically, an unsuspecting vehicle traveling in the opposite direction found navigating around the weaving bus precarious at best. Each time the passengers thought they were about to experience a head-on collision the bus driver managed to narrowly avoid catastrophe. Approaching the second summit, it became evident to all on board that the driver was in no condition to continue the remainder of the journey without some immediate intervention.

From the back of the bus, a local Macedonian man approached the driver and engaged him in conversation. The longer they spoke, the louder the conversation became. An argument in any language is unmistakable, and there was no doubt the man was speaking on behalf of all the passengers. He was animated yet direct with the driver. Soon a second man joined him and continued the debate with the driver. Pointing to a set of lights up ahead that illuminated a small cluster of buildings, the second passenger motioned to the driver to pull over. It was a gas station with a small café. Turning to the passengers, the first man announced, "We stop here ... briefly. The driver must drink some espresso so he can continue driving ... Okay?" The passengers were relieved as the bus finally came to a halt and the driver shut down the engine.

As the colonel stepped from the bus, a blast of subzero air hit him in the face like the firm fist of a boxer landing a solid blow on his opponent in the ring. It momentarily shocked his system but also encouraged him to move quickly to the café, which was warm and welcoming.

Passengers took up their places at various tables, sipping

warm beverages while engaging in small talk. The two men who had intervened on behalf of their fellow passengers stood on either side of the driver at a small bar conversing while forcing him to drink more miniature cups of the steaming-hot black espresso. Meanwhile, outside one of the team members had successfully made contact with the TOC to update their position and tried to make accommodations for them overnight in Skopje. Returning to the café, he informed the team leader and colonel that the TOC was already working on reservations for the team at a Holiday Inn in Skopje. It was one of the few American-owned hotels in the city and one that they knew would have a measurable standard of upkeep. From there, a bus would pick them up in the morning and deliver them back to the FOB.

The driver left the bar and stopped briefly in the café entryway. In a booming voice he announced he was ready to depart. Leaving the café, he made his way around to the side of the building to relieve the pressure that had built up in his bladder from the shots of espresso. Pulling up firmly on the zipper of his pants, he returned to the bus and started the big diesel engine, letting it idle as he watched his passengers board one by one and take their seats. Closing the door behind the last one, he pushed down on the clutch pedal, disengaged the brake handle, and slipped the gear shift lever into first gear. Letting out the clutch pedal while accelerating, the driver eased the bus back onto the highway and continued the journey down the windy mountain toward his final destination.

It was just short of three in the morning when the bus finally came to a halt in the city center of Skopje on a vacant, dimly lit street. Relieved the trip was over, most of the travelers gathered up their belongings and scattered into the night. Having no sense of where they were in the city, the team leader asked the bus driver if he would mind dropping them off at the hotel for a little extra money. The response was a firm no—not because the driver didn't want to or didn't need the money ... he did, but he was still intoxicated. He had done all he could to make it down the mountain to the final stop without passing out, and he wasn't in any condition to continue. Grabbing their duffles, the team set out in the night cold to find their hotel.

Their search took just under an hour before the familiar yellow-and-green sign appeared in the distance. It was a welcome image guiding them to their temporary accommodations for the night where for at least a few hours they could find some peaceful rest.

As they entered the hotel lobby, the clerk behind the marble-top check-in counter gave them a warm welcome. "Good evening, Americans. We've been expecting you," he said. "I have temporary rooms for each of you tonight ... well, this morning." He laughed briefly at his own mistake. "Is there anything else you need?" he asked as he passed out room keys to each member.

"Do you know of any place that's open at this hour where we might find something to eat?" one member asked. "We're starving!"

"Yes ... we will open our dining room for you." The clerk could tell the men were weary, and a good meal might help them forget at least for a while the ordeal they had just been through. Their last meal had been in Frankfurt before boarding the flight. On board the plane they had received the customary soda pop and peanuts, expecting the flight to be short. While tasty, the snacks had done little to appease their appetites. "Please ... follow me; I will show you." The clerk was eager to assist his new customers.

Finishing his meal, the colonel wiped his mouth with the linen napkin, folded it neatly, and placed it next to his plate. Glancing briefly at his watch, he made a mental note of the time – 5:30am – Christmas morning. He paid his bill and retreated to his room to relax for what was left of the night.

Tossing his duffle next to the desk, he threw himself backward onto the bed, sighing as he glanced up to the ceiling, wondering what he was missing back home. Feeling relieved for the moment, he intended to lie there only briefly as he recounted the ordeal they had just been through, but after he closed his eyes, he drifted off to sleep still fully clothed.

It felt as if only minutes had passed since he'd lain down when the phone on his nightstand rang with the red message light flashing. It was the front-desk clerk. "Good morning, sir. This is your wake-up call." The cheerful voice on the other end was annoying and did little to help welcome the colonel to a new day ... to Christmas morning.

"What time is it?" the colonel asked groggily, trying to wake himself from his sleep.

"It is 11:00 o'clock in the morning," the clerk replied.

"Thank you," the colonel said, fumbling with the receiver as he tried to hang up the phone. He'd been asleep just shy of five hours. Correspondingly, his head and body ached from the short night and long trip that had preceded the ordeal in the bus. Knowing the remainder of the team would be ready and waiting, he quickly showered, shaved, dressed, and headed for the hotel lobby. It was no surprise to any of them that they all looked and felt as if they'd been run over by a truck after a rowdy night in a cheap bar. Fortunately, none of them was working on either the best-dressed or best-appearing award.

"The bus is waiting," one team member reported. "But before we leave, we have time to grab a quick breakfast or coffee."

Making his way to the coffee bar in the lobby, the colonel poured himself a cup of the black brew, adding his usual amount of cream and five teaspoons of sugar to sweeten it and sipped it slowing, savoring the taste and allowing the liquid to slip freely down his throat to his awaiting stomach. Finishing the last drop, he placed the cup next to the carafe, grabbed his duffle bag and headed towards the hotel lobby entrance.

In the drive-through entry of the hotel was an olive-drab army bus. Once boarded, the team departed for their final leg back to their forward operating base. Making its way along the highway, the bus traveled northward on its three-hour trip through the Macedonian and Kosovar countryside. The cold outside was harsh and blew steadily through the crack between the middle seal of the front door.

"Any chance of turning on some heat?" the colonel asked the driver.

"No, sir," the driver replied as he navigated his way along the highway. "We don't have any heat." He wasn't kidding.

"What do you mean we don't have any heat?" the colonel asked. "We're in Kosovo in the dead of winter, and we'll freeze our asses off before we get back to the camp."

"I know," the driver said, holding up his gloved hands momentarily to reinforce his remarks. "It kinda sucks, sir, but it's the only working bus we've got. They wanted to get you guys back to the base as soon as possible, so someone made the command decision to use the bus."

Leaning back in his seat, the colonel put on his winter gloves and readjusted his jacket in a vain attempt to keep as warm as possible. His actions were mostly psychological and did little to add to his comfort or warmth.

Leaving the highway, the driver executed a right turn onto a side road that led to the back gate of the FOB where the bus and its passengers went through the checkpoint and the routine inspection by the security guards. "Welcome home to Kosovo," the colonel muttered under his breath. He had yet to fully accept the idea that the Department of Defense had wasted so much of the taxpayers' money deploying two armies to Kosovo, Iraq, and Afghanistan. The real one served as peacekeepers while the civilian force was paid twice as much to guard the real army. It made no sense but was indicative of bureaucratic insanity at its best. For now, it was beyond his pay grade to try to make any sense of it.

After arriving back at his headquarters, the colonel made his way to his office. Throwing himself in his desk chair, he glanced around his office. It was Christmas. In fact, it was Christmas nearly over. He had missed the one reason why he had returned to Kosovo: to spend Christmas morning with his soldiers. That hadn't happened. Instead, he was now alone, experiencing what was left of the most sacred day in all of Christendom. On the wall next to his desk he had hung a Christmas quilt before he had left for Washington. One of his closest friends back home had hand sewn it with care, and it reminded him of days gone by. More importantly, it reminded him of the season. In his absence, his staff had erected a small artificial Christmas tree with lights. It was a nice touch to the otherwise plain room.

Lost in reflection, he hadn't noticed the chief nurse enter his office. Stopping short of his desk, she said in a cheery voice, "Welcome home! We were all worried sick about you when we learned your plane had vanished."

"It's good to be back," the colonel replied. "I missed all of you, and I too was a bit worried, wondering if we were ever going to land."

"I made you a plate of Christmas dinner from the mess hall," the chief nurse said as she set the plate and utensils on the colonel's desk. "Here, eat this before it gets any colder." Her charisma was contagious, combining her motherly skills with her nursing talents. "Merry Christmas!" she said as she disappeared back through the colonel's office door and down the hall.

Glancing down at his plate, then back to the tapestry, and finally toward the Christmas tree, the colonel whispered to himself, "Merry Christmas." He lifted his fork and downed a bite of mashed potatoes.

★ 21 ★

THE PENTAGON

The general drummed his fingers on the polished conference tabletop as he sat alongside a fellow general of equal rank listening to a third general speaking on the videoconference screen. The three generals were deep in a serious conversation, each mentally processing what the others had said and trying to determine what his next move might be.

"Well, gentlemen," the first general said. "it appears to me we have ourselves a little problem down in Kosovo that needs to be resolved a little sooner than later I'd suspect."

"We've been trying," the general on the video screen replied. "I initially sent my deputy down there. I thought that would be enough, but it wasn't." The general appeared genuinely concerned. "I've sent several IGs down there hoping to persuade them through intimidation. When that didn't work, I followed up with several more unannounced general officer visits. Each one leaned a little harder on the general and colonel, ratcheting up the pressure. I thought the one-on-one interrogations would be enough to break them, but it hasn't fazed them in the least. They really believe in that leading-by-example-and-doing-the-right-thing shit. I think that is truly what this is all about."

"What else have you tried since nothing you're doing

appears to be working?" the first general asked, still drumming his fingers.

"The colonel continues to send us reams of documents that his investigative team has discovered. To date, we've secured them all and simply told him he has insufficient evidence for the army to act. What does concern me is that they have managed to obtain some sensitive and potentially damaging documents that I thought had all been destroyed the last time this issue raised its ugly head," the general on the video screen said. "I'm thinking if we keep telling him he doesn't have a case, then maybe he'll just give up."

"Is it working?" the first general asked.

"Not yet. Perhaps we just need to give it a bit more time."

The second general at the conference table had been quiet throughout the conversation, listening carefully to what his two colleagues were saying. Now, slamming his fist on the table, he said, "Listen! I've heard enough!" It was clear from his tone that he was irritated by how the conversation was going. "They're fucking guardsmen and reservists for God's sake! How hard can it be to control them?"

"Let me remind you, General," the general on the video screen warned. "They *are* soldiers first! We're a total army—one army, one force. My army consists of commands from all three components blended into one army—"

"I don't give a damn about your army and what those assholes in the White House or even our SecDef have to say on that topic!" The second general was clearly fired up. "We're fuckin' in charge here, mister, and you"—the general paused and pointed to the television screen—"had better do something to figure this shit out now and get this mess turned around and under control, or you can start planning your retirement!"

"General," the general on the video screen said. "I know the seriousness of the situation, but I do have to admit, this group of senior officers are some of the best that I have seen in a long time. They are truly professional and among the best the army has to offer, and I don't give a damn about what component they come from!" The general was firm. "I'd take these soldiers anytime, anyplace, anywhere with me over any other command, especially that general, the colonel, and their chief." The general was passionate. "Besides, if it weren't for the fact that their investigation is striking a little too close to home, I think we'd be congratulating them for their effort."

"Have you lost your fuckin' mind?" the second general at the table asked.

"No, sir, but there is one thing you should know."

"What's that?"

"The president recently selected the colonel who's commanding the medical task force for promotion to the general officer rank."

"Fuck ... that's just dandy, isn't it? Does the colonel know that?" the first general at the conference table asked.

"I doubt it," the general on the video screen replied. "It's still close hold."

"Can we stop that promotion or use it to convince the colonel it's not worth his career to continue his quest?" the second general asked.

"Or at least use the threat of withdrawing it?" the first general asked. "That just might be the key to our little problem."

"No, it's out of our hands for the moment. Besides, as I said, the list has not been published as of yet. For now the White House has it; at some point we can regain control of it, but we'll have to be patient," the general on the video screen replied.

"Listen, goddamn it! Don't you two get it?" The second general's anger and panic was ablaze. "There's too much at stake here! Shit! If they're allowed to complete their investigation, too many of our fellow generals could be screwed, not to mention some of our friends in Congress. We have been very successful to date in burying this issue with two other general officers. Why suddenly is it so damned difficult with this one?"

"The last two generals were truly concerned about their careers and future opportunities to advance. These folks truly believe in the army system. They believe that it is their duty to do what is right. The others simply wanted to avoid conflict; thus, we could make it work our way. These guys seem to think duty and honor take precedence over their careers ... It's just fuckin' odd."

The first general at the conference table leaned forward in his chair. "Now understand this and understand it clearly, General." His voice deepened, and his speech slowed as he directed his comments to the general on the video screen. "This is a fragile house of cards. If they succeed in completing this investigation, the ramifications are far reaching. Do you understand? You do not want to know just how far."

"Yes, sir," the general on the video screen replied.

"You've drawn enough attention through your botched-up plan so far. I thought we'd put this matter behind us the last time it reared its ugly head, but apparently I was wrong. This new situation happened on your watch; now fix it, or as I've already said, you can start looking for a new career." The general was exercising his authority to the maximum extent possible. Reaching for the video screen, the general pushed the off toggle and leaned back in his executive chair. "What do you think?" he asked, looking across the table at his associate.

"Joe's a good commander. He's one of our best," the other general replied. "He'll do whatever he needs to do to make it right."

★

KOSOVO

The colonel rose early in preparation for his meeting with the general and the remainder of the commanders and staff. It was to be the first in a series of briefings when the task force would start putting into place the transition plan in preparation for the next rotation of peacekeepers who were due to arrive in the spring. The colonel poured a cup of steaming black coffee from his instant coffeemaker and added in his usual cream and sugar, taking after the British customs inherited from his mother. Sipping the smooth, steamy brew, he sat down briefly at his desk to scan his e-mails before setting out to the general's headquarters conference room. Starting the day with emails was not quite the way the colonel preferred to begin his morning, but he was resigned to the fact that it was simply all in a day's work in Kosovo.

Completing his tasks, the colonel headed to the conference room, where the briefers lined up one by one and presented their portions of the plan. The briefing was performed in the army's grand style of getting the job done, and for now the job was a necessary one. By ten o'clock, the last presenter was wrapping up his presentation as the colonel slugged down his last gulp of coffee. He'd skipped breakfast but was thankful that he'd had at least three or four cups of coffee to help tide him over. He'd make up for it at lunch, which was only two hours away. As a holdover until then, he'd stop by his office to down a few of his favorite snack food—peanut M&M's, which he bought and consumed by the pound. He'd then continue visiting his troops, which was his favorite passion.

Gathering his papers and notebook, the colonel departed the headquarters and leisurely walked across the parade field to the hospital. He made a point to round through each department to greet his staff and ensure each department's needs were being met. Leaving the intensive care unit, the colonel continued down the hall enroute to the physical therapy department. Trailing behind him, the ICU head nurse followed him through the ICU doors.

"Excuse me, sir; do you have a moment?" the young captain asked. His looks were deceiving. Although young in appearance, he was experienced, professional, and committed to the care of his patients.

"Of course," the colonel replied. Turning to face the captain, the colonel suddenly staggered back against the wall. Bracing himself against it, he glanced around. Strangely, the hall was moving around him, but he knew that was impossible. He glanced back at the captain. Something was wrong, but what? The colonel fought hard to apply his clinical knowledge to discern what was happening, but his mind was betraying him.

"Sir, are you okay?" the captain asked as he reached out to steady the colonel.

"I'm fine," he said. He noticed his words were slow and slurred and echoed in his ear. "I think my blood sugar is a little low. I skipped breakfast and was going to eat later."

"Can I help you sit down?" the captain asked, still supporting the colonel. "I can call for some help right now."

"No!" the colonel ordered. "Just get me a cup of coffee, and dump a lot of sugar in it stat. I'll feel better in a minute." Pushing himself harder against the wall, the colonel struggled to maintain his stance and consciousness, but both were slipping beyond his control.

Disappearing through the ICU doors, the captain soon reappeared with cup in hand. "Here, sir, drink this," he said, passing the cup to the colonel.

Taking it, the colonel fought to steady his hands as he took a small sip to ensure he would not burn his lips on the hot liquid. Finding the coffee comfortably warm to the touch, he took a large gulp, waiting for the strange feeling to stop. It didn't. He closed his eyes momentarily, anticipating the symptoms would resolve given a little more time, but that didn't help either. Meanwhile, the captain waited, expecting to resume their conversation. It didn't happen.

The cup slipped freely from the colonel's grasp as he slumped to the floor, unresponsive. Kneeling beside him, the captain checked the colonel's carotid artery on the side of his neck for a pulse. It was shallow and barely palpable. Recognizing the colonel was in serious trouble, the captain burst into the ICU and shouted, "Code blue in the hallway! It's the CO." Returning to the unconscious colonel slumped against the wall, the captain began CPR, hoping the emergency team would arrive in time.

Waking briefly in a fog-like state in response to a tugging on his arm, the colonel watched a nurse working feverishly to establish a peripheral intravenous line as the doctor stood by waiting to order some critical drugs through it. "We're in!" the nurse exclaimed.

Standing to the right of the colonel, the doctor conducted a quick exam of her new patient lying on the gurney. As she barked orders to her team, the colonel interrupted her. Still disoriented, he looked up at the ICU monitor above his head. "Hey, Doc ..." he muttered. "That rhythm strip ... it looks like shit. Don't you think you should be paying more attention to that patient than me? I think I'll be all right now."

"That *is* you!" the doctor replied. "And I'm going to fix it right now." In a split moment, the colonel was no longer in charge. He was now at the mercy of the attractive female captain who stood by his bed giving orders and guiding her team as they worked rapidly to stabilize him. Drifting back into unconsciousness, the colonel lost awareness of the organized chaos occurring around him.

Hours passed since the colonel had been officially admitted to the intensive care unit with an uncontrolled tachyarrhythmia and runs of ventricular tachycardia. Untreated, the abnormal rhythm was lethal. Wakened by the soft, repetitive beeping of the monitor, the colonel scanned the room where he lay. His chest ached from cardioversion. At the end of his bed sat the commanding general.

"Hey, sir, I'm sorry to interrupt your day," the colonel said softly. "You really didn't have to come over. I think I'll be okay as soon as I'm feeling better; I should be back to work by tomorrow or the day after at the latest."

"I can't afford to lose my medical commander," the general said with a smile. "Take all the time you need, but do get better soon." He walked to the top of the bed and patted the colonel on the shoulder. "You're not returning to duty until your doctor says you can … understood?"

"Understood, sir. By the way, I don't want a Red Cross message sent back home. I don't think anyone back there needs to know what's going on out here, if that's okay."

"Let's see for now how things go," the general said before leaving.

After three days in the ICU, the colonel had grown weary of being wakened every three or four hours for blood pressure checks, blood draws, nursing checks, and doctor visits. Being a patient for the first time, he quickly appreciated how awful it was to be on the receiving end of medical care and understood why patients disliked being in the hospital. Hospitals weren't patient centered, as administrators purported, but process driven. They were designed to accommodate the needs of the medical staff and the operational efficiency of the hospital, not the patient. Despite all the testing, there still was no explanation for what had occurred in the hallway three days previously. Tired of the pampering and unwarranted attention, the colonel decided he'd had enough. Climbing out of bed, he slipped into his hospital-issued slippers and donned his hospital robe. Opening the door to his room, he scanned the ICU. A lone nurse sat at the nursing station working her way through the charts and doctor's orders. It was a perfect situation for the colonel.

Entering the station, the colonel took up a position behind the nurse. "Where is my chart?" the colonel asked.

Startled, she jumped. "Oh, uh, sir, what are you doing here?"

"I'm leaving," the colonel said. "Now, where is my chart?"

"Here, uh, it's here," the nurse replied, unsure of what she should or should not be doing.

"Good." The colonel took the chart and began writing on it.

"Uh ... sir, what are you doing?" the nurse asked.

"I'm writing a discharge order," the colonel said without hesitation. "Like I said, I'm leaving."

"Sir, you can't do that. You're a patient." The nurse was gaining her confidence back as an ICU nurse.

"I was a patient ... *Was* being the operative word here," the colonel replied without looking up. "Who is going to override my order?" he asked, somewhat confident.

"Well, I guess the doctor could," the nurse said, unsure if her response was correct.

"Wrong answer, Lieutenant. The captain is on my staff, not me on hers," the colonel said. "Now take this IV out of my arm, or I'll do it myself."

The colonel departed the ICU and carefully made his way undetected from the hospital and down the short hill to his quarters. Picking up his phone, he dialed his operations center.

"Get my driver and long-and-short-rifle security detail, and have them meet me at my quarters ... now!" the colonel ordered. He changed into his uniform and combat gear.

Before stepping from his quarters, the colonel paused in front of the mirror that hung next to the front door. "It's good to be out of hell and back in the saddle. I'm ready to resume my duties," he said, looking at his reflection. "So ordered," he concluded as if he were dialoging with himself. As the vehicle came to a halt in front of his SEA hut, he stepped from the porch and walked around to the open door on the passenger side where the colonel's driver stood saluting. Returning the salute to the sergeant, the colonel took his place in the right front.

"Where are we going?" the driver asked.

"Anywhere," the colonel said.

"Excuse me, sir?" The driver was baffled.

"Let's get out of the camp, and we'll just start driving for now. From there, I'll figure out where we're going," the colonel said. He had grown tired of being confined to the ICU and simply needed to be somewhere, anywhere, other than where he was.

Arriving at the main gate to the camp, the security guard approached the vehicle and held his hand up, not lifting the gate rail that stopped traffic from proceeding.

"Good afternoon, sir," he said in a polite tone. "Are you going somewhere?"

"Yes, I am," the colonel said with some confidence. "Now open the gate."

"I can't do that, sir," the guard said.

"Why can't you do that?" the colonel asked.

"I have orders not to let you pass."

"What the hell are you talking about, son?" The colonel was short with the sentry. "The only one who can give you such orders is the general, and I doubt seriously he would or has done that. He has more important things to attend to."

"Well, sir, there is someone else."

"Like who?" the colonel demanded.

"Sir, the captain …your doctor."

"If you hadn't noticed, the captain works for me. She has no authority to issue such an order," the colonel said, admonishing the guard for what appeared to be an obviously ridiculous statement.

"Well, sir, it looks like the general has given her full authority to act, and she has." The guard stepped away from the vehicle. "You'll need to take it up with her. Have a good day, sir."

The driver turned the car around and returned the colonel to his quarters. The chief nurse, the colonel's physician, and a soldier were standing on his porch.

Approaching the colonel, the chief nurse chastised half seriously and half jovially, "Trying to escape, were you?"

"If I were sick or dying, I would have stuck around. Since I'm neither and hospitals are for sick people, I felt I ought to leave and make room for someone who met one of those criteria."

The nurse knew he couldn't or, more appropriately, *wouldn't* do anything about the situation, so it was safe for her to take the lead in directing his care. "Well, since you wouldn't be a good patient, you're now confined to your quarters by order of the commanding general until the captain says you can leave." The lieutenant colonel was taking great satisfaction in issuing the order to the colonel.

"I'm not dead!" the colonel protested.

"Just to ensure that you comply, the general has authorized a guard be stationed outside your quarters to enforce this directive."

"That's not going to work," the colonel said, pleading his case. "I've got some work to do, and … I still have to eat." He was hoping that alone would be enough for the lieutenant colonel to consider modifying the general's order.

"Well, let's see … you do have a command staff consisting of the XO, deputy commander, and command sergeant major, which will tend to your duties along with me. So that part is taken care of. And for your meals, I'll be bringing those to you each day to ensure that you're eating and staying healthy."

"So, Doc, when will I be cleared to return to work? This restriction to quarters stuff alone is going to kill me," the colonel said.

"Sir, I'm working on that," the captain replied. "I'll have more info for you in the morning."

The first day of confinement had been tolerable, but it was rapidly beginning to wear on the colonel's patience. There was only so much he could do in his ten-by-twelve-foot room. Besides, he was chomping at the bit to be back at his desk and with his troops. The colonel was sitting in his easy chair reading one of his favorite Tom Clancy novels when he was interrupted by a solid series of knocks on the door.

"It's open," the colonel said, looking up briefly from his book.

Opening the door carefully, the chief nurse entered, followed by the doctor. "Good morning, sir. How are you feeling?" the chief nurse asked.

"How should I be feeling?" the colonel retorted. "I'm going stir crazy. Isn't that a diagnosis?" He was feeling sarcastic. "How do you treat that, Doc?" he asked, laying the book facedown on his desk with the pages spread as to not lose his place.

"Sir, you're being medevaced to Germany," the captain said.

"That's horseshit and a total waste of resources! There's nothing wrong with me, so cancel that and get me cleared back to duty," the colonel ordered.

"I've been consulting with the cardiologist in Landstuhl at the army medical center. He's in agreement; you have to go there where they can better determine what happened to you." The captain was clearly operating in her doctor-patient role.

"Like I said before, Captain, that's horseshit! I trust my team here and you as my doctor. I don't need some prissy physician up at the MEDCEN second-guessing what you're doing here. I'm not going," the colonel said with some finality to his comment.

"Too late," the chief nurse said. "The general's already signed your orders. The medevac plane will be here tomorrow morning to pick you up." She handed the colonel the paper containing his orders.

★ 22 ★

ARMY COMMAND, GERMANY

The general listened pensively from behind his polished cherry wood desk as his JAG briefed him on the proposed charges against the general and colonel in Kosovo. The general was clearly uneasy as he shifted occasionally from one position to the next. He kept telling himself it wasn't him. It wasn't anything he'd done to create this mess, but he too was a soldier, and like any soldier, he had his orders. For now, it was his responsibility to clean up the mess that someone else had created.

"Based on what you have shared with me, I think you can charge them with dereliction of duty, conduct unbecoming an officer, failure to comply with a lawful order, and issuance of an unlawful order against a fellow senior officer," the JAG informed the general. "This is pretty serious stuff."

"You're right, Colonel ... it is," the general muttered.

"That should be enough to scare the shit out of them and get them to comply with whatever you're trying to get them to do."

"I hope so. I don't want any of my fingerprints on these proceeding," the general said, strategizing.

"Who do you have in mind to be the convening authority?" The JAG was oblivious to what the general was scheming.

"I don't know yet. We have several of our subordinate commands we can use. I'll review those and get back to you." The general was doing his best to play Pontius Pilate. "But I want to be the final reviewing authority on any potential appeal." The general had set the trap and now had checkmate on whatever moves the general and colonel might have left. There was no turning back. The futures of two senior officers with impeccable careers were being held in the palm of his hand, and he alone now had the power and authority to destroy them with the stroke of his pen. Once the deed was done, the situation would all be over forever, and everyone could go on with their lives. In a sense, it was a simple solution to a rather convoluted problem. The sacrifice of two officers at an isolated outpost was a small price to pay for what was at stake. On the other hand, was he truly protecting a matter of national security or simply covering for his fellow generals and for congressmen who might be less deserving of such protection? What if the colonel and general were right? Either way, it didn't really matter; there was so much at stake. Covering his mouth with one hand, he pinched his lips as he contemplated the consequences of his decision.

PRISTINA INTERNATIONAL AIRPORT, KOSOVO

Standing on the tarmac with his arms crossed, the colonel looked on as the large four-engine air force C-130 cargo plane taxied slowly to where he stood. He'd refused to be transported on a stretcher by ambulance to the airport, which was customary for medevac patients. Coming to a halt, the pilot feathered his engines and shut them down. The forward hatch door lowered, and two female flight nurses emerged, followed by their two medics, one carrying a folded stretcher.

Approaching the colonel, the first nurse saluted. "Good morning, sir. I'm Major Tara Johnson, and this is Captain Abigail Kuper. We're flight nurses here to transport your patient. Where can we find him?" They were typical air force nurses—slim, cute, no sense of what a combat environment was, and sporting tailored uniforms.

"You're looking at him," the colonel replied.

"Excuse me, sir; we're looking for a cardiac patient," the major replied.

"Yep, I'm your cardiac patient."

"Okay then," the nurse said a bit surprised. "We need to get some quick vitals and get you to lie down on the stretcher so we can get you aboard the aircraft."

"How about if we simply walk to the aircraft and you do my vitals on board?" the colonel suggested. "Note: I'm not dead yet."

"Okay, sir, your call … We'll still need to assist you," the nurse said, smiling.

"That works for me," the colonel said, matching her smile.

Taking a hold of his arms on either side, the nurses escorted the colonel to the aircraft. The pilot restarted the engines and guided his plane back to the active runway and lifted off for the short journey back to Frankfurt.

"What's your next stop?" the colonel asked as the nurses took his blood pressure and listened to his heart under the roar of the engines.

"Landstuhl," one of the nurses replied. "You're our only patient today."

"You're kidding me of course?" the colonel asked, somewhat surprised.

"No, sir. We'd been told you had suffered acute runs of v-tach and were in the ICU, so we brought our cardiac nurse and ICU monitoring set along."

"Well, that part is true, but you know … the ICU thing is overrated. I wasn't dying, so I decided I didn't need those services anymore," the colonel said, knowing he hadn't been a very compliant patient.

"Well, sir, you're just going to have to humor us on this trip."

We have a job to do, and for now, you're our patient," she said with a grin.

"What a waste of plane and crew," the colonel muttered as he leaned back into the red vinyl interlaced-cargo-strap bench. Every quarter hour the nurses took great pleasure in checking their patient's vitals, recording them carefully in the medical transfer record and querying him about life in Kosovo. It helped pass the time as the plane made its way smoothly northward.

The whine of small motors running overhead awoke the colonel. Looking up, he could see the movement of exposed cables running along the ceiling as the wing flaps responded to the pilot's controls in the cockpit. The adjustment of the engine speed and the lowering of the landing gear indicated the pilot was now on final approach to the airport. As far as landings went for cargo planes, the touchdown was smooth. After taxiing to the plane's assigned parking on the tarmac, the pilot shut down his engines as the crew chief lowered the rear cargo door on the aircraft. A ground crew awaited the plane along with an ambulance with its red light on top flashing and a black Chevy sedan.

"What's with the ambulance?" the colonel asked, turning to the major.

"It's for you. That's how we were planning to transport you up to Landstuhl," she replied.

"No way in hell am I'm getting in that thing. As I said earlier, I'm not sick or dead."

"I kinda figured you'd say that, so I also requested the sedan. We'll escort you to the hospital. After that, you're on your own."

The colonel's experience at the Landstuhl Regional Medical Center was no more pleasurable than the one he had encountered in Kosovo, with one exception—the customer service had been better in Kosovo. It was not that the staff in Kosovo was any better, although the colonel was biased toward his troops; the issue was Landstuhl had become the main triage center for the combat wounded from the Iraqi, Kosovar, and Afghan theaters. Exacerbating the problem, all the other military hospitals in the region had been closed, leaving the staff at Landstuhl severely understaffed, overwhelmed, and burned out with the sheer numbers of troops being treated.

It had been nearly a week since the colonel had been admitted; his patience as a patient was relentlessly tested and was rapidly wearing thin. He'd undergone every blood test, poking, prodding, imaging, and examination that the chief of cardiology could think of. Still the colonel sat in the hospital wondering what would be next and how he could check himself out and return to his troops. In Kosovo, he'd had the power to do that. In Landstuhl, he had nothing.

The colonel was once again sitting on the edge of the exam table, waiting for the cardiologist. The doctor entered the room and reviewed the test results in the colonel's medical record. He looked serious. Tossing the chart on the small table in the corner, he took up a seat next to it. "The good news is I think I have figured out what happened to you down there in Kosovo," the doctor said.

"I'm glad to hear that," the colonel replied. "Does that mean I can leave now?"

The chief of cardiology retrieved a page from the colonel's chart and held it up. "I was just reading about this the other day but had not seen a case until now. You have a rare condition."

"What is it?" the colonel asked.

"There's a substance in regular coffee not found in any other caffeinated drink. For now, no one really knows what it is, but what I do know is that you've developed an allergy to it. When you drank your coffee that morning, it set off an arrhythmia in your heart."

"That's nonsense!" the colonel blurted out. "First, you do know we're both physicians, so you can level with me. I've been drinking coffee for years without any issue."

"I know. According to this article, patients can drink coffee for many years without ever having an episode; then suddenly they have an unexplained acute event just like the one you had. Some can be mild; others can be lethal. In this case, you were either lucky or had a guardian angel looking out for you. Being at the right place at the right time when you had your event saved your life."

"I doubt that I could have such an allergy." The colonel was in denial.

"I hate to break it to you, but you do. From here on out, I'm recommending that you avoid all caffeinated drinks to prevent having another episode." The doctor was firm. "Since we don't really know what the substance is and any lay person would not understand the complexity of this allergy, I'm having your medical records tagged with an allergy-to-caffeine identifier."

"Well, that truly sucks," the colonel said, feeling somewhat defeated. "What will that do for my career?"

"Nothing … I'm clearing you to return to Kosovo and to a full-duty status. Just avoid regular coffee and you'll be fine. When you return to the states, check in with your cardiologist just to be sure all is well. Good luck and be safe down there."

The return flight to Kosovo stopped briefly in Vienna before continuing on to Pristina. To help pass the time during the layover, the colonel decided to do some exploring around the concourse with the captain who had been assigned as his aide to escort him back to the FOB. Rounding the corner, the colonel spied the familiar green-and-black iconic mermaid of

Starbucks. Surprised to see it in a foreign country, the colonel paused. It had been a while since he had tasted a freshly brewed cup of coffee from the vendor whose headquarters was in his home state.

"C'mon, I'll buy you a cup of real coffee," the colonel said, motioning to the captain.

"Sir, I don't think that is a good idea. I'll pass ... I heard you shouldn't be drinking that stuff."

"Captain, I'm not sure that doc back at Landstuhl really knew what he was talking about. Besides, I'll get a small cup, and if anything happens, well ... you're here. Just start thumping on my chest," the colonel said with a grin.

The colonel bought a cup and sipped slowly on the steaming, fresh java as they returned to the departure gate. The smell alone was intoxicating; the taste exquisite. It felt good to be out of the hospital, heading back to where his command was waiting and once again sipping a good cup of coffee. Taking another sip, he suddenly staggered, fighting to steady himself. He'd consumed less than a third of the cup.

"Are you okay, sir?" the captain asked, reaching to steady the faltering colonel.

"I'm fine. Just help me over to that chair."

Easing the colonel into the boarding-gate lounge chair, the captain took the cup of coffee and tossed it in a trash can. Then he said, "Sir, you're looking pale." The captain checked the colonel's wrist for his pulse. "Your pulse is rapid and somewhat weak. Let me ask for the paramedics," the captain said, growing increasingly concerned.

Grabbing hold of the captain's forearm, the colonel ordered, "No! Just sit here with me, and keep me awake. No matter what happens, you must get me on that plane. Is that clear?" The colonel was adamant.

"Yes, sir but –" The captain looked surprised.

"Listen here! Once I'm on board, I'm sure things will

subside. I didn't drink that much coffee, so it should burn off after a short while. Do you understand?"

"Yes, sir. Got it." The captain replied.

When it was their turn to board, the captain took hold of the colonel and assisted him to the Jetway. Stopping them short of the entry to the gate, the gate agent asked with a concerned look, "Is he okay?"

"Oh, he's fine, ma'am," the captain replied. "He recently got discharged from the hospital and is just feeling a little tired, weak, and you know, flying is not his thing. I was assigned to escort him home. I think once I get him in his seat, he'll be just fine." The captain was working hard to sound convincing.

"Would you like some assistance?"

"Thank you, but no, ma'am. I can manage him. I'm a trained professional," the captain said, unsure of what type of professional he was referring to. After strapping the colonel into his seat, the captain took up the seat next to him. "Are you sure you're okay?"

"I'm sure."

The trip back to Kosovo was uneventful, ending with a smooth landing under clear blue skies at Pristina airport. The colonel retrieved his luggage from baggage claim, and he and his aide crossed the tarmac to the awaiting Black Hawk helicopter, which transported them back to the forward operating base. Like the flight from Vienna, the short flight was also without incident. Back in his quarters, the colonel wasted no time in dropping off his bags and heading up to his headquarters where his staff waited, eager to bring him up to speed as to what had transpired in his absence.

At the conclusion of the brief, the XO approached the colonel and said, "Sir, there is one more issue that arose during your absence, but the CG wants to discuss it with you personally. He's expecting you in his office."

★ 23 ★

The general sat relaxing on his sofa, thumbing through the latest copy of the *Stars and Stripes*. Outside his office the colonel knocked on the doorframe and politely requested permission to enter.

"Welcome back," the general said, motioning the colonel in. "Glad to have you back to duty. We missed you while you were out."

Taking the empty seat next to the general, the colonel said, "It's good to be back. I understand you wanted to see me?"

"Yes," the general replied quickly. "While you were gone, we had an unfortunate incident take place. One of our five-ton trucks accidently hit two nine-year-old girls, killing one and critically injuring another on the main highway to Pristina."

"What were the circumstances?" the colonel asked.

"From what I've been told, they were walking home from school along the lip of the road. As you know, there is no shoulder out there. There was an oncoming bus in the opposite lane and nowhere for the truck to go. They all unfortunately arrived at the same time and same place. He was traveling about sixty miles per hour when he struck the girls." The general became emotional. "One little girl died instantly; the second one was dragged about a hundred feet before the driver could stop."

"What's the condition of the survivor?" the colonel asked.

"I don't know. They took her to the university medical center, but we haven't heard anything since."

"How can I help?" the colonel asked.

"I believe we should be doing something, but I don't know what. I was hoping you might be able to go check on her and offer whatever assistance you think we should be providing," the general said.

The university medical center stood just off the main highway near the center of the city. Like the other hospitals in the region, the term *medical center* was a misnomer. The hospital had been built in the early 1960s during the Russian occupation, and in the past forty years, the hospital had received little to no maintenance. Like the other hospitals in the region, broken windows remained broken, floors and walls remained dirty or unpainted, children were housed with adults, and sterility was virtually nonexistent. Surgical instruments were in poor repair, bandages were rinsed and reused, and medications were limited to adults who could afford to buy them on the black market. It wasn't due to a lack of knowledge or caring but more because of a lack of leadership and resources.

Arriving at the hospital main entrance, the colonel observed that the elevators, like the rest of the facility, were nonfunctional. So he made his way up the concrete service staircase to the fifth floor. Exiting through the fire door, he continued down the dimly lit hallway to the room where the little girl lay. It had been four days since the accident, and the colonel wasn't sure what to expect. He hoped she'd at least been to surgery where she would have been stabilized and her wounds debrided.

When the colonel entered the room, the nurse caring for the girl greeted him. "Good afternoon, Doctor," the nurse said in perfect English with a beautiful smile. Like most women of Kosovo, the nurse was astonishingly radiant with her deep-blue eyes, long blonde hair, and soft milky-white skin. Her natural features made her a shoo-in for a Cover Girl magazine advertisement. "I was told you would be coming. I am sorry the doctor could not be here to greet you himself, but you're just in time to see the wounds for yourself. I'm about to change her dressing."

The girl's father and mother were in the room as well. The colonel shook hands with both of them and said, "I was so sorry to learn about your daughter. I am here on behalf of the American general to see what we can do for her."

"Thank you," the father said in broken English. "Thank you for being here."

Lifting the girl from her bed, the nurse carried her to the spartan treatment room on the opposite side of the dingy hallway. Laying the child on a gurney, the nurse began removing the blood-soaked bandages from the girl's right leg. As she approached the devastated tissue, the bandages took on a darker red hue, adhering more to the shredded tissue below. As the nurse pulled gently on the remaining bandage, the girl could not contain herself any longer; bursting into tears, she let out a chilling scream.

"Stop!" the colonel blurted out in a commanding voice as he reached out to hold the nurse's hand in place. "Did you give her something for pain before starting this?"

"Yes, Doctor, I did," the nurse replied softly.

"What did you give her?" the colonel asked. "It doesn't seem to be working, or it hasn't kicked in yet."

"I gave her a dose of Tylenol."

"You gave her what?" The colonel was stunned. "That's nothing! Certainly it's not enough pain medication to do squat for her! Why didn't you give her something stronger like Demerol?" The colonel was angered by what appeared to be an unconcerned attitude toward the little girl.

"Sir, we don't have any of those medications. This is all we have, and we're lucky to have that," the nurse said. Removing the last of the bandages, the nurse exposed the entire wound.

The damage was significantly greater than anything the colonel could have imagined. If it hadn't been for the fact that he had witnessed battlefield trauma firsthand, he would have without hesitation thrown up at the sight of the injury. The impact of the five-ton truck striking the small nine-year-old girl at sixty miles per hour and dragging her along the asphalt for nearly one hundred feet had inflicted the maximum amount of damage to her without killing her. While she was more fortunate than her cousin, the net result was horrific. A large gash ran along the lateral side of her right hip and extended the length of her femur to the ankle. The flesh and muscles had been torn from her bones. Embedded in the wound were bits of dirt, rock, bone fragments, shredded muscle, and blood vessels. The wound was raw and infected and smelled with early signs of gangrene. The colonel was horrified, knowing the little girl had suffered for four days without any definitive medical treatment or pain medication to help comfort her. Instead, she had lain on her hospital mattress without saying a word.

"Why didn't she go to surgery for the wound debridement?" he asked, trying to regain his composure.

"She is not a priority patient," the nurse answered bluntly as she rinsed the bandages in the corner sink.

"She's not what? It's been four days! Is she on any antibiotics?" The colonel's anger grew; the nurse's responses clearly irritated him. "What are you doing with those bandages?"

"First, she is a child. She does not have a priority status in the operating room." The nurse tried to educate the colonel on the realities of Kosovo, equating it to what it must have been like to live in the early days of the American Wild West. Wringing out the bandages, she continued, "If there is room on the OR schedule after the adults have had their surgeries, then the surgeons will take her. No, she is not on any antibiotics; we don't have any. And … oh yes, I'm washing the bandages because we reuse everything." The nurse was equally irritated with the colonel's lack of understanding of the spartan Kosovar health-care delivery system. "Unlike you Americans where everything is disposable, we don't have any extra bandages. She's lucky we have these. If she didn't need them, then they'd go to someone who did." It was clear that the nurse was equally unhappy that she didn't have anything to use for her patients. Squeezing out the last drop of red-tinged water from the bandages, she began reapplying them to the wound.

Stroking the little girl's forehead and hair, the colonel turned to the parents. "Okay, I've seen enough. I'm truly sorry your daughter has had to suffer like this. I promise you I will bring bandages, pain medication, and antibiotics tomorrow for her." Turning to the nurse, he said, "Please ask the doctor to get her wounds debrided as soon as possible if she is going to have a chance of making it."

The return trip to the camp was somber as the colonel struggled to understand why, in a modern-day world, medicine was still practiced in such a barbaric way. The girl's wounds haunted him throughout the night as he tried to determine how best to ensure she would receive the best care possible. Rising earlier than usual the next morning, the colonel dressed quickly and made his way to the general's office and waited for his boss to arrive.

Entering through his private side entrance, the general caught a glimpse of the colonel waiting in his anteoffice. "Good morning, Steve," the general called out. "C'mon in ... What did you find out in Pristina?" He was anxious to receive an update.

"Sir, her wounds are far more extensive than I could have possibly imagined. She needs debridement of what's left of the tissue, which is rapidly becoming gangrenous. There is a good probability that she will lose her leg or worst case, die. She needs antibiotics, pain meds, and bandages." The colonel expressed the growing compassion he felt for the little girl.

"Can you arrange for her to receive those items?"

"I can, but I have some reservations about doing that."

"What do you think we should do?" the general asked.

"I was originally thinking of taking all the meds and supplies she'd need to the hospital, but thinking it through, I realized she'd never receive them. Most likely those supplies would go to someone else who the hospital staff deemed a higher priority or, even worse, end up on the black market. So instead, I'm contemplating something that is far more on the margin of meeting our rules of engagement with regard to civilians."

"What's that?" The general's interest was piqued. "You're not thinking of breaking the law?"

"Well … not exactly. It boils down to how you choose to interpret it. I'm thinking she needs to be transferred to our hospital. If she has any chance of making it, it will be here, not there." The colonel's had already made the decision in his own mind, but he waited to see how the general would react to his idea.

"You're the medical commander. I trust you'll do whatever is right, not what is necessarily politically correct. Whatever you decide, you have my support." Breaking into a smile, the general said, "You may be the craziest medical commander I ever met, but I do know this: you're the best I've ever seen anywhere in the army. I think it's in part due to the unorthodox background you've had in the army. Too bad there's not more of your kind."

The colonel gathered his ambulance crew and set out for Pristina to retrieve his patient. After arriving at the hospital, he retraced his steps to the little girl's room where the nurse and the girl's parents again greeted him.

Taking a seat at the edge of her bed, the colonel began to lay out his plan. "I am sorry that I did not return today with any medicines or bandages for your daughter." The colonel was emotional.

"Doctor, she has a fever," the nurse pleaded. "We have no more Tylenol to give her."

"I know," the colonel said, "but the more I thought about it, the more I realized that if I brought those supplies here, the chances of her receiving them would not be good."

The girl's mother's heart sank. "I understand," she said. "We were hoping that there might be a small chance you could help." Her tears flowed as she held her daughter, rocking her gently. "I suppose now ... we just wait for ..." The mother could not contain herself knowing that her daughter was now going to die. She was inconsolable.

Leaning forward, the colonel put his hand on her shoulder and paused. "Instead of bringing the supplies to her, I have decided to take her to the supplies, if of course, that is okay with you." he said, gathering his composure.

"What is this you say?" her father asked, looking perplexed.

With the nurse's translation help, the colonel said, "With your permission, I would like to take your daughter to the American hospital. However, it is important for you to know I do not believe we can save her leg, but we may be able to save her life. At least we'll give it our very best, if you're willing to let us try."

Looking up from her handkerchief, the mother said, "You think you can do this thing? You can save her life?" She was desperately clinging to any words of hope the colonel could offer. "We are not allowed to go to this American hospital. Who can make this thing happen?"

"Yes, ma'am, I know you're not allowed. This is an unfortunate and unusual situation. I am the medical commander, and I can make this happen. I also have the American general's support. I do believe we can save her life."

"Yes, please take her now," the father said, moving toward

his daughter to help lift her from her bed. Her body was limp and unresponsive. Her forehead beaded with sweat from the rising fever and spreading disease that was rapidly taking its toll on her fragile body. Her father gently laid her like a rag doll on the stretcher that the medics had laid out next to her bed.

The colonel took one last look at her. "Once you've got her in the ambulance, start an IV of LR," the colonel ordered the medics, referring to Lactated Ringer's solution. "Run it at 100 cc per hour, and dose her with some Tylenol and ibuprofen based on weight or age. Notify the ER of your ETA, and request the surgeon to meet you in the ER. Get any additional orders from the ER staff." The colonel then tapped one of the medics on his shoulder, and the two soldiers lifted her up and began their journey back to the army hospital.

Arriving back at the camp, the colonel wasted no time in making his way to the emergency room. The little girl had captured the attention of the emergency room staff and was receiving their undivided attention. Having cut away the blood-soaked, foul-smelling bandages, Captain Nguyen, the hospital's general surgeon, was already tending to the wounds, along with the emergency room physician and staff. As a young surgeon, he was good at what he'd been trained to do; he was an even better doctor because he'd yet to be tainted by the so-called rules of medicine that for many experienced physicians clouded their ability to be open to new ways of doing medicine better.

"What do you think?" the colonel asked as he took a position alongside the surgeon.

"Well, it's as bad as it gets, to put it mildly. She's got some pretty extensive gangrene, along with a very dirty wound. It hasn't been debrided in five days, and she's septic." The captain's assessment was grim.

"I told her parents that we would do our best but that I

didn't think we could save her leg. I made no promises or guarantee to them. They've accepted the odds," the colonel said. "Do you think we can pull her through?"

"It'll be touch and go, but if it's okay with you, I'd like to be aggressive with antibiotics, rehydrate her, and take her to the OR this afternoon to start debriding the wound." The captain had already formulated his plan on how he'd manage her care. "I'd give her about twenty-four hours before making the decision to amputate her leg. There's not much left to work with, but I'd like to try something I've never done before to see if we can save it ... if you're okay with that, of course. It's not the orthodox way of doing surgery, but I think we have nothing to lose here." The captain paused for a reply. Knowing his commander was equally unorthodox in his command style, he was banking on a favorable decision.

"Tell me more," the colonel said.

"We would do a daily debridement of necrotic tissue to help revitalize the remaining tissue. While most of the muscle has been destroyed, the major blood vessels and nerves are remarkably intact. Each day I can reconstruct what muscle is left and, by harvesting from existing good muscle tissue, reconstruct destroyed muscle. If that process is successful, then I can begin to do some closure by doing a series of skin grafts." The captain was feeling hopeful. "Just in case we're successful, she'll need some extensive rehab therapy."

"I wouldn't worry about rehab; we have a great team here. What's the risk?" The colonel was laser focused on the proposed plan.

"High risk, sir. No question, the odds are stacked against her."

"Would the chief of surgery back home allow you attempt this?" the colonel asked.

"Quite frankly, sir ... no. Because she has about a thirty percent chance or less of keeping her leg and forty to fifty percent chance of surviving, He'd simply have me amputate the leg and get on with closure and rehab."

"If you do nothing other than a simple debridement, then what?"

"I'd most likely in the end amputate her leg, but her chance of survival would improve just over fifty percent." the captain replied.

"If you do what you've proposed, then what?"

"I'd say we have about a thirty percent chance or less of saving the leg, and about the same in her survival. Like I said, it's a huge gamble."

"Well, I know this sounds a bit counter-intuitive, but I suppose it's a good thing we're not back home and don't have your chief of surgery to contend with. For now, all we have is you. Here in Kosovo, if she remained in Pristina, she'd have only a five percent chance of surviving this accident and a zero percent chance of keeping the leg. So I say we should take those odds and see if we can make this long shot work ... don't you agree, Captain?" the colonel said. The colonel had learned much about his colleagues during his short time in medicine. He had observed that physicians in general were either too lazy or too afraid to do what's right—it wasn't that they didn't want to, it was they were simply afraid of the lawyers who couldn't make a real living, so they waited like a bunch of vultures for doctors to screw up. Unlike the rest of their attorney colleagues, they were the bottom-feeders of the legal profession who were encouraged by financial greed. As such, many people who could benefit from the science of medicine remained ill or died because no one is willing to take the risk.

The colonel clearly had his opinions, but he fought hard not to let them overshadow his decision making in doing his job. He knew not all attorneys were the so-called bottom-feeders. There were those who did do good deeds for their clients and did what is right. They were simply not among the ones who did malpractice for plaintiffs."

"Well, I think the OR is calling and you have a patient who is waiting for your skilled hands, Doctor."

The first surgery had taken a little over an hour. Emerging from the operating room, the surgeon jerked his mask from his face. Wiping his forehead with his arm, he said to the colonel, "I don't know about this one. Maybe I was a bit premature in my assessment."

"Remember, you're just the surgeon. Give it your best, and then leave the rest to God to manage," the colonel replied as he left the OR scrub area.

★ 24 ★

Back in the colonel's office, the major waited patiently for the arrival of his CO. It didn't take long before the colonel entered and took a seat opposite the major.

"Hi, Augy, how's everything going at your end?"

"Couldn't be better, sir," the major replied.

"What do you have for me?"

"Sir, while you were gone, I got a boatload of information to share. First, we cannot verify this guy ever went to medical school. No one, not even the medical school he reportedly went to, can confirm he was there. While there was a student with a similar name, the time frame doesn't match our good colonel's record. Second, I now have four generals and two congressmen who signed off authorizing Colonel Weston to draw hundreds of thousands of dollars from the army. Each of them verified it was their signatures on the documents, but none of them admitted ever knowing the colonel or authorizing any payments of those amounts. One congressman has sent you a letter advising you to stand down. One command I spoke to thought the colonel had been thrown out of the army two years ago for fraud. They were stunned to hear he was still in. I have several more documents to support this guy is a fraud, but I think we've stumbled into something even bigger. I have found all his letters of recommendation to be fraudulent. The signatures are real, but somehow he managed to transfer the signatures from real letters to the forgeries. He has a track record of suddenly disappearing from time to time up to weeks at a time and then suddenly reappearing in strange places like Vienna, other places in Europe, and Russia. I've confirmed his credentials are bogus, although the credentials specialist swears she prime sourced those. I personally think she's lying or covering up something, but what … I don't know. Whatever it is, it's really big. I know we have a real case!" The major was energized.

Not wanting to affirm what the general and he already knew, the colonel took a more neutral tact. "We really have nothing until the army says we do." The colonel was trying to keep the major's excitement contained. "Good work, Augy. Keep digging, but for now it's business as usual around the headquarters. I don't want to arouse his suspicions."

The major left, and in the quietness of his office, the colonel contemplated how best to proceed. Leaning forward, he typed out the name of the deputy commander at MEDCOM, paused, and then quickly deleted the line. What he was contemplating was audacious and could jeopardize his relationship with his colleague and, more importantly, his career. He leaned back in his chair and carefully assessed the risk-to-benefit ratio of doing something versus doing nothing. The passing moments were agonizing, but at last he felt doing nothing made him no better than the officers he criticized. He had spent a career telling himself that if he were ever in charge, he'd do things differently. He would do what was right following the basic tenants of being an officer in the United States Army. He had arrived at that moment as fate would have it, and now he had to make the decision to put up or forever shut up. Leaning forward again, he typed out his message.

Dear Bob,

The events that are occurring here in Kosovo have given me great cause to pause and take note of my purpose and mission, not only as the med task force commander, but also as a senior officer serving in the United States Army. It is my hope in writing you that my remarks will not put at risk the relationship that we have forged during my tenure.

When I joined the army over twenty years ago, it was a different time. The spirit of our army was broken, as was our leadership. During the Persian Gulf War, I observed firsthand that soldiers who trained well, fought well. Those who trained poorly, fought poorly. I made a promise to myself as a young lieutenant and later as a major that should I ever find myself in a leadership position, I would do what the army demands of us—lead from the front and by example, even if it disadvantaged me; at all times take care of my soldiers; and always accomplish the mission. As leaders we answer to a higher calling, holding ourselves to a greater level of accountability and standards.

The army values of loyalty, duty, responsibility, selfless service, honesty, integrity, and personal courage define who we as leaders must be and how as soldiers we must live. These values are not empty rhetoric but words to live by in all that we think, do, and say. I embrace those values and live by them. It disheartens me to think we have senior leaders who, as proven by their inaction, do not adhere to those values. For several months now we have been conducting an investigation of an alleged fraudulent officer, yet despite the overwhelming amounts of documented evidence that we have forwarded, the only response I have received from you and the others has been a simple reply of "insufficient evidence." My general and I have endured one IG investigation after another alleging the same seven complaints against us, all of which have no validity, and intimidating interrogations from a string of general officers in response to what we have discovered, reported, and in the end know to be wrong. Each time we have been warned to stand down, disregard the facts, and ignore the truth or face the consequences.

I am tired, discouraged, and, for the most part, ashamed to call myself a senior leader in the United States Army. It embarrasses me to think we represent the same values, the same army, and the same country when the main effort from all of you is to cover up something, whatever that may be, that each of you knows to be wrong. I have repeatedly requested support from your command to address this matter, which to date I have not received. I have continued to receive complaints from several of my department chiefs regarding the care this individual is rendering. In addition, the majority of the patients he is caring for are not getting better, but worse. Yet you have elected to ignore my repeated requests for a person with greater qualifications to conduct a peer review. I have denied colonel Weston's request to remain in theater for an extended tour of duty, only to have my authority challenged by your command. I once again find myself defending my decision with another IG investigation.

I am forwarding to you this correspondence as final plea for assistance from your command with hopes that you will see it fitting to have a change of heart and do what is in the best interest of the army as an institution. The soldiers who serve it and the American people who support it deserve better. I await your reply.

V/R

Steve
STEVE FRANKLIN
COL, MC, FS

Leaning back from his computer, the colonel hesitated again, reconsidering what he was about to do. The die would be cast, and there would be no turning back. His inner voice called out to him, asking if in fact it would be worth it in the end. He fought back the urge to withdraw, feeling compelled to stay true to his beliefs, knowing how tenuous the situation had become. He stretched out his hand and clicked send. He closed his eyes. It was only a matter of time before he would know whether or not his voice had been heard or if it was the end to what had been a great military career. For a moment, he felt a huge burden lifted from his shoulders, but he also realized the feeling would only be transient.

The tires of the glistening white Cessna UC-35A Citation jet gently kissed the Pristina International Airport runway with a light puff of white smoke as the rubber came into contact with the concrete. On board, the jet carried a brigadier general and his aide, both who were new to the Kosovo Theater. Taxing to a halt in front of the makeshift control tower, the pilot shut down the twin engines and lowered the left front passenger door that doubled for a stairway. Stepping from the cabin, the general and his aide crossed the tarmac, and boarded the awaiting Black Hawk UH-60 to continue their journey to the American forward operating base. The general detested being in Kosovo, but found comfort in knowing he would be there only briefly. He had been hand-picked and sent by the commanding general in Europe to do the dirty work, which if successful, would positively impact his potential for future advancement in the army. It didn't really matter that he knew nothing about either the commanding general in Kosovo or his subordinate medical task force commander nor did he care. He had a job to do and for the moment, it was simply a matter of business and nothing more.

In the ICU, the colonel stood quietly alongside the bed of the little girl as she slept. Sitting at her side, her parents looked on with devoted love for their daughter and immense admiration for the medical staff that were working tirelessly to save her life. It had been a week since she had arrived at the American military hospital, and in that brief time she had undergone seven surgeries, each one slightly improving her odds of living ... at least for the moment. Her fever had subsided, and the pain medication had done its job, giving her some reprieve from the excruciating pain that gnawed at her, allowing her for the moment, to forget the horror of the accident.

"Do you think she will be okay?" the father asked. "What about her leg? Are you going to cut it off soon?"

"It's still too early to tell," the colonel replied. "Her fever has broken, and the surgeries seem to be working for the moment. We'll know more in a few days."

Before the colonel could finish his conversation, the S-1 interrupted, "Sir, there is someone who wishes to see you in the conference room."

"Who is it?" the colonel asked.

"I don't know, but he's a general. I've never seen him before." Her lack of details did not surprise the colonel, but it still irritated him, knowing that a member of his staff lacked the proficiency to gather even basic information regarding a distinguished visitor.

Taking his leave, the colonel made his way to the conference room. The general sat patiently as the colonel entered the room. In the corner, the general's aide sat awaiting instructions from his boss.

"Good morning, sir," the colonel said, extending his hand in greeting. "Welcome to Kosovo."

Without reciprocating the greeting, the general said, "Colonel, you have the right to remain silent. You have the right to an attorney. Anything you tell me will be used against you at your courts-martial. Do you understand?" The general concluded in a monotone voice without any expression. Turning to his aide, he motioned for him to leave the room.

Startled by the general's comments, the colonel said, "Sir, do you mind telling me what this is about?"

"Sit down, Colonel," the general ordered. "It's not your place to be asking the questions here. That's my place." He was blunt and direct.

"I have done nothing wrong, so I'm not quite clear as to why we're having this conversation." The colonel was still trying to recover from the general's opening salvo. "Does General Moore know you are here?"

"He'll know when he has a need to know," the general replied. "For now, do you waive your rights, or do you wish to have an attorney present?"

"I've been through several of these interrogations lately. Is this one of the same or something new?"

"Like I said in the beginning, Colonel, it's not your place to be asking any questions. Do I make myself clear?"

"Yes, sir."

"Now, do you waive your rights?"

"I'll waive, since I have nothing to hide."

The general then read the charges against the colonel.

"That's horseshit! These are bogus charges!" the colonel said, raising his voice. "You know these charges have all been concocted, so please, just tell me what you really want from me." He was careful not to cross the line of insubordination with the general or call him an outright liar.

The general began interrogating the colonel. For nearly two hours the general fired questions that made little sense and did not even relate to one another. The string of incoherent questioning led to only one thing: Why wouldn't the colonel simply leave the fraudulent psychiatrist alone to do his own thing? The general recorded the conversation and supplemented his questioning with scribbled notes on his yellow legal notepad.

In return, the colonel fired back each time with his own questions. "As the commander in the field, is it not my responsibility to ensure the competency of my subordinates?" the colonel asked.

"Like I said earlier, it's not your role here to ask the questions." The general was unnerved by the colonel's persistence.

"Why don't you ask me about the investigation or whether or not this guy is a real colonel or doctor or, worse yet, some sort of spy?" The colonel wasn't backing down. "How do you explain his ability to get generals and congressmen to approve unauthorized payments to him in the hundreds of thousands of dollars or how he's able to gain access to top-secret information and attend those briefings without any security clearance? General, you know this whole thing is wrong, so why are you choosing to be a part of something that is bigger than you or me? What are you trying to cover up?"

"That's not for you or me to answer. I have my orders, and I'm carrying them out," the general said tersely. "Keep this up and I'll add more charges to you!" The general had become agitated and was frustrated with himself for allowing the colonel to turn the interrogation around.

"If you're charging me with these phony allegations, I have a right to know ... and now! This whole process is a sham! What are you hiding, General?" the colonel asked.

The general shut off his tape recorder. "You have nothing!" the general said firmly as he slammed his open palm on the table. "You don't have the right to know shit! Don't you get it, mister?" The general's tone matched the redness in his face and the bulging veins in his neck. "You fucked up big time, buddy! You and your fuckin' general had a chance to do the right thing and walk away from this and go back to the holes you crawled out from back home, but no, you assholes had to be a bunch of fuckin' heroes. You think you're part of this army. Well, get this ... you're not! Besides, do you really think this shit you're pulling is going to give you a chance of ever having another command or, better yet, being a general? Huh … Let's see how many fuckin' Indians have ever been a general in this army … Oh, I fuckin' forgot—none! The only way to succeed is to play the fuckin' game! Don't you get it, or are you two just too stupid to figure that out?" The general was losing it, yet he felt so in control. "I reviewed your record. Your advisor at the War College told you that your kind didn't belong there, but did you listen? Fuck no! You just had to go prove some idiotic point that you could do it. You don't stand a fuckin' chance, so you should have stopped while you could have. Better yet, why don't you go back to that shit hole of a reservation where your relatives waste away their days getting drunk or back to some fuckin' minimart? Did you or your general really think you could take on those who are more senior and have more power at their fingertips than you could ever imagine and win? What kind of funny stuff are you guys smokin' out here? As for your general, he's done too! He had it all, but somehow he just had to stand with a loser like you. If you were one of my officers, I would have fired your ass a long time ago. It wouldn't be worth risking my career for some shit like this. So now you and your boss are here, and I'm going to put this mess behind us all once and for all!"

The general's eyes blazed with contempt, but he was on a roll and couldn't contain himself. "Hell, I don't really know what you did, how you did it, or why you did it. I personally don't give a shit and don't want to know. But what I do know is you both have a boatload of senior leaders pretty pissed at you. Now, you have been formally charged, and I have to proceed. So find yourself a fuckin' lawyer, because, buddy, you're going to need one who has God on his side before this is over," the general said, slamming his notebook shut and gathering up his recorder. Stopping at the doorway, he turned back to see the colonel still sitting at the conference table motionless. "I'm told you still have a lot of documents in your possession regarding this situation. Those are considered sensitive items, and as far as I'm concerned, they're not yours to keep. I want every document you have in your possession."

"I don't have them readily available," the colonel said, knowing that once he surrendered the documents, there wouldn't be any evidence remaining to prove the investigation had ever happened. "It will take some time to gather them up and forward them to you."

"You just be sure you get that done ASAP. Consider that an order, colonel," the general said as he departed.

Retreating to his quarters, the colonel sat on the edge of his bed processing the latest turn of events. Weighing his options and reflecting on his passing career in the army, he realized he was quickly running short of options as the increasing weight of the situation continued to crush down on him with no means to stop it. This was truly David versus Goliath, but in this case, "David" had nothing to bring the giant down. The colonel felt profoundly lonely as a cold sweat broke out over him. He clung to the thoughts of the person he loved and missed back home, but in a moment like this, even those thoughts could not hold him up. He sensed in his gut that it might be only a matter of time before those feelings would betray him just as the army he knew and valued had.

Lifting the receiver on his phone, he placed a call stateside. "Good evening, Sarah," he said. "I realize it's late there, and I hate to bother you." The colonel spoke slowly and carefully. "This is Steve. I'm here in Kosovo with a small problem, and I need your help ..." The call lasted just under ten minutes. Hanging up the phone, the colonel sighed and said to himself, "God ... if there ever was a time, I need that miracle from you now."

★

The colonel's crushing stress was reaching its zenith rapidly as he entered the general's conference room. The JAG, chief, and general were already waiting. Motioning to the colonel, the general said, "C'mon in and take a seat." His voice was soft and welcoming as he patted the armrest on the chair. "I see you recently had an unexpected visitor."

"Yes, sir. I wanted to inform you, but the general would not allow it."

"I know. I had a similar visit. How are you doing?" The general appeared tired but caring.

"I'm not sure anymore," the colonel replied, feeling the insurmountable pressure intensifying.

"It looks like they've turned up the heat to maximum. As I told you in the beginning, if you were going to hang, we'd all hang together. Well, it looks like they're preparing the gallows for us now."

"I'm so fuckin' pissed right now I can't see straight!" The chief was keyed up. "This is so wrong. We have a fraud and most likely some sort of criminal in our midst, and they're fuckin' charging you both with bogus crimes? Tell me what's wrong with this picture? Isn't there something we can do?"

Looking to the JAG, the general asked, "What are our options?"

"As I see it, until they start the article thirty-two proceedings to determine if there is sufficient evidence to proceed to a courts-martial, there's really nothing we can do. From the looks of things, I seriously doubt there is a cavalry coming to the rescue either," the JAG replied.

"There has to be something," the colonel insisted. "I'm not sure how much more of this stuff I can take."

"If we had something bigger than what we have so far on this guy, we could possibly submit an appeal to the Fifth Circuit Court of Appeals in Germany." The JAG's remark was calming but not reassuring.

"We've proven he's committed fraud with government funds, has accessed top-secret information without authorization, and has fraudulent credentials along with his medical degree. What more do we need?" The colonel was confused. "What ever happened to *res ipsa loquitur*?"

"We would have more than enough evidence to prosecute if this were a civilian court, but for whatever reason, the army will not accept what we have provided so far. So in order for us to have the ear of an appellate judge, we'll need to have more."

"I don't have anything more!" the colonel blurted out.

"Can't we bump this up to the chief of staff or SecDef or at least someone higher?" the chief asked.

"I think what we need for the moment is for cooler heads to prevail," the general said, trying to de-escalate the situation and lessen the emotions. "I think we need to keep turning over every stone we have until we find something … anything. I suppose we also need to start preparing for a strong defense. While the army doesn't have a case, that's not to say they can't make one up that will stick."

★ 25 ★

The ride from the camp to a smaller FOB in Gnjilane should have taken only a short thirty minutes. In the front seat of the Mitsubishi SUV, the driver focused hard to navigate the road while keeping a watchful eye out for suspicious devices or activities along the roadside. In the right front seat, Lieutenant colonel Bachmeir, commander of the mental health detachment, took in the passing scenery and contemplated what work he had to do when he arrived at the smaller camp. In the backseat Colonel Weston sat with the long rifle guard to his left as if he were Douglas MacArthur out to visit his troops.

Breaking the silence, the colonel said to the guard, "Let me see your rifle."

"Excuse me, sir?" the young sergeant said, taken somewhat by surprise by the odd request. "I'm supposed to keep my weapon to—"

"Give me your weapon," the colonel repeated, a bit more sternly.

Not knowing how to respond, the young soldier passed the colonel his weapon. Taking it, the colonel began examining it, rotating it as if he were inspecting the weapon for serviceability.

"Is it loaded?" the colonel asked as he continued his inspection.

"Yes, sir. That's protocol when we're out on the roads," the sergeant replied.

"When did you last clean it?"

"This morning before we left, sir."

Turning in his seat to view the commotion in the backseat, the lieutenant colonel castigated the colonel. "Sir, with all due respect, the weapon is for security. It belongs to the soldier; please return it to him. It's not a toy."

"I can see that," the colonel said, still gripping the weapon. Pulling back on the charging handle, the colonel chambered a round. Pointing the rifle at the young soldier's chest, he slowly flipped the safety switch off and gently rested his finger on the trigger. The soldier suddenly became pale as he gasped; his eyes opened wide in fear at the gravity of the situation. Realizing the circumstances had rapidly deteriorated, the lieutenant colonel demanded the driver bring the vehicle to a quick halt and demanded that the colonel put the weapon down.

"You want to grab the weapon ... don't you, Colonel?" the senior colonel said with a cynical smile. "Why don't you?" he coaxed Lieutenant colonel. Turning to the soldier, whose emotions had now turned to terror, he said, "Do you feel afraid of me, or do you trust me?" His smile broadened, becoming a devilish grin.

"I ... I ... I ..." The soldier struggled to get words out.

"Well, what is it?" the colonel barked, pushing the barrel closer to the terrified soldier's chest.

"Tru ... tru ... trust ... you, sir," the soldier said. "I trust you! For God's sake ... please!" The soldier was trembling.

Pausing, the colonel slid the switch back to safety and laughed out loud. "You choose wisely," he said, looking directly at the lieutenant colonel. "None of you will breathe a word of this. Is that clear? You do know this could affect your careers, and besides, if you tried to do something foolish, it would only be your word against mine." The colonel was cold and calculating. "Who are they going to believe ... a pathetic sergeant ... a lieutenant colonel ... ha ... or a full colonel? Gentlemen, if you value your careers, I would not risk it if I were you."

"Colonel, you're out of line," the lieutenant colonel snapped. "This incident, along with you locking two of my soldiers in a closet the other day until they would sign letters of recommendation for you, is inexcusable. I don't mind risking my career. You can count on me reporting this to the CO."

"Like I said, I would think twice if I were you. Remember, if you do, your soldiers will only have you to blame if, let's say, an accident were to occur. After all, we are in a war zone. Besides, I'm not sure how much longer your colonel will be commanding. After he is gone, I will be the new commander, and then what?"

Back at his headquarters, the chief poured over the stacks of documents laying on his desk, determined to find a shred of new evidence that the major may have overlooked in his investigation that would be enough to garner the army's attention. He knew he was searching for a needle in a haystack, but he also knew it was worth the effort. Too much was at stake, and he wasn't about to stand by and watch those with more power destroy lives and careers of innocent men just to protect themselves from some huge mistake they had made. He also realized no general or congressman would ever admit to being accessories to a major crime or risk his or her own career. No, it was easier for them to sacrifice a general and colonel that no one knew or cared about in some godforsaken outpost in Kosovo.

Two days had passed since the unfamiliar general had arrived in Kosovo, leaving in his wake a command in mayhem desperately trying to understand the motives and intent of those with greater authority. He had summarily upped the stakes and was effectively tightening the noose about the necks of the general and colonel. He was hoping that, like the two previous senior commands who had foolishly attempted to conduct the same investigation, the general and colonel would feel enough pressure that they would abandon their pursuit before it truly came to a head. His orders were clear: while the two officers were on a collision course with their superiors, he was to ensure there could be only one victor, his bosses.

Perusing his e-mails, the colonel noted one in particular from Colonel Bob James, whom he had written previously. He had not gotten a reply … until now. Reading it, the colonel recognized quickly that the message had not been intended for his eyes.

Gentlemen,

It is apparent we have a colonel in Kosovo who is somewhat disappointed with all of us and is of the belief that we are failing to embrace army values or lead by example by ignoring the present finding of his investigation of what he alleges is a fraudulent colonel and a potential threat to our national security. While it is only his opinion that our conduct is not commensurate with our positions, it is also important to note that he is not satisfied with how we have handled this situation.

I think in order to appease him we might toss him a bone. He requested some time ago a peer review of this colonel. While I seriously doubt we will find anything worth noting, we at least might consider doing this. That way we will prove that he's misguided, and it should be enough for him to back off and forget this nonsensical quest. If we do nothing more, we will at least have some solid ammunition to use against him. Either way I see it, it's a win for us.

Best,
Bob

Filing the note away, the colonel now knew the game plan was to humor him, not to vindicate his position. He savored the experience of being on the offensive for the moment, knowing that whichever way the game played out, he would soon be back on the defensive. He simply needed a new plan … hopefully one that would allow him to turn the tide once again for good, but there was nothing that he hadn't already thought of that would change that. It was fourth down, less than ten yards to go to score in the fourth quarter, with the second hand ticking down the time on the clock. There was no play in the playbook, and the colonel couldn't turn to the coach on the sideline for any help. He was truly looking for the Hail Mary play, but there wasn't one to be found.

Looking down at the framed photograph of his entire family on his desk, he thought how much he wanted to trade his current situation for any chance to be with them all back home partying it up in their usual fashion. Lifting the frame from the desk, he paused as he studied each individual in the picture. How wonderful it must be back in his beloved Washington State and how deep the contrast to here in Kosovo. Drifting off with his thoughts, he envisioned how they had all spent their summer basking in the sun along the pristine shores of Lake Chelan, enjoying the coolness of the fresh mountain runoff water by day and drinking it up in the bars by night. He thought of how they had celebrated holiday after holiday—Labor Day, Thanksgiving, and Christmas—without him and how little they had probably stopped to think of him and troops half a world away. It was a paradise unparalleled by anything he could have imagined in the bowels of Kosovo.

He was cut short in his thoughts by the sharp ring of the phone. Setting down the photo, he picked up the receiver. The general's aide said, "Sir, the general wishes to see you right away."

Knowing it had to be related to the investigation and the

subsequent charges, the colonel gathered the message could not be good news. He grabbed his camouflaged field cap from his desk and made his way to the general's office.

"Steve," the general said, "I need you to do me favor. I have a request from the French senior medical officer in the NATO task force to use your medevac helicopter to transport what appears to be a very sick young woman at the medical center in Pristina to Albania where she is to receive some sort of specialized surgery." He paused.

"What kind of specialized surgery is he referring to? Do we know what her diagnosis is?" the colonel asked.

"I don't know. I figured you medical types can figure that stuff out. Would you mind talking to this guy to see if that is something you can do?"

"Before I commit to that, I'd like to see the girl myself. From past experiences, I've learned to rely on our own judgment and not that of the Kosovar doctors—not because I don't trust them; I just don't think they have an in-depth understanding of which conditions are serious and which ones are not."

"Do what you need to, but keep me posted as to what you decide, so I can keep the NATO commander informed," the general said.

"No problem, sir," the colonel replied. "I'm headed into Pristina now, so I'll stop by and take a look."

Leaving the Forward Operating Base, the colonel's driver, with his passenger and security team made the forty-five minute drive to the city that lay north of their position without incident. The colonel once again stood at the hospital's entry and surveyed the dilapidated condition of the structure and wondered how and where they would start in rebuilding a new health-care delivery system when they received their final independence approval from the European Union. Making his way through the front entrance, he climbed the five stories to the familiar ward where the young woman lay. Somewhat winded by the climb, the colonel asked himself the rhetorical question of when the elevators that had not worked in years might be repaired. It was the second time in two months that he had journeyed to the worn-out facility, and somehow in his gut he knew this could very well be a repeat of the previous venture.

In the dimly lit hallway the French colonel warmly greeted him. "*Bon après-midi, mon ami!*" the French colonel said with a broad smile, extending his hand in a friendly gesture.

"*Bon après-midi, le colonel*," the American colonel replied. "Where is our patient?"

"*Ici*," the colonel replied excitedly, motioning the colonel to a room on his right. "I am so glad you have come to see for yourself." He was enthusiastic ... perhaps a bit too enthusiastic for the colonel's liking. "I have already told the father of the girl you would be here to approve her transfer and all would be well with his girl."

In the room a young woman in her early twenties lay on a mattress on the floor covered by a simple blanket. Like most Kosovar women, she was naturally beautiful. She didn't move or speak as the colonel looked down at her for a glimpse of what could be a potential patient for his medevac crew. Her eyes were sunken and her face expressionless as she looked up. Kneeling next to his daughter, her father looked on, stroking the top of her hand and feeling helpless to make her feel better. His face appeared rugged and tired. It had been a long ordeal for him since his daughter had been admitted. He had slept little as the doctors tended to whatever it was that was ailing her. His hands told a story that he was no professional or businessman. They were rough from years of work in a factory or field. Like most Kosovar men, he was stoic, concealing his feelings behind darkened, weary eyes and tightly drawn lips. Standing behind the father was another man, younger than the father and wearing a long white lab coat. His thick black hair combed neatly back blended well with his suspicious dark-brown eyes and heavy brows. He looked like a stereotypic Russian doctor, except he was Albanian.

"You see, Colonel," the French doctor said, "I need your medevac helicopter to transport this lovely patient to Albania for a lifesaving surgery."

Kneeling next to the young woman, the colonel gave her a friendly smile. She struggled to reciprocate, but beneath her graciousness he could make out the pain she was trying so desperately to conceal.

"What type of surgery?" the colonel asked, not looking back.

"She needs a bowel surgery," the Kosovar doctor said.

"Yes, I'm listening." The colonel glanced upward at the doctor.

"She has had a surgery here for an infection of her large intestine, but we cannot do the second surgery; it is complicated and can only be done in Albania."

"Are you the surgeon?" the colonel asked.

"Yes, I am," the doctor was quick to reply.

"I need to take a quick look at you," the colonel, still smiling, said to the young woman. "May I?"

She nodded slowly. The colonel gently pulled back the blanket and pushed up her blouse to expose her abdomen. He was stunned by what he saw. Glancing up at the French colonel looking over his shoulder, he tried to telepathically communicate, *What the fuck!* Trying not to show his emotions, the colonel studied the woman's stomach carefully while he gathered his thoughts.

Her abdomen was bloated and stretched like a tight leather skin over a drum. It was thin and waxy and glistened with a bright-red hue. On her left side pus and feces oozed freely from where the tissue had begun to break down. The stench was repugnant. When he lightly touched her stomach, the young woman winced from severe pain. Her abdomen was hot, rigid, and unyielding.

Standing, the colonel turned to face the two doctors. "Can either of you explain this mess to me? Have either of you examined this girl recently?" He was again enraged at the lack of care patients received at the hospital.

"No!" the French colonel replied, as if he'd just been scolded by his school nun. The expression on his face had changed suddenly from lighthearted and jovial to utter shock. "I took the doctor at his word." He pointed to the surgeon, who was somewhat surprised by the French colonel's actions.

Turning to look the father straight in the eyes, the American colonel said, "I'm sorry. I am deeply and truly sorry." This was the second time in two months he'd had to speak to a parent of a seriously ill child. In this case, it was a bad news message, and the colonel became choked up. He could see himself in the father's eyes, and in the eyes of the young woman, he could see his own daughter. He dreaded what it must be like to hear what he was about to say. "I cannot take your daughter to Albania."

"No!" the father wailed, holding his hands up in a prayerful motion. "No ... no ... please!" The father could not contain his emotions any longer. Grabbing hold of the colonel's arm, he held on to it firmly, pleading with the colonel. His tears flowed freely. "No ... please!" His voice faltered. "I beg you! I will give you anything I have ... just tell me what you want. Please ... take my daughter to Albania! It *is* her only hope! I'll do anything. Please do not leave her, sir! Oh ... please!" He was inconsolable.

Prying the father's hands free, the colonel simply said quietly, "I cannot take her. She would never make it."

Eyeing the young woman again, he gave her a broken smile and departed the room. He made his way quickly back to the stairs and out of the building. In the empty hallway, he could hear the echo of the father's wailing ... It was gut wrenching.

★ 26 ★

Retracing his steps back down the five flights of stairs and exiting the front door of the hospital, the French colonel and the father followed at a quick pace behind the colonel a short distance behind him, with the Albanian doctor bringing up the rear of the entourage.

"*Mon ami*, you need to reconsider your decision," the French colonel said hopelessly attempting to persuade him. "I promised them you would help!"

Coming to an abrupt halt, the colonel spun around. "Promised?" He glared at the French colonel as he closed the distance between them. "Promised? You son of a bitch! That woman is dying! She's septic, has peritonitis, and God only knows what else!" the colonel shouted as he pointed skyward toward the young woman's room and then at the French colonel. "She has no antibiotics, no pain meds, no IV. Her pain level is easily a ten out of ten or higher! She'd never survive the flight. Never! Who in the hell do you think you are, setting the Americans, my boss, and the NATO command up for an international incident involving a failed mission? Are you out of your fuckin' mind, *mon ami*?" The colonel was shaking and wasn't holding back how he really felt.

As the verbal altercation escalated between the two colonels, the father collapsed along the outside wall of the hospital building to a crumpled position, weeping harder as he repeated his pleas.

"You're right," the surgeon said, finally breaking his silence. "Besides, I will not let her leave here. I have every right to detain her. It was her father's and the French colonel's idea for her to leave, not mine." He had realized the blame was rapidly descending on him, and he was determined not to allow that to happen. "She will not leave here … I will see to it, and that's final."

Overcome by mixed emotions from the encounter, the colonel spent the somber return trip to the camp agonizing over what had just transpired and what he should or should not do. He was angry about being set up by the French colonel, but overriding his resentment was the extremely poor condition of the young woman. It haunted him with an unexplainable intensity. He had never witnessed an extreme case of an abdominal infection in his entire career in medicine. In the world of modern medicine, it was unfathomable. He attempted to rationalize that her situation for now was none of his concern. It was up to her doctors, her parents, and the Kosovar government to determine her fate. After all, he had only been requested to transport her and nothing more. The transport couldn't be done, so his job was done. Despite his attempts to absolve himself of any responsibility for the young woman, his conscience wouldn't let him.

Returning to the general's office, he reported his findings and shared his thoughts on how best to move forward. "Sir, I have decided to deny the request to medevac her to Albania. Her condition is critical, and her body is too fragile to consider her a candidate for transport for such a distance. She'd never make it, and we'd be on the hook for whatever transpired in flight. It's potentially a political hot potato, and I don't think it is wise for us to engage in this mission request." The colonel took a deep breath.

Leaning back in his chair, the general clasped his hands in a prayerful manner. "What do you think we should do?" he asked inquisitively.

"Well, if we follow the established rules of engagement regarding civilian personnel that we're required to operate by, we should simply leave her there and let the situation take care of itself. After all, it's not really our problem," the colonel replied, giving the standard military response. "We received a medevac request. It can't be supported, so we can easily walk away from this one—no harm, no fowl."

"But is it the *right*, moral thing to do?" the general asked.

"No ... I think we both know it's not, but as far as army policy goes, it doesn't really matter. It's out of my hands," the colonel answered matter-of-factly.

"Then what *is* the right thing to do?"

"If it weren't for these rules of engagement that we have to live by, I'd say we bring her here to the FOB and treat her as we'd treat any other patient back home that was in this situation. It's the only chance she has at the moment," the colonel said.

"Then I'll trust that you'll do what's right, and we'll figure out the rest later. Sounds like you've had two moral dilemmas lately. How are you doing with the first one?" the general asked, referring to the little girl.

"She's making slow but steady progress, but I do have to tell you that the MEDCOM general is pretty pissed with me at the moment for allowing the girl to be treated here. Having said that, I believe it was the right thing to do," the colonel said with a smile. "The surgeon mentioned yesterday that it's looking like we might get lucky and save that leg, but it's still tenuous at the moment."

Smiling, the general replied, "Then I suppose you already know what you're going to do."

Electrified by the thought of conducting such an operation, the colonel worked through the night, along with his ops staff, the chief, and the general's staff, as they put together the details of their plan to retrieve the young woman.

It was late in the morning when, clad in full combat gear, the small contingent consisting of the colonel's SUV, three Humvees with a squad of infantrymen, and an ambulance with four medics rolled past the security guards at the main entrance to the camp. Their attire made it clear to anyone who saw them that they were all business. The convoy drove to the medical center, stopping just short of the front entrance in an open gravel parking lot. Dismounting, the soldiers took up their position, forming a secured half ring around the entrance as the colonel, a corporal with an infantry rifleman, and the four medics with a stretcher entered the structure. The team moved quickly up the dark staircase closing in on the room where the young woman whom the colonel had seen the day before lay. The operation appeared formidable and was meant to be. The colonel intended to send a clear message to the surgeon and anyone else who might try to stop the evacuation of the young woman that they would not succeed no matter how tough they thought they were. Two Black Hawk UH-60s—the first was a gunship flying over watch and the second was a medevac aircraft—circled over the hospital, awaiting their cue.

Arriving at the young woman's room, the colonel was again greeted by the French colonel and the patient's doctor, who was surprised to see the return of the American. Without looking up, the young woman's father remained kneeling beside his dying daughter.

"Ah … good morning, *mon* colonel! I did not expect to see you, but I do see you reconsidered." The French colonel grinned broadly. "I knew you Americans would do the right thing. You just needed a little time, yes?"

"Yes, I did," the colonel replied, firing a quick glance at the

Frenchman. Kneeling next to the father, he said in a soft, comforting voice, "Sir, I'm here to take your daughter."

Lifting his head to make eye contact with the colonel while still gripping his daughter's hand firmly, he whispered softly, "Thank you ... thank you ... thank you ..." as tears welled up in his eyes.

The colonel said, "Sir, you need to know that I am not going to take her to Albania."

Recoiling slightly, the man appeared surprised and confused. "What?" he gasped, looking back at his daughter.

"I won't be taking your daughter to Albania. I'm taking her to the American hospital instead."

No sooner had his words escaped his lips than the surgeon moved quickly, positioning himself between the colonel and the girl. He raised his hands as if he were protecting her and puffed his chest slightly as if to exert whatever authority he thought he had as a surgeon. He said sternly, "She's not going anywhere! I am in charge, and she is my patient. You will have to go through me to take her. Now leave!"

"Doctor ..." Anticipating the surgeon's foolishness, the colonel responded calmly, not impressed by the physician's sudden interest in protecting his patient. "I know you are a smart and intelligent man. So as I see it, you have two choices. You can voluntarily remove yourself from in front of me and step away from the patient, or my soldiers here will do it for you the army way." As if on cue, one soldier immediately pulled the charging handle on his M16A2 rifle, chambering one round as the second soldier closed the distance on the doctor.

Standing firm, the surgeon said defiantly, "What are you going to do ... shoot me? Is that your American army way?"

"Only if you took too many stupid pills this morning and you're now stuck on stupid. And only if you want to be some sort of idiotic hero ... which you're not by the way," the colonel replied, "The soldiers have authority to take whatever measures necessary to protect themselves or their patient. As I see it, you're threatening them and their patient." Glancing toward the French colonel, he added, "Do you agree, Colonel?"

Pausing momentarily, the French colonel replied excitedly, "*Absulement!* I too see the surgeon threatening everyone."

Pausing and looking around the room to assess the situation, the surgeon knew it was not worth risking his life to prevent the colonel from removing his patient. He had played his only card and lost. Defeated, he stepped aside.

As the medics lifted the young woman from her bed like a fragile China doll, the colonel said, "Doctor, I'm sure the family has appreciated your care, but your services are no longer required." Laying her gingerly onto the stretcher, the medics took up their assigned positions to carry their delicate patient from the room. As the team approached the staircase, the young woman's father pushed his way towards the colonel.

"Colonel, I must help move my daughter ... please. She is my daughter; I am her father. I must help." After exchanging glances with the medics, the colonel stepped aside and ordered one of the medics to yield his position on one of the litter handles to the father. They made their way down the five flights of stairs. Exiting the hospital, the squad of infantrymen formed a tight perimeter around the stretcher, escorting it toward the parking lot where the medevac helicopter had set down to pick up the young woman. Lifting her into the aircraft, the giant bird took off and returned to the forward operating base, escorted by the gunship. Following the departure of the helos, the security team reassembled in their Humvees and, as they had come, made their way back to their base.

Nearly as soon the young woman arrived, the surgical team transported her to the OR to prep her for surgery. Slipping under the anesthesia, the young woman for the first time in three weeks escaped from the imprisonment of her excruciating pain.

Dressed in his scrubs, Captain Nguyen greeted the colonel at the entry to the surgical suite.

"Have you seen what we got here?" he asked, surprised at what he had discovered on his initial exam of his new patient.

"Yes. It's the worst peritonitis I have ever seen in my life," the colonel replied.

"She needs to be decompressed and cleaned out. I've got a bad feeling about this one, Colonel," the surgeon said.

"Well, let's see what we can do for her." Donning his surgical scrubs, the colonel joined the surgeon in the operating room.

The surgery lasted nearly two and a half hours as the surgeon and colonel labored to salvage what they could of the woman's bowels. The stench of dead and decaying colon and tissue and overt amounts of pus and feces permeated the room, causing the OR staff to gag and even vomit into their sterile masks. The Albanian surgeon had butchered the young woman's abdomen, creating gangrenous flesh and organs. Without antibiotics, the infection had rabidly consumed the cavity, leaving behind little to nothing for the surgeon to work with to save her life. Without medications, she had been left to endure pain that exceeded any normal person's tolerance. At twenty-one, she was just six months shy of graduating law school but now stood little to no chance of ever seeing her dream fulfilled. As the surgeon worked fervently to save what he could, her life, like sand in an hourglass, was slowly slipping away.

With the initial surgery complete, the colonel returned the waiting room where he found the young woman's father sitting quietly by himself staring off into the distance. Taking up an empty chair next to him, he said, "We've done all we can for your daughter. At least with some antibiotics and pain medications, she won't be suffering anymore."

"Thank you for saving my daughter's life," the father said softly, still staring off into the distance.

Sitting in silence, the colonel turned, fixating on the gracious father, he said in a soft tone of voice. "I'm sorry ... We cannot save your daughter."

"I know," the father said without changing his position.

"Do you understand what I just said?" the colonel asked. "She's going to die ... How long from now? I don't know. It depends on how she responds. She has no stomach or bowel, so we have improvised with some tubes." Knowing no human being should have ever suffered like she had, the colonel was heartbroken and tearful.

Taking hold of the colonel's hand, the father turned and looked at him. "Colonel, it is you who does not understand. You see, it doesn't really matter anymore if she lives or if she dies. Today ..." The father was overcome by his emotions. "Today, when I saw those American helicopters come down and lift my daughter up into the sky, it was like watching angels descend from heaven, and I knew ... I knew ..." The father spoke with conviction and resolve as he clenched his fist. "God had sent an angel to look over her. She is in his hands, and I ... am now at peace." The father sighed and took a deep breath. "What I will never forget ... *never forget* as long as I live ... was when no one would come to help her ... to help my little girl ... it was the Americans who came." Grasping the colonel's forearm, the father said, "Don't you see ... it was the Americans! I will *never* forget you or the Americans. Thank you ... thank you ... thank you, my friend." Standing up, he walked slowly through the waiting room door and disappeared outside.

★ 27 ★

A blue haze and the smell of cheap tobacco hung heavily in the district health director's small office. Sitting at the end of his conference table, he listened intently to the dialogue taking place between his underlings, the colonel's operations major, and the colonel with regard to the condition of the health-care delivery system in Kosovo.

The director took a final draw on the remaining butt of his cigarette and leaned forward, extinguishing it amid the pile of discarded cigarette remains in the ashtray in front of him. "Colonel, you must understand, we are doing the best we can with what we have here in Kosovo," he said with a heavy Balkan accent. The director was relatively young for the position he held and had little experience with regard to how to run a health district, yet he had become a quick study. Under the Russian occupation, he, like his fellow health directors, had learned it was better to take orders and not question them. He hadn't considered the idea of thinking for himself and had instead found job security in letting the Soviets think for him. It was the only way he knew, but, more importantly, it had become a method of self-preservation. Inaction had produced a failed system with little collaboration between his colleagues and none with the minister of health.

"Unlike your people in America," the director said, "we do not have the resources to make everything ... how do you say ... like new all the time. We make do with what we have."

"It doesn't have to be new, but it has to be clean and functional," the colonel rebuffed. "It's about taking care of what you have and taking pride in what you do. For example, you have two ambulances outside. Neither has been washed, started, or driven in months. They're dirty, nonfunctional, and unappealing. Your emergency department lacks a working EKG machine, bandages, antiseptics, or monitors, and it too is dirty."

Eyeing the director, the major interjected, "Sir, Kosovo was given thirty-three million euros to spend on health care. Instead, the Kosovo government returned every penny to the European Union because they couldn't find any health-care-related projects to spend it on. That's absurd when you look at the needs of your district and the others. There is so much you could be doing, but you're not." The major was careful not to insult his host.

"This thirty-three million euros you speak of. I knew nothing of it."

"There lies the problem," the colonel said. "There is so much need here, yet none of the leaders speak to each other, and therefore, no one ever knows what is going on. You each operate in your own worlds. Russia is gone, and now you must function as a country, or you will fail."

"Sir, if we could only get everyone on the same page, I believe we could then get a good start on turning this health system around," the major said.

The colonel said, "I am going to host a summit at my hospital for all of the health directors and the minister of health. I want you to see what a hospital can be, and at the same time I want each of you to start talking to one another and begin working together to fix your health-care delivery system."

It took a little over a month for the colonel to pull together the pieces of his plan, send out invitations, and convene the first

Kosovo health summit. The colonel entered the large conference room and took the extra time to greet and acknowledge each of the directors who'd come. They represented all the regions in Kosovo and were from the Serb and Albanian communities. The colonel had deliberately organized the seating in a circle, ensuring no two Serbs or Albanians sat next to each other. It also symbolized that each director was important and equal. Next to each director was a large flip-chart writing pad on an easel with an interpreter to help capture ideas and ensure the Serb and Albanian directors could communicate with one another. The colonel and the minister of health took their places in the circle.

Standing, the colonel said, "Good morning, gentlemen, and welcome to the first ever Kosovo health summit. In my travels around the country, I have seen a great need and opportunity for Kosovo to rebuild its health-care system into a great system. I know you have many needs—from building new hospitals to training medical staff on preventing the spread of disease in hospitals to replacing obsolete or nonfunctioning medical equipment. Before we can do those things, we must first decide what the top priorities are for each district, determine how much money these things require, and then collectively identify the top ten priorities for Kosovo. Once we have done that, each of you will present to the minister, who will take your ideas and apply money to fund them. He has requested the monies be returned from the European Union, so we should have an opportunity to get a good start."

The colonel was excited to begin laying a foundation from which future health leaders would build upon. During his tenure, he had come to realize Kosovo was a diamond in the rough, just waiting to be reshaped into a new democracy. While politicians haggled over the political structure and function, the health-care infrastructure lay decaying and ignored. He believed in the people of this historic region and in their dream of becoming the newest nation in the Western world. As the senior

American medical commander, he knew he had the support of the general, the chief, the resources, and the chance to make a difference, and he was determined to achieve success on his first meeting with the directors and the minister.

"To ensure we are not interrupted in our work," the colonel said, "I have ordered that the doors be closed and locked until we are finished. The security team will not let anyone in or out of this room during our meeting. I have also provided plenty of espresso and snacks to eat during our work, so now we can begin. It is important that you all begin talking to each other very soon." The colonel had intentionally provided the espresso coffee as a ruse. Knowing it to be a potent diuretic, he was counting on the black brew to do its duty and serve as a compelling motivator to the unsuspecting health directors.

The colonel took his place again next to the minister, and the two looked on as each director sat in silence. The directors stared at one another, sipping their espresso and eating the provided muffins and cakes. Ten minutes passed without any dialogue. The silence was deafening. Realizing his strategy was not playing out the way he had anticipated, the colonel said, "Gentlemen, the minister and I have all day to be here with you. So it is important that each of you starts talking to your colleagues and work on the problem."

"But, Colonel," one director said, "I must use the bathroom soon."

"No bathroom breaks. No one is leaving the room until our task is done." It was imperative that the directors begin talking to one another. It felt like a group of first graders on their first day of school. Maybe the group was too shy, or maybe no one wanted to be first. The colonel was betting on the latter to be true.

"I do not understand this thing you want," another director finally said. "My colleague here is Serb. I am Albanian. We do not speak to each other."

"Exactly!" the colonel exclaimed as he shot from his seat. "That is the problem with each of you. You want to be a country. You want to provide health care to Kosovars. Yet you as leaders will not talk to each other. Health care knows *no* ethnicity. You, my friends, have a responsibility to take care of everyone! Not just Serbs ... not just Albanians ... but everyone!" The colonel was animated. "Today—*now*—you are the future of Kosovo. You will start health care moving in a new direction, not just for your people but for all Kosovars!"

"Colonel, we are used to being told what we should do," another director commented.

"Well, that may have been in the past. Today, you will need to start thinking for yourself. I have been to each of your hospitals and shown you how to improve your facilities. If that is important to you, then start talking to each other and sharing what you have learned and what your needs are. There are interpreters to help you. Use them." The colonel was resolved to the success of the summit and could not have been more pleased to deny bathroom breaks to the men gathered in the room as a means to ensure the fulfillment of his plan. As the espresso flowed, it didn't take long for them to comprehend that the sooner they finished their task, the sooner they could relieve themselves of the growing pressure in their bladders as the strong liquid accumulated. Nature was pure magic as a motivator, the colonel thought as he took his place once again beside the minister.

It took the directors just over an hour to identify their most important issues, select the top three priorities for their districts, and then compile a list of the top ten priorities for Kosovo on the white flip charts. Completing their task, the directors presented their conclusions in quick succession to the minister, sparking some brief yet lively interaction between the minister and the group. In terms of a celebrated chapter in the new Kosovo, it was a historic first of its kind for the health leaders. The colonel was content, knowing he was no longer needed to continue the effort. The wheels of progress had been set in motion, and the first hammer and chisel had been applied to remove the barriers and carve out a new start between the Serb and Albanian health-care leadership.

"I am pleased with this meeting today," the minister said. "We start now rebuilding the Kosovo health-care system for all Kosovars. We thank the Americans for helping us begin this process." The minister was cautious yet gracious with his remarks.

"We are not used to this process, but I like it," a director said.

"Back in America, we use this process routinely to conduct business. Collaboration with our peers is how we get things done," the colonel replied. "For you, the minister, and everyone here, this is not the end but the beginning. Next year, we will all meet again to see what each of you has done with your priorities and the money the minister will give you. While I cannot be with you in person, I will be in spirit. My successor will be here in my place. We will again set new priorities. We will build on the past and plan for the future." The colonel took comfort in knowing they had now achieved what no one had been able to do.

"We use the bathroom now?" one director asked, squirming in his seat.

"Yes!" the colonel replied. "Yes, we can use the bathrooms now."

★ 28 ★

The drive to Kacanik was peaceful as the convoy of army trucks and Humvees meandered along the narrow, southwesterly, winding country road through the valley of scattered farms shielded by the steep, rugged, snowcapped mountain peaks on either side. Entering the outskirts of the small town, the procession moved slowly past a heavily fortified checkpoint that served not only as an outpost for the task force but also as security for those who lived within the town's limits. The township was a known enclave for Serb rebels who without provocation would strike impertinently against the NATO forces and innocent Albanian civilians. A recent reminder of their ruthlessness still smoldered at the far end of the village where two rivers joined, making their way down from their headwaters high up in the surrounding mountains to form a single ribbon of water. At the wide portion of the fork in the river a small group of Albanians had built their homes. Each home faced one of the rivers, and the community formed a football shape with each home's backyard contributing to a common area that all the residents shared. In the middle of the night, the Serb rebels had attacked the small neighborhood, gathering up and separating the families. The women and girls had been sequestered in the central portion of the backyard. Once gathered, the rebels had taken their time executing them one by one until their bodies lay in a heap in the center of the lawn. Then they tied the men and boys to chairs on the first floor in each of their homes and lit a single candle in each attic. Before departing, they had turned on the gas in the kitchen stoves. It had taken only a few minutes for the invisible fumes to make it to each attic, but it was long enough for the rebels to escape. Once the gas reached the high point of the homes, the lone candle ignited in a massive fiery explosion, killing all the remaining Albanians.

In its heyday, Kacanik had served as a Russian ski resort. It was beautiful, majestic, and peaceful, tucked into a natural bowl of the mountain. Remnants of the primitive ski lifts and lone hotel wasted on the slope above the town. The right entrepreneur could probably see an opportunity to rehab the site and turn it once more into a thriving tourist attraction. Most village inhabitants hoped that the occupying NATO forces would be such an investor to host troops and possibly visitors from Europe, bringing money and business to the struggling town. It was, at best, a wishful prayer.

Passing through the village along the main road, the contingent took note of the people who had gathered along the sidewalk like spectators watching a parade. While most of the inhabitants welcomed the presence of the troops, not all shared in such sentiments; some viewed the troops as no more than another occupying force in their territory or another reason to provoke the Serb rebels. Little did they realize it was a force not sent to occupy but to provide healing, hope, and goodwill to an otherwise demoralized community.

Aware of the convoy of troops and medical staff passing through their town, a moderate-size crowd had gathered near the town center to watch. Observing the onlookers, the colonel decided to make a brief stop and engage the crowd. Exiting his vehicle, he hesitated, surveying the people to determine whether or not they posed a threat. Satisfied that the benefit outweighed the risk, he decided to proceed. Before the colonel entered the thick of the crowd, the lieutenant responsible for security expressed his concerns, saying, "Sir, I'd advise against you going into that crowd. You have no idea whether they are friend or foe."

"I understand," the colonel said. "However, are we not here to win their hearts and minds? If we hide from them, how will we ever accomplish that task? It's important for the people to know we do care about them, their town, and their future."

"I'm not sure I can guarantee your safety if you do that," the lieutenant said.

"I know," the colonel replied. "Just give it your best. I won't hold you responsible."

"Sir, we'll need to provide a 360-degree perimeter around you. Please maintain a three-sixty situational awareness and a visual on us at all times. If something goes wrong, signal." The lieutenant was clearly uncomfortable with the colonel's decision to mingle with the locals but knew it was the colonel's call in the end.

"Will do. The sooner we get this done, the sooner we can be back on the road to our destination."

As the colonel reached the crowd, the people began cheering and waving. The colonel returned the gesture. They were friendly and welcoming to the Americans, which reassured the colonel that he had made a good judgment call. Entering the small gathering, he planned to mix with only a few as he smiled and shook hands. Within minutes the security team had blended with the crowd, eyeing every individual as if everyone was suspect. Suddenly, the colonel was face-to-face with a man in his thirties. He wore a black, short-sleeved shirt that was not tucked in his denim blue jeans and a pair of white tennis shoes, giving him a casual appearance. His dark eyes; short, black, wavy hair; and neatly trimmed five o'clock shadow gave him a buff model look, but unbeknownst to the colonel, he had stumbled upon one of the most wanted Serb terrorists in Kosovo.

Extending his hand in a friendly gesture, the colonel smiled, greeted the man, and stepped to the left. The man matched his move.

"Excuse me," the colonel said politely, stepping again to the left. Again the man blocked the colonel.

"I'm sorry," Surprised by the encounter, the colonel stood fast, quickly assessing his options. His security team was too dispersed in the noisy crowd to call for help. Besides, whatever weapon the man had, it would be too late for one of them to come to his aid should he manage to get their attention. He thought about drawing his weapon, but there were too many civilians around him. Was it a gun or a knife the man had, or was he a suicide bomber? The colonel wasn't willing to risk it to find out.

"You've made your point, so what do you want to do?" the colonel asked staring the man down.

The man said nothing at first. "Nothing today … I know you have come to help my people. But next time, I *will* kill you." Turning, the man slipped back into the crowd and disappeared.

Moving quickly toward the lieutenant, the colonel informed him the visit was terminated. It was time to return to the vehicles and continue on the journey.

Beyond the town of Kacanik, the road narrowed to a single dirt lane as it rose along the ledge of the mountain. In some places the dirt changed to mud where streams of mountain run-off crossed the road, cascading over the edge and forming small walls of water and streams below. It was treacherous at best for any driver traveling down the mountain to navigate past the larger trucks making their way up. Yet with patience and skill by both drivers, the vehicles managed to make a safe passage. It took just over an hour on the earthen road before the trucks pulled into a wide clearing and came to a halt. Beyond the wooden guardrail that marked the road's termination, a path continued farther up the mountain, leading to a smaller village that had little to no employment, running water, electricity, or food. The meager hamlet's inhabitants were among the poorest of the poor, having next to nothing to protect themselves from the elements. Their sustenance was what they grew, cut, and stored during the warmer months. They derived some income from what they could sell from crops or scrap wood.

The straw-colored grass and low-lying green vegetation had vanished, buried beneath the mounds of snow that covered the ground. Leaping from the lead vehicle, the team leader signaled to the rest of the soldiers of the contingent to do the same. With frost forming from his exhaled breath, he announced with a beaming grin, "This is the end of the line ... at least for the trucks." He turned to the colonel, looking for further guidance. "Sir, how do you wish to proceed?"

"How far are we from the village?" the colonel asked.

"About two clicks up that path," the lieutenant replied, pointing to the path beyond the barricade.

"Well, son, I suggest we grab our gear and head up that path. I don't think these supplies are going to get there on their own," the colonel replied in a somewhat-sarcastic tone.

Appearing more like a band of climbers and Sherpas on an expedition with their large and small boxes and bags of supplies, the team ascended the path through the snow. Arriving on the outskirts of the village, the team was greeted by a small cluster of children clad in ragged T-shirts playing outdoors in the snow and freezing temperature. The children had no toys or jackets. From a Westerner's perspective it appeared cruel and abusive, yet the children were happy making do with what they had. Making their way further into the village, the Americans were welcomed by some older members who escorted them into one of the stone buildings. It was dark and dank inside, lighted poorly by some scattered candles and heated by a single wood-burning stove that sat in the center of the rather large room. It was spartan at best, yet the villagers complained little.

Without losing a moment of time, the team went about their

business unpacking the boxes they had hauled up the mountain. Each one contained something of importance for the villagers, including medical supplies, clothing for infants to adults, and ... toys—all donated from people living half a world away in Ohio and from close friends of the colonel's living in Michigan. The donors had assembled the care boxes in hopes of touching the life of someone whom they would never know but who had been affected by this senseless and pathetic war. The team had scored big with this village as young and old gathered coats, shoes, shirts, pants, and dresses for various family members. After distributing all that they had brought, the team then turned their attention to tending to the villagers' medical needs. It was good for the people being treated but better for the members of the team who treated them. Surveying the crowded room, the colonel took note of the lives they were impacting and the misery they were alleviating, even if it were only temporary.

At the entrance to the room, a small, barefoot boy stood looking in on the bustling activity. His small build, round head, and dark eyes made him appear like an orphaned character in Charles Dickens's *Oliver Twist*. Like the other kids, he too was clad in a dirty, ragged T-shirt and worn-out pants. Reaching into a box, the colonel retrieved a coat, a pair of shoes, pants, and a bag of Lego toy men. It was the perfect opportunity. Approaching the boy, he knelt down before the lad and placed the items in his arms. Pondering the situation, he wished the left-wing politicos back home who saw the military as a global killing machine could truly understand that there was so much more to serving in the army, fighting a war, and winning hearts and minds. If they could only see what they were doing here to help heal broken hearts and mend the deep scars, would they be so quick to criticize or condemn the military? But then again, did such people even care? Shaking his head as if in response to his own question, the colonel returned to his work.

Putting the final touches of medicine and clean bandages on

an elderly man's arm, the colonel noted their work was done. His hands burned from the bitter cold, but it wasn't his place to complain. His discomfort was only temporary. He surveyed the room filled with villagers who had huddled inside to either seek treatment or find shelter from the light flakes that fell outside. Their suffering would continue long after the team had departed.

Trudging through the snow, the team made their way back toward the path that led down to their vehicles. In the open field, the older children, wearing their new shoes, played happily with their new soccer balls. Rounding the corner of the stone building, the colonel paused to observe the small boy that he had encountered earlier wearing his "new" clothes and jacket playing alone in the snow with his Lego men. For the moment, all was right with the world.

It had been a long day but a good one. The colonel sat alone in the mess hall consuming his evening meal and reflecting on his trip to the village nestled in the rugged mountains above Kacanik.

"Hey, Colonel!" the mess steward said as he approached the colonel. "I see you have a new doc in town."

"I think you're mistaken," he replied dryly, taking a bite of his honey-glazed ham.

"I don't think so," the steward said convincingly. "He's a colonel like you and sitting over there eating alone." The steward gestured to the far end of the mess hall.

"If there was a new doc coming to Kosovo, I would have been the first to know," the colonel said without hesitating. "I'm not expecting any new staff, so I think you're a bit confused." The colonel took another bite.

"Sir, with all due respect," the steward said, determined to make his point, "that man sitting over there has the same rank as you and wears the same branch insignia as you. No doubt in my mind he's a colonel and a doctor."

"Well, let's just check him out," the colonel said, rising from his chair. Throwing his napkin on the table, he walked the short distance to the soldier who sat alone with his back to the colonel. The colonel was taken aback when he came around the table to confront the soldier. He was old for a colonel, not a warrior type. The wrinkles in his face gave him a human bulldog-like appearance. His thinning gray hair and pudgy gut gave the colonel the distinct impression this doctor was far past his prime and seriously misplaced in the army.

"Good evening, Colonel," he said, pulling up a chair opposite the more senior officer. "I'm Steve Franklin, the med task force commander. I wasn't expecting any new docs here in Kosovo—"

"You're right, Colonel," the elder officer interrupted without looking up. "You're not expecting me, and I'm not here to be your doc. I'm here at the request of the Department of the Army to conduct a peer review on one of your officers. I anticipate being here tonight and gone by tomorrow."

"Thank God you're here!" exclaimed the colonel. "I thought they had changed their minds and chosen to ignore my request. I'm the one who requested the peer review. Let me fill you in on the details before you get started." The colonel was elated.

"I'm not interested in you or your details." The elder colonel was curt and in no mood for cordial collegialities. "I simply want to review twenty charts, and I'll be on my way."

"Colonel …" Colonel Franklin's attitude had suddenly changed to be more formal to match the lack of any friendly conversation from the elder colonel. "I don't see how you can render a fair assessment without knowing the facts."

"Like I said, I don't need you or your details to guide me. I'll draw my own conclusion without your help if you don't mind."

The elder colonel wiped his mouth with his napkin. "Now, if you'd be so kind to show me where his records and office are, I'll get to work, and you can leave me alone."

The encounter had not been what the colonel had hoped for. Walking the elder colonel to the clinic where the records for the patients were maintained, he had a gut feeling the so-called peer review would be more perfunctory than fact-finding.

Returning to his office the next morning, the colonel soon found himself lost in the routine of the paperwork that had accumulated on his desk.

"Hey, sir," a voice called out from the hallway just outside his door, "looks like someone likes you." It was the mail clerk making his daily rounds with the mail. Every deployed soldier looked forward to mail call with great anticipation. Knowing that someone, anyone, cared about what he or she was doing a half a world away carried more meaning than anything. It was the highlight of a soldier's day. Conversely, mail call without a letter was sometimes equally disappointing, as were the Dear John or Jane letters.

"What do you mean?" the colonel asked, glancing up briefly over the top of his glasses.

"Sir, you got a box ... a big box!" the mail clerk said eagerly. "Were you expecting something?"

"No ... not really," the colonel replied.

The clerk wheeled the box in on his hand truck and off-loaded it next to the colonel's desk. "Well, I hope it's a good surprise ... whatever it is," the clerk said as he departed.

Rolling his chair with his feet from behind his desk, the colonel repositioned himself next to the box. He pulled the carton closer to get a better look at the return address label. As he had told his mail clerk, he wasn't expecting anything from anyone stateside. Recognizing the sender's name, he was baffled. It had been mailed from the State of California Board of Medical Licensing. *Oh my God! Was it possible his friend had found something meaningful that he could use?* The colonel thought as he tore open the lid, revealing reams of documents. On the top of the stack was a scribbled note: "*I hope you find what you're looking for.* ☺ *... Sarah.*"

The colonel quickly realized as he perused the reams of documents that they were the answer to his prayer for a miracle. Leaping to his feet, he snatched some of the papers and his hat from the corner of his desk and hurried from his headquarters to the chief of staff's office. Racing past the chief's assistant, as if he were late to a fire drill, he shouted over his shoulder to summon the JAG immediately to the chief's office.

"Sam!" the colonel called out as he burst through the chief's door. "You're not going to believe what I just received in the mail." The colonel gasped for air.

"I have no idea what that could be," the chief replied. "Catch your breath before you keel over on me. I don't want to play doctor on you."

Holding out the papers he had brought with him, the colonel began sharing his discovery. The JAG entered the room behind him, listening intently. "I just received a large box from the medical licensing board. In it are reams of documents pertaining to our good Colonel Weston." The colonel was more than simply ecstatic. "As it turns out, he's wanted in at least eleven states, the latest being New York. He's here in Kosovo because he's on the lam. As long as he remains deployed, the states can't touch him." The colonel couldn't convey his newfound information fast enough. "In California and several other states, he was convicted of theft, forgery, fraud, and four other counts. We also learned today that the credentials clerk in Germany who signed off on completing a prime-source verification of his credentials for the army never—I mean *never*—did it. As it turns out, our good colonel paid her a visit and, through his charm, convinced her that his credentials were impeccable, so she took him at his word and approved them. This guy is a bona fide fraud and wanted criminal!" The colonel couldn't contain himself, finally feeling vindicated.

Flipping through the documents, the chief said to the JAG, "It all looks official to me. What do you think?"

"I think we may have a strong argument for our position. If the army doesn't accept this new evidence, then nothing we have will," the JAG replied somewhat cautiously. "I'll forward these new documents to the JAG up the food chain and see if they'll not only stand down but give us the authority to apprehend this guy. Congratulations, Colonel, I think we may have just turned the table on this case."

Three days had passed since the colonel's encounter with the elder colonel in the dining facility, and he assumed the man had departed Kosovo without further comments. It was disheartening yet predictable to believe that the elder colonel had performed his obligatory duties and vanished. Sitting on the edge of his bed, the colonel removed his boots with a tug and tossed them softly on the ground. It had been an exhaustingly long day, and the idea of a good night's sleep was tugging at him. For once, the colonel believed the tide had truly turned in their favor, and it felt good. As he reached to undo the first button on his battle dress uniform blouse, the phone rang. Lifting the receiver on the second ring, he took note of the time, eleven o'clock. It was the elder colonel at the other end.

"Colonel," the elder said slowly, "you've got a problem, and I need to speak with you tonight."

"I thought you departed Kosovo already," the colonel replied.

"I should have, but I didn't. Would you mind coming down to my quarters now? I'd rather discuss this matter with you in person."

Standing outside the elder colonel's door, Colonel Franklin took a deep breath. Puzzled by the cryptic message and his colleague's serious tone, he tried to process what possible bad news he was about to receive. He raised his hand to knock on the door, but the elder opened it before the colonel could strike it. Turning his back to the colonel, the elder walked away from the door, motioning to the colonel to follow. Sitting on his bed, the elder patted it, indicating for the colonel to follow suit and sit down.

"Colonel, like I told you on the phone, you've got a very serious problem on your hands. The question is ... what are you going to do about it?" Clasping his hands around his crossed knee, the elder leaned back. He waited like a mentor speaking to his apprentice, expecting the colonel to offer up an immediate solution.

"Well, sir, can you share with me what sort of serious situation I'm facing?" The colonel was probing for a hint. "I think I know what the problem is, but I'd rather hear from you what you either believe or know it to be."

"You see, I came here to evaluate only twenty charts. Instead, I did a review on all of them. After the first twenty, I found a pattern but had to confirm it. In short, your colonel psychiatrist is a fraud!" the elder stated harshly, looking for a reaction.

"I already knew that," Colonel Franklin said. "Unfortunately, despite my many attempts to convince MEDCOM and higher-ups, no one would believe me. What makes you think he's a fraud?"

"To begin with, none of his chart notes make any sense. They are all incoherent. Second, his clinical acumen doesn't measure up to a first-year medical student's performance, and last, he's doing more harm to the soldiers than good," the elder stated matter-of-factly.

"I think what you say is all well and good, but are you simply verbalizing your findings, or are you willing to commit those remarks to writing?" the colonel asked.

"My report is already done," the elder said, somewhat irritated by the colonel's doubt. Holding up a single-spaced, typed report, he said, "I'll be filing it with both the MEDCOM and DA when I return to Washington."

"I don't mean to question your integrity, and I hope you'll forgive me," Colonel Franklin said. "But I think that when you file that document, it, like the rest of the documents that I've filed to date, is going to simply disappear as if you were never here. Is it possible to get a copy of that before you leave?"

"I didn't think you'd ask," the elder said, breaking a small smile. "I see you have potential, and I do agree with you. So here's your copy." The elder handed over a second piece of paper to the colonel. "I will presume you have no idea where that came from, of course," he added, ensuring the colonel understood the risk associated with sharing the document.

"I have no idea what you're talking about," the colonel replied, folding the paper and tucking it in his pocket. Breathing a sigh of relief, the colonel rose from his place on the bed and shook the elder's hand. "Thank you for coming to Kosovo. I have just one more question of you, if I may ask?" the colonel said, hoping again not to offend the elder.

"You may; go ahead."

"This colonel is smart ... no, he's very smart; one of the most cunning men I've ever met," the colonel said. "He's going to try to discredit your report by claiming your credentials are not equal to his and thus you have no standing to question or review him. So would you mind sharing your credentials with me?"

"Well, I suppose he might try to do that. I admit my

credentials are not all that impressive against his. The only difference is my credentials are genuine. On the other hand, I'm just a professor emeritus at Princeton University." The elder made his point crystal clear in an unpretentious manner.

"Okay, sir, that works for me," the colonel said, feeling surprised and somewhat sheepish.

★ 29 ★

The clouds hung heavy and low in the distant northern sky, concealing the mountains. Studying the winds pushing the clouds across the heavens, the colonel determined that it was only a matter of time before snow would fall again on the camp. The cold penetrated his uniform, and he pulled his olive-drab scarf snug about his neck and headed back toward the hospital. His first stop was the ICU, where he enjoyed visiting his two favorite patients. The little girl who had survived the accident with the five-ton truck had completed her fifteenth surgery and her first skin graft. Despite the monumental challenges that she had faced, she was progressing exceptionally well. With the help and encouragement of the physical therapy staff she had taken her first steps since the accident, learning to walk again on her newly constructed leg.

"Show the colonel what you can do," the therapist said, coaxing the little girl on. With a big smile, the little girl slowly stood from her chair next to her bed and put one foot ahead of the other as she made her way slowly toward the colonel with her arms extended. Kneeling, the colonel reached out to her, urging the little champion to come to him. With sheer determination she pushed herself until she could fully embrace him.

"That was totally awesome!" the colonel exclaimed, giving her another hug.

Crossing the ICU to the opposite side, the colonel made his way to the other occupied bed in the far corner. The feeling was much different at this bed with the privacy drapes drawn around it. It was quiet as he approached. The colonel pulled the drapes back slowly. The young woman's father sat alongside her on the bed, holding her hand. She lay motionless with her eyes closed. Standing on the opposite side of the bed the nurse made adjustments on the IV pump while checking the cardiac monitor from time to time. Glancing up at the screen, the colonel observed the severe bradycardia.

"What do we have?" he whispered.

"We're losing her," the nurse replied softly. "She's been bradying down for the last hour."

Standing behind the father, the colonel placed his hand on the father's shoulder as the beeping and illuminated wave recording the heartbeat on the monitor continued to slow. Her respirations became progressively more prolonged and shallow. Suddenly, the red light on the monitor flashed, and the alarm sounded. She had flatlined. Reaching up to silence the alarm, the nurse turned off the monitor and IV pump, waiting in silence for the colonel to speak.

Squeezing the father's shoulder, the colonel said, "I am sorry ... She has gone to be with the angels."

Leaving the ICU, he sighed heavily. The passing of the young woman was a heavy toll on his spirit, and tears welled up in his eyes. She had fought the good fight, but in the end, it had been simply too much for her to overcome. All that remained now was the memory of her beautiful smile and her amazing courage. Continuing down the main corridor of the hospital the colonel retreated to a place where he felt he could find some peaceful solitude to reflect—the med task force's ops center.

As he entered his TOC, he was greeted by his operations major.

"Sir, I have the general on the line. He wishes to speak to you."

Taking the phone from the major, the colonel acknowledged his boss on the other end of the line.

"I have a political request and opportunity for you tonight," the general said. "There was an assassination attempt this afternoon on a local politician in one of the small towns in a neighboring sector. Apparently he was shot several times but is reportedly stable in the local hospital. The Kosovar president has requested that he be transferred to our hospital so that he can recover in a neutral facility, thus avoiding any more political unrest in the town. I just got off the phone with the NATO commander, who has concurred. Can you take care of that?" the general asked.

"Sir, what do you mean by 'stable condition'?" The colonel asked, knowing from his past experiences, that "stable" had many meanings in the Kosovar medical community.

"I don't know. You may want to call the doctor up there and get more details from him," the general replied.

"I'm on it," the colonel said and hung up the phone. He had a gnawing gut feeling, unsure of what the real situation was with the victim. The experience of the young woman who now lay dead in his ICU was still stinging and fresh in his mind.

Lifting the receiver on the civilian phone, the colonel dialed the hospital in town where the incident had occurred. "Good evening, my name is Doctor Franklin," the colonel said. "I am the American doctor. I need to speak with the doctor who is caring for the man who was shot today." He paused.

"Oh, yes, Doctor," the voice on the other end of the line said euphorically. "I am the doctor. You come to take patient now?"

"Maybe ..." The colonel was exercising extreme caution. "What can you tell me about your patient? How stable is he?"

"He's very stable," the doctor replied.

"Can you tell me more about him and his condition?" the

colonel asked, wanting a better understanding of the circumstances before committing.

"No problem, Doctor. He was shot twice early this afternoon while drinking coffee at the café—once in the stomach and once in the shoulder. Neither was life-threatening. The shoulder wound is a flesh wound and not very serious. We have not treated that other than to place a dressing on it. The stomach wound was repaired in surgery this afternoon. The bullet must have passed through since we could not find it," the doctor said.

"Anything else I should know?" the colonel asked.

"No. He's doing fine resting in recovery. How soon will you be here?" the doctor asked.

"I don't know. It looks like it may snow, and if it does, it could be two to three days before we can get there. Will your patient be okay until then?" The colonel was still trying to gauge the patient's condition.

"No problem," the doctor replied. "We can handle him until you can come. Like I said, he tolerated the surgery well and is pretty stable."

"Okay, we'll keep you posted as to when we can fly. It should be clearing in the next two days," the colonel said and hung up the phone.

Turning to his major without hesitating, the colonel ordered the TOC to plan for a DV, a distinguished visitor medevac mission. Knowing the major had a firm grasp of the significance of the mission, he departed his ops center.

Less than a minute after the colonel left the TOC, the Dust-off pilot in command on call for the evening walked toward the colonel. The chief warrant officer 4 was a crusty, old, seasoned aviator with more experience in the cockpit than any other aviator on the FOB. He was methodical in how he went about his business and drew respect from all the soldiers in the command.

"Hey, sir, I just got off the phone with the three. He tells me we might have a DV medevac mission."

"Yes, depending on weather of course."

"I just wanted to let you know that we have a weather break for the moment that will give us a four- to five-hour window of opportunity tonight if you still want to fly that mission."

"Do you think we can get there and back before it closes in on us?" the colonel asked.

"I'm pretty certain of that. We can take the new J-model Black Hawk with the beefed-up avionics, equipment, and engine for some added insurance." The chief felt confident yet cautious.

Returning the TOC, the colonel told the major. "Change to the plan. Inform the local hospital and the CG's TOC the mission is a go for tonight with an ETA of approximately twenty hundred hours. The mission will consist of the pilot, copilot, flight medic, crew chief, and me."

"You, sir?" the major asked.

"Do you know of any other qualified flight surgeon or doc on the FOB willing to go out in this crappy weather?"

"Uh … no, sir."

The colonel donned his flight gear and walked briskly to the helipad where the chief warrant officer 4 and crew waited aboard the Black Hawk with its engine turning. From the outside, the new Black Hawk appeared like any other helicopter on the base, but the interior was far sexier as army aircraft went. In the cockpit, the analog avionics had been replaced with digital, simplifying the clutter on the instrument panel. In the nose a forward-looking infrared (FLIR) system had been added. The state-of-the-art FLIR camera sensed infrared radiation being emitted from a heat source to create a "picture." It could also be used to help pilots navigate their way at night and in fog or to detect warm against a cooler background if they were searching for someone. In the main cabin, the aircraft had likewise been upgraded with the latest emergency medical technology and equipment, including a built-in suction apparatus, EKG monitor, and trauma crash cart. In essence, it had been built to be a flying emergency room and every ER doc's dream.

The wind created by the whirring rotor blades increased the wind-chill factor but served as a strong motivator to the colonel as he quickly leaped aboard the aircraft. He was pleased to see the flight medic chosen for the mission was the same young sergeant who had accompanied him previously during the mountain rescue of the Macedonian soldier. After buckling himself into his seat behind the pilot and opposite the medic, the colonel gave a thumbs-up, indicating they were good to go for departure.

The liftoff from the pad was powerful, more so than the other Black Hawks produced, revealing the added thrust the aircraft had with a newer and larger turbine engine. The Huey UH-1H that the colonel had once flown had never been able to do that.

With the nose pointed slightly down, the pilot pulled pitch on the collective while applying a slightly forward effort on the cyclic, forcing the helicopter to rapidly ascend with greater speed and moving it in a northwesterly heading. Within seconds, the helo was climbing hard through five hundred feet as the medic leaned forward to close the open door. She couldn't reach it. Undoing her seatbelt, she leaned harder and grasped the handle on the opened door. She was tugging firmly on the handle when the aircraft unexpectedly banked left. The door slid quickly rearward along its rollers. Fighting against the weight of the door, the medic's hand became pinned between the door and the fuselage as it locked in the open position, flinging her forcefully out of the aircraft. Dangling by her arm like a rag doll, she struggled desperately to pull herself back into the cabin, but her efforts were futile as her body slapped hard against the skid.

Across the cabin on the starboard side, the crew chief scanned the landscape below with his back to the cabin, unaware of the situation evolving behind him.

The colonel pressed firmly on the press-to-talk button on his headset. "Chief, set down now … We have an emergency back here with the medic! She's unsecured outside the aircraft." There was no reply from either the pilot or crew chief. Pressing the button harder a second time, the colonel repeated his urgent message. "Chief, abort! We have an emergency on board!" Still no response as the helo climbed higher. Realizing his headset was nonfunctional, he jerked it from his head and threw it on the floor while pulling the release on his seatbelt. Moving to a prone position on his belly, he extended his right hand and arm as far as he could with hope of grabbing the medic's flailing hand. While their fingertips touched at times, he was inches short of her grasp. Again he tried, but her thrashing hand failed to connect. The terror in her eyes was horrifying as she desperately tried to reach his hand. Once more the aircraft banked left, slinging the medic away from the skid and causing the colonel to slide forward toward the opened door. He hooked his boot on the leg of his seat and held tight with all his might, dangling partially out of the Black Hawk as his heart pounded hard within his chest.

Feeling the helicopter level out in flight, the colonel cautiously pulled himself back into the cabin, securing himself again in his seat. He glanced around the cabin frantically to find something he could throw at the crew chief with hopes of gaining his attention. He grabbed a black roll of electrical tape lying between the seats and launched it forward, but the breeze in the cabin was too strong and blew it out of the aircraft. In the meantime, the situation was becoming dire. Yelling had done nothing to gain the attention of the pilots or crew chief; his voice was lost amid the whine of the turbine, the blowing wind about the cabin, and the SPH-4 helmets the crew wore. The colonel was desperate as time worked against him. Exasperated, he struggled to turn in his seat to tap the pilot's shoulder, but like his other attempts, it was useless. Knowing he had no other options, the colonel again unfastened his seatbelt, hoping a second attempt would prove to be more successful than the first, but just then the crew chief momentarily looked back. Pointing to the empty medic's seat, the colonel tried to mouth the urgency of the situation while using hand motions to alert the crew chief of the medic's precarious situation outside the aircraft.

Recognizing what had happened, the crew chief quickly informed the pilot of the situation. Reaching up, the crew chief gave a hard tug on the cable, secured in the eyebolt on the roof of the cabin that tethered him to the craft. He moved quickly to the opened door to assess the situation. Bending as far down as he could, the crew chief grasped the medic's arm firmly and pulled her back into the helo. After freeing her hand from the doorjamb, he strapped her into her seat. Grabbing the cargo door handle, he gave it a hard tug, pulling it closed, and moved back to the opposite side of the aircraft to his seat. Rummaging through his flight bag, he retrieved a new headset and passed it to the colonel. The ordeal had clearly shaken the medic up badly. Staring at her hand that had been trapped in the door jam, she studied it as she massaged the bruised tissue. Tears flowed from her as she withdrew into herself, looking down at the floor. Unbuckling his seatbelt, the colonel moved towards her and patted her knee. Taking her injured hand, he delicately examined the hand. It was bruised with multiple abrasions, but not broken. The medic had been lucky despite the traumatic experience. The colonel reassured her she would be okay. Returning to his seat and securing himself with the seatbelt, he leaned back into his seat, realizing the situation could have been much worse.

It took forty-five minutes for the Black Hawk to reach the

narrow valley that led to the small town. The dark shadows of the mountains rose sharply on either side, closing in on the helicopter as the valley narrowed to a long, tapered canyon. Below, lights from the scattered clusters of homes and buildings spotlighted the snow that blanketed the area, giving the landscape a pristine and serene appearance. Glancing out the side window of the aircraft, the colonel caught sight of a light snow beginning to fall in the brightness of the strobe lights. As a former aviator, he recognized the conditions were beginning to deteriorate and wondered if the mission was really worth risking their lives for. He was, after all, the commander, and he had options like aborting the mission, that he could exercise anytime he needed to. He also had a duty and responsibility for the mission and the safety of his crew.

Farther up the canyon, the density of the ground lights gradually thinned until there was total darkness. Without the illumination of the moonlight to outline the mountain range, pilot and copilot suddenly found themselves flying blind in an unfamiliar airspace. Activating the FLIR, the pilot continued to make his way up the canyon as the snowfall intensified. The lack of visibility was now a major factor, and the colonel knew he no longer had a choice. Pressing the button on his headset, he said, "Chief, abort the mission. I'm scrubbing it for now. Let's turn back and get out of here while we still can. We can give it another try when the weather breaks."

"Sir, before we abort, I believe we can still make it," the pilot quickly replied. Going against his instincts as a senior pilot in command, the pilot knew he was too close to the town to turn back now. He knew as a medevac pilot, there was a seriously wounded patient counting on him to get to the small hospital where the patient was and bring him back to a safer place.

"I'd rather not sacrifice the safety of the crew and this aircraft for a politico who I'm told is stable for the moment," the colonel said.

"By my calculations we are approximately three Mikes from our target," the pilot said. "I think we can make it. If I'm wrong, I'll turn back." The chief warrant officer was counting on the colonel to defer the final decision to the more experienced pilot as he tried to make his case.

"It's against my better judgment," the colonel said. "Three Mikes. No town, we turn back." Leaning back in his seat, the colonel second-guessed his decision and imagined the worst-possible scenario of losing the aircraft against the invisible canyon wall.

"Roger that, sir," the pilot said.

Holding out his wristwatch, the colonel began the countdown, trying to keep his mind off of what was happening with the weather outside. Three trips of the second hand around the face of the watch seemed to take an eternity. When the third sweep had been completed, the colonel pressed his mic button. "Okay, Chief ... abort," the colonel said calmly yet firmly.

"Sir, I've got lights at twelve o'clock one-half mile ahead," the pilot replied. "Looks like the snow is easing."

As they approached the town, the orange glow of the incandescent streetlights grew brighter until they could see the entire town nestled against the steep mountainside.

"Do you know where the hospital is?" the pilot asked the colonel.

"Negative," the colonel responded. "I'm presuming it's like any other town around here. It should stand out from the rest of the buildings. No coms with them either."

Circling the town slowly, the pilots and crew searched for the hospital. On the third attempt, the crew chief called out, "Hospital-like building at three o'clock!"

"Got a visual," the copilot said, narrowing the circular pattern over the structure.

"No helipad," the pilot said.

"Crap!" the colonel said. "Do we have an alternate site?"

"There's an empty field about a quarter mile down the road," the copilot replied.

"Roger ... Let's set her down there, and we'll hike up from there," the colonel said.

The pilot brought the large Black Hawk to a hover as he began a slow descent to the vacant field. To the rear of the helicopter a tall grove of trees waved in unison from the intense rotor wash, to its front was a row of power lines, and to either side, wooden fences that bordered the field.

"All eyes open," the pilot commanded as he slipped the helicopter into the tight space. When the wheels touched down on the snow-covered ground, the helo didn't stop descending but instead settled deeper into the icy snow.

"How deep is this stuff?" the crew chief asked.

"I don't know just yet," the pilot said sarcastically. "I suppose when it stops settling I'll know."

As the wheels disappeared beneath the snow, the belly of the helo broke through the crust of the frozen snow and came to a rest. Powering down the turbine engine, the pilot said, "Okay, sir, I think we're here."

Throwing open the side cargo door, the crew chief jumped from the aircraft, turning to assist the medic and colonel. Retrieving a stretcher and medical bag, the colonel and medic set out on the dark, narrow road, hiking up a small hill toward the structure that had been identified as a possible hospital from the air. Ice had formed on the black asphalt surface, making it difficult at best to negotiate the slight incline. Slipping and then sliding at times, the pair finally made it to what appeared to be the front of the yellow cement building. In the center of the portico that marked the entrance, a single dimly lit lightbulb hung by wires, illuminating a pair of tall, dirty-white doors.

Pulling on the doors, the two entered a brightly lit, smoke-filled room packed with people standing wall-to-wall yelling and screaming as they waved their arms above their heads. To the casual observer, it was as if they had stumbled into the local Friday-night cockfights. But to their bewilderment, they were standing in the hospital. Pushing their way through the crowd, the colonel shouted, "Doctors … where are the doctors?" No one understood or paid attention to what he was saying.

As if on cue, a pair of doors on the far side of the room flung open, and a hospital bed entered the crowded room like the Mad Hatter's Disney ride emerging from the tunnel. Led by a man in a long, white lab coat, the bed, containing a motionless patient, made its way slowly through the crowd. Another man similarly dressed sat on the bed squeezing an Ambu bag, indicating the patient was intubated. On a pole attached to the bed, an IV had been hung, transferring a unit of blood into the patient's left arm. Two more men were behind the bed, pushing it along. Hopeful the men in white coats were physicians, the colonel pushed his way toward them, intercepting the entourage at the midpoint of the room.

"Are you a doctor?" the colonel shouted above the noise in the room to the man walking alongside the bed.

"Yes, I am doctor," the man shouted back.

"I am the American doctor. I am here to pick up a patient," the colonel said.

"Yes, this is your patient," the doctor said, smiling.

"No!" the colonel said. "The patient I'm supposed to pick up is stable. This patient is not stable."

"Yes, patient is stable," the doctor said.

"No," the colonel said. "Tell me what you've done for him, and before we agree to take him, I want to exam him myself."

"We have given him twenty units of blood and made him stable. The bullet in his abdomen cannot be found, but we have stopped the bleeding." The doctor's tone was serious.

"What about these people?" the colonel asked.

"They are here for this man. They love him!" the doctor said.

"Twenty units of blood, intubation, and comatose is *not* a stable patient, Doctor!" the colonel yelled.

Turning to examine the patient, the colonel was startled to see the bed had disappeared into the crowd. "Where's the patient?" he asked.

"He has gone to the helicopter," the doctor said, breaking into a smile again.

"Oh no he hasn't!" the colonel blurted out. Turning to the medic, he ordered, "Catch up with that patient, and stop him. Do not let him on the aircraft!" The colonel turned back toward the doctor but noted he too had disappeared into the crowd.

Working his way back toward the front entry of the hospital, the Colonel emerged, searching desperately for any signs of the medic or patient. Neither was to be found.

★ 30 ★

It had rained all morning, and by ten o'clock it still showed no signs of easing. The general stood staring out of his Pentagon window with his hands clasped behind his back, unaware of his secretary's presence behind him.

"Excuse me, sir ..." She paused, awaiting his acknowledgement.

Without turning around, the general who had previously led the conversation with a second general and a third on the video conference said, "Anna, it's not everyone who gets that once-in-a-lifetime opportunity to be a general. Do you know how rare generals are? They represent less than point one percent of the army. They are the crème de la crème of leadership. As a young soldier, you enter this army believing in everything it stands for ... power, justice, duty, and honor." The general paused only long enough to draw a breath. "You spend a career scratching and clawing your way from the muddy, rain-soaked trenches in the field as a snot-nosed lieutenant who doesn't know shit to one day being here in the center of power. Do you know what that's like? At your fingertips, you wield unimaginable power." He paused again as if to gather more of his thoughts. "Our historians make us out to be larger than life ... and rightfully so. You know, everyone needs something to believe in, and these days, everyone needs a hero. We're that hero. Then out of nowhere a band of some goddamn assholes who believe in the Cinderella version of the army show up and threaten to take it all away." Turning around to face his secretary, he continued, "Somehow, it just doesn't seem right, does it? One would think that by the time we make these guys senior leaders they should know the world isn't perfect. All this crap about doing the right thing and leading by example. What in the hell are they thinking or smoking out there? They work for us. Their job is to obey and execute our orders ... our will! As soldiers, they are not to question but to obey and execute what they are told to do ... without question! Power isn't what's given to you; it's what you take!" His eyes burned with disdain as he spoke of the men in Kosovo. Clenching his fist, he slammed it in the palm of his other hand. He was clearly agitated by the unraveling situation but was at a loss as to how to contain the issue. "It's a matter of national security, and all they keep telling us is they're trying to do the right goddamn thing! Who do they think they are? How dare they question our orders!" The general could feel his ability to influence and control the situation slowly slipping from his grasp. "If they succeed, it will become a national—no, *international*—embarrassment for us all. Too much is at risk. Our glass house is very, very fragile at the moment."

"Sir, the ARMYCOM commander is on the line for you," the secretary said politely referring to the Army Command Commander in Europe, without acknowledging the general's emotions.

Lifting the receiver on his desk, the general dismissed his secretary with a wave of his hand and took a seat behind his desk. "What do you have, Joey?" the general asked.

"We have a little problem out here," the general on the other line replied.

"You told me that last time we spoke. I thought you were going to take care of it. What is it now?"

"General Moore's JAG has submitted some new documents that confirm the alleged fake colonel is wanted in eleven states."

"That's all we need—just let this thing blow out of control with eleven stinkin' states getting their noses involved where they don't belong. Can you mitigate that situation?" the general asked.

"I can, but there's more. The professor we sent to pacify the colonel has confirmed in his report this guy is a fraud and a danger to soldiers. In his report, he is recommending this guy be relieved from his duties immediately."

"What's the problem? You're the commander over there ... aren't you?" The general's agitation intensified. "Use the fuckin' authority you have, and make the report go away like the rest of the crap they've sent you. Shit, do I have to do your job and mine? Let me remind you again of what's at stake here in case you've forgotten—the careers of distinguished soldiers, congressmen, and the reputation of the army is on the line. We simply cannot afford to let that happen. Once this little matter is taken care of down there in Kosovo, I don't give a damn if the states draw and quarter the little shit, each taking their piece of him. He is becoming a great liability for us, but for now, you have some work to get done."

"Sir, this isn't about national security as I was led to believe; it's about a criminal who's infiltrated our system and hoodwinked individuals to participate in his scheme without their knowledge. All we need to do is come clean and support this investigation. We'll all look like heroes doing the right thing. We can say one of our commands uncovered a spy or mole that had threatened our national security, and in the end, we'll all be winners," the ARMYCOM commander said.

"Have you been drinking their Kool-Aid? Congress will eat us alive for our incompetence in allowing this guy to walk out of the Pentagon with all of that money and top-secret information, not to mention implicating some very senior-ranking members of Congress," the Pentagon general replied. "Before the ink had dried on the paper, key congressional leaders would have resigned, and we would all be facing some form of UCMJ," the general said, referring to the military Uniformed Code of Military Justice from the *Manual for Courts-Martial*. "It would be the biggest embarrassment for the army, and you know shit always rolls downhill, so it wouldn't just stop at the flag level. Our enemies would exploit this disaster. No, this *is* a matter of national security. In the meantime we're counting on you to see this little matter through to completion. Don't get waylaid in the details. That's what you have a JAG for."

"But, sir, what about the careers of the general and colonel down there in Kosovo?"

"Collateral damage. It's a small price to pay for what's at stake," the general said and then hung the phone up.

Hanging his phone up delicately at the other end, the ARMYCOM commander leaned back in his executive leather chair and thought about the conversation. He walked across his office and said softly to his aide-de-camp sitting attentively outside his door, "Get me the JAG."

KOSOVO

The chief and JAG sat quietly at the conference table poring over the documents they had just received from the ARMYCOM headquarters. "It appears as if our boss and fellow colonel are about to have that opportunity to swing from the gallows," the JAG said softly.

"I don't get it," the chief said. "We have provided them with reams of documentation supporting our case, yet each time they have ignored it. What's really going on?"

"Well, according to their JAG, we have failed to provide them a shred of evidence to support our case. In their mind, our command is incompetent, and we have aided and abetted a subordinate rogue commander who functions much the same way, in their opinion, as we do."

"The evidence ... it's all been destroyed, hasn't it?" the chief asked, looking up at the JAG.

"I'm afraid so. Nothing exists to prove our case, so it's now our word against the mystery machine up the chain, and you know they have all the horsepower behind them. We're in essence the bastard stepchildren who may have been too dumb to know it or let go. After all, if we'd simply walked away and swept this whole thing under the rug, who would have cared one way or another? Instead, we chose to do what was right, and now we don't have a leg to stand on," the JAG said flatly.

"I wonder if Steve kept any copies of those documents we handed over. If not, we're screwed. If he did, we just might have a chance ... don't you think?" the chief asked.

"I think it's a wish and a prayer at this point," the JAG said. "I believe he forwarded everything he had. If he did keep any documents, we might have a small hope in heaven by filing an emergency appeal through the United States Fifth Circuit Court of Appeals in Germany to block the article thirty-two hearings, but with what we currently have, I'm not sure they'll hear it. It's our last chance, and time is definitely no longer on our side. As you know, we've lost every battle up to this point. If we lose this one, then we're truly done."

"As the general once said, this really is our Alamo. I don't like the odds, but you'd better start setting the wheels in motion for the last stand. In the meantime, we'd better go see the old man and lay out his options," the chief said with a heavy tone.

"Where's Franklin?" the JAG asked.

"On a mission, but he should be back soon."

★31★

Reaching the crest in the road that led from the hospital back to the Black Hawk, the colonel saw that a crowd had gathered around the helo. Breaking into a trot, he continued down the icy road, slipping as he went, until he reached the fringes of the crowd. Forcing his way through the multitude, he reached the olive-drab-painted bird, hoping to board and depart the village, but it wasn't possible. Seeing the crew chief standing alongside the door of the aircraft, the Colonel wasted no time moving toward him, barking orders as he went.

"Chief," he shouted, tapping on the copilot's side glass and twirling his index finger in the air, "start cranking her up, and let's get out of here!" He moved toward the side cargo door to board and strap himself in but was instead taken aback to find the helo overloaded with civilians. Looking to the crew chief, he demanded, "What the hell is going on here?"

"They told us you had authorized them to go with us," the crew chief replied innocently, shrugging his shoulders.

"Hell no! Now get them off this aircraft *now*!" the colonel ordered. "I can't find the medic or the patient," he added.

"They're on board," the crew chief said, tugging to remove the newly added passengers. They resisted as he forcefully pulled them from the Black Hawk until they were down to the man in the white lab coat still squeezing the Ambu bag.

The main rotors were now turning at a full idle, causing the crowd to back away from the aircraft as the colonel asked the man, "Just what do you think you're doing on my bird?"

With wide eyes, the man broke into a broad grin and replied, "I go with you ... yes?"

"Wrong answer, friend ... No!" the colonel shouted as he clutched the center of the man's white coat. With one jerk, he yanked the man from the helicopter. Leaping aboard, he shouted, "Take off *now!*" as he pulled the door closed.

Pulling up on the collective, the pilot slowly lifted the Black Hawk from the snow. At ten feet, he called out to the colonel through his headset, "Sir, we have some strap hangers on the wheels."

"Shake them free if you can," the colonel said, "but I don't want anyone hurt."

Moving the cyclic slightly back and forth sideways, the pilot rocked the aircraft sufficiently to cause the individuals to fall free into the snow below.

"All eyes open," the pilot said as he guided the large helicopter clear of the trees and power lines. Setting a new course, he began the return trip to the forward operating base.

Kneeling alongside his new patient, the colonel began a quick assessment. The unit of blood connected to his IV was running low. The bandage over his right shoulder was soaked with blood, and fresh blood flowed freely from around the endotracheal (ET) that was taped in the patient's mouth. Having taken over the rhythmic squeezing of the Ambu bag, the medic awaited further orders from the colonel. Pulling up the patient's shirt, the colonel noticed the abdominal bandage was equally blood soaked. He wasn't simply bleeding from his wounds; he was hemorrhaging.

"Shit! This patient isn't just unstable; he's fuckin' trying to die on us! I hope to hell we're not dealing with a botched surgery or, worse yet, DIC!" the colonel yelled. DIC, disseminated intravascular coagulopathy, was a blood disorder caused by the sudden formation of small blood clots inside blood vessels. The small clots consumed coagulation proteins and platelets, disrupting normal coagulation and causing bleeding from any site where the skin had been disrupted or through the skin itself, resulting in a profound and diffuse hemorrhage. Rechecking the ET tube, the colonel yelled to the medic over the sound of the turbine engine, "Damn it ... it's a pediatric tube! I need to reintubate him. Change places with the crew chief, and pass me a number seven French ET tube."

Grabbing a pair of bandage scissors, the colonel cut the tape that held the ET tube in position. Using a 20cc syringe, he attached it to the small tube that dangled freely next to the ET tube and attached to the small air bag at the base of the tube that held it in place. Pulling back on the plunger, he deflated the bag and attempted to remove it slowly. Just as he began to withdraw it, a large amount of fresh blood rushed from around the ET tube.

"Damn it!" he shouted again. If he pulled the tube out, he'd lose the only established airway he had. "Cancel that; I need suction stat!" Frustrated, the colonel gently pushed the tube back into position and re-inflated the air bag.

Reaching for the built-in suction apparatus on board, the medic pushed the toggle to turn it on. Nothing happened. She tried again ... still nothing. Inspecting the apparatus closely, she tried again. Still nothing ... "The suction's not working," she said.

"I need something ... anything. Do we have a back-up manual suction?"'

"No. We were counting on everything working due to this aircraft being new."

"Damn it ... Okay ..." the colonel said, trying to quickly gather his thoughts and implement a plan C on the fly, he directed, "Get me some IV tubing. Recalling his days in obstetrics and pediatrics, he frantically grabbed the tubing and cut it into lengths of about eighteen inches. Fashioning a makeshift Delee suction, typically used to suction newborn infants, he pushed one end of the tubing around the endotracheal tube in the patient's mouth and attached the other end to a connector at the top of the jar lid.

"Keep bagging!" the colonel ordered. Taking a second piece of tubing, he connected one end to the second connector at the top of the lid. Then he put the other end in his mouth and began sucking. Blood flowed freely into the jar.

"Sir, his pressure is falling."

"Start a second IV with Lactated Ringer's solution, and run it wide open. Add some Dopamine beginning with five micrograms per kilogram per minute—titrate to effect at ten- to thirty-minute intervals." The colonel moved to the patient's feet and elevated his legs, resting them on a medic bag. Noticing his and the medic's hands were rapidly stiffening from the cold temperature in the cabin, he called out to the pilot on his headset, "Chief, we need a little heat back here, please."

"Sir, you've gotta make a command decision. We can heat the rotor blades and keep them from freezing, or we can heat the cabin, but not both," the pilot replied. "Crazy, I know … but that's how they built this aircraft."

"Rotor blades it is," the colonel said. "When you're clear of the canyon, put some speed on this bird back to camp. I'm losing our patient. Notify the med TOC I need the trauma team on the pad and the OR open and standing by when we land." The colonel continued working to stabilize the critically ill patient, giving more orders and taking more interventional measures. Despite everything they tried, the patient's condition continued to deteriorate.

"Roger that," the pilot replied.

"Sir, I'm not sure we're going to keep this guy alive," the medic said. "He's slipping."

"No one dies on my bird!" the colonel yelled. "What's our ETA?" he asked into his headset. Despite the chaos unfolding in the Black Hawk, he kept cool and calm.

"Wait-one," the copilot said. He pulled a map of the area out from the map case and quickly studied it with his red-lensed light. "I believe we're here, just five thousand feet below the peak," he said to the pilot, pointing at a position on the map.

"Are you sure?" the pilot asked.

"Yes, I'm sure," the copilot said.

"Okay ... I say we take the shortcut back to camp. It'll cut twenty minutes off of the flight, and we can be on the pad in under thirty-five minutes," the pilot said. "Let's start climbing along this wall. Do you have visibility?"

"Limited," the copilot said as the helicopter began a slow climb into the clouds.

"Let's keep her steady," the pilot said calmly. "Call out our climb until I've added five thousand feet to our present altitude. Once we clear the peak, we'll cross over the mountain and then straight line to the camp."

"Roger that ... Clearing one thousand," the copilot announced. "Two thousand ... three thousand ... four thousand ... clearing five thousand."

"Let's go another five hundred for good measure," the pilot said. "Do you have any visibility on the mountain?"

"Negative ... just clouds," the copilot responded. "Clearing five hundred ..."

"Okay, let's start a slow right turn and see what happens."

Bracing for impact against the rugged mountain, the colonel, medic, and crew chief pushed themselves hard against the seats and bulkhead while they continued to work on their patient, but it didn't happen.

Soon the pilot said calmly to the copilot, "I think we've cleared the peak. Let's try a slow descent." The pilot slightly lowered the collective, and the Black Hawk descended slowly.

Nearly five minutes had passed when the helo finally broke through the clouds.

"Awesome, we're clear of the mountain, I believe we can go VFR now," the pilot reported, indicating he was changing from following instrument flight rules to visual flight rules. Within seconds of clearing the clouds, the pilot shouted in a panicked voice, "Oh shit!" as he pushed forward on the cyclic, putting the Black Hawk into a steep dive.

"Wha—?" the colonel asked as equipment and crew rolled uncontrollably forward in the cabin with the sudden change in the aircraft's attitude.

As the helo nosed hard toward the earth, the pilot struggled desperately to regain control, pulling back on the cyclic with all his strength and up on the collective while applying pressure to his right pedal to counter the torque on the tail rotor. The avionics on the dash reflected the aircraft in a sudden critical and precarious position. The helicopter was plummeting out of control to the valley floor below. Simultaneously, an unfamiliar, deafening roar violently shook the helicopter. Overhead, the silhouette of a Boeing 737 jetliner appeared out of the darkness and flashed past the window on its final approach into Pristina International Airport. Leveling out, the pilot once again regained control of the aircraft, resetting his course to the forward operating base.

"Holy crap, Chief!" the colonel said. "That was way too close for comfort."

"Sorry, sir. I never saw that one coming," the pilot said, trying to maintain his composure. "We apparently exited the clouds in the midst of Pristina's final approach pattern."

Understanding the urgency of the situation on board his Black Hawk, the pilot pushed his helo to maximum performance in flying back to the hospital at the camp. Approaching the helipad from the north, the chief swung the helo around and touched down. The trauma team quickly ran to the aircraft and removed the wounded victim. After placing him on a gurney, they rushed him to the operating room, still bagging the man with the Ambu bag as they went. The colonel followed the team. He changed quickly into his scrubs in the men's locker room and joined the surgeon, who was already prepping the patient, in the OR.

"Glad you're scrubbing in, sir," the surgeon said. "I'm sure I'll need a second pair of hands tonight. What do we have besides a train wreck?"

"He's a fifty-something-year-old politico who barely survived an assassination attempt this morning after being shot twice. According to his surgeon, the shoulder was a flesh wound with the abdomen being the major wound. They supposedly did surgery on the abdomen, although they didn't find the bullet. The doc could not provide any details on what procedure they performed. I consider that alone suspect."

"He's bleeding badly," the surgeon said. "Let's get an x-ray to locate the bullet. In the meantime, I recommend we crack his chest and clamp the aorta. That should buy us a little time to open the abdomen and repair whatever is there that has failed from the first surgery and then come back and fix the shoulder wound," the surgeon said.

"Let's do it," the colonel said as the surgeon made his initial incision with the surgical knife. The surgeon applied the chest spreaders to expose the patient's heart and lungs.

"Change in plans!" the surgeon said. "Sir, the flesh wound isn't a flesh wound. It looks like the bullet took out the left subclavian artery and the entire apex of the lung. There's not much left here other than Swiss cheese. This may be the lethal wound, not the abdomen."

The doctors labored to control the hemorrhage, but the harder they worked, the more futile it appeared. After six units of blood, the anesthesiologist informed the colonel the hospital was out of blood for the patient. The precious red fluid was running out as fast as it ran in.

"If we can help it, we don't want this guy dying on American soil. Contact the German hospital, and ask them to send us whatever blood they can spare. Dispatch the medevac to secure it," the colonel ordered.

The team worked in the operating room for nearly three and a half hours, and still they were unable to control the hemorrhage.

"Damn! I can't get ahead of this bleeding!" the surgeon blurted out in frustration.

"Patience," the colonel replied. "Let's apply more Surgicel to the bleeding ... What do you think?"

"I suppose ... we really don't have anything to lose," the surgeon said.

Another hour passed, and the anesthesiologist hung the last of four units that he had received from the Germans. "Gentlemen, we're on our last bag. What would you like to do?"

Looking up at the colonel, the surgeon said, "Sir, there's nothing more we can do to control the hemorrhage. The Surgicel applique is not holding."

Glancing at the clock on the wall, the colonel said, "We'll continue working through the last bag. Let us know when it runs out."

They turned their attention back to the chest wound until the IV bag collapsed as the last few drops of blood flowed into the patient lying on the surgical table. It was now five o'clock in the morning as the second hand ticked off the time. The thought of a civilian politician dying in an American hospital was unfathomable. Such an incident was all it would take to incite riots or, worse yet, rekindle the flames of war in Kosovo. Recognizing the seriousness of the situation, the colonel turned to the circulating nurse in the OR, "Get a message to the TOC to awaken the general and chief, and have the general or both meet me in the ER conference room stat."

"Sir," the surgeon asked, "what do you want us to do?"

"We're calling it," the colonel said, stepping back from the table. He broke the sterility of his surgical dress by tearing the disposable blue gown that he wore. "There is nothing more we can do here other than make him comfortable and say a prayer."

"Sir, the patient's brother is out in the waiting room. Do you wish to speak with him?" the nurse asked.

"Not yet," the colonel said, watching his worst nightmare unfold before him. "First things first."

It took another fifteen minutes for the exsanguination to effect the heart.

Watching the monitor, the OR team stood in silence as the bradycardic rhythm continued to slow before finally flat lining. "Time of death is 0516," the colonel announced. Pulling back the sterile drapes that covered the remainder of the patient's body, the surgeon and colonel began a final study of the blood-soaked gauze that protruded from a surgical wound at the mid-portion of the abdomen.

"That's a strange looking dressing," the colonel said.

"Indeed it is," the surgeon agreed, pulling on the bandage. It soon became more evident as an entire roll of gauze had been packed within the abdomen through the opening just below the belly button. Taking a pair of surgical scissors, the colonel cut it.

"Those assholes didn't operate on him. They did nothing more than pack the belly with this gauze, creating a tampanode," the surgeon stated. Studying the x-ray on the wall, he pointed to the right lower quadrant of the abdomen. "Aha! I also found the missing bullet. They must not have even looked for it."

"They probably just used what they had. I doubt it was intentional malpractice." Removing his gloves, the colonel then tugged at his surgical mask, removed it from his face and left the operating room. He made his way to the conference room, where he found the general sitting quietly with one of his majors.

"I didn't think this was going to be good news, based on your message," the general said. "What do you have?"

"Sir, the DV died on the table."

"Oh, that's just great," the general said, slapping his field hat on the table and not knowing whether to kick the chairs or shout.

"I thought I'd better tell you before the word gets out ... It's only a matter of time. His brother is in the waiting room," the colonel said.

"Let me get the camp on full alert and inform NATO head-quarters before you break the news," the general said mordantly. "We're also going to need a good PR plan and should get a statement out from the PAO." The general continued referring to his Public Affairs Officer. "This is one screwed-up morning, and it hasn't even begun yet," As he got up to leave the general concluded. "Thank the team for doing all they could."

It took the camp just under an hour to put its emergency plan into motion to address any type of unrest that might arise from among the local population. The camp was on high alert, as evidenced by the flurry activity by soldiers preparing their weapons and equipment for any adverse activity that may occur outside of the camp and by those who manned the main and med ops TOCs where personnel waited for what might happen next. By six thirty in the morning everything was in place. Taking up a position next to the victim's brother, the colonel gathered his thoughts. The younger brother was a solid, large, heavyset man who looked to be in his mid to late thirties. With dark, curly, short-cropped hair and rugged facial features, he appeared more intimidating than he perhaps was. The travel from his hometown to the camp had been exhaustive. Combined with the events of the day and a lack of sleep for the past twenty hours, as revealed by his stubbly beard and disheveled shirt and slacks impregnated with the strong smell of tobacco, the man had little reserve left to do much more.

"Good morning," the colonel said. "I'm Colonel Franklin, the commander here at the hospital and one of the doctors who worked on your brother last night. We operated through the night to save him, but I regret to inform you that he passed away peacefully this morning." The colonel paused, waiting for the brother to respond. "We did all we could, but his wounds were just too much for him."

"I understand," the brother replied. "When can I take him home?"

"As soon as his body has been prepared," the colonel said. "With your permission, we would like to do an autopsy to determine his real cause of death."

"No," the brother said abruptly, turning to face the colonel. "I must take him home now."

Perplexed by the younger brother's insistence and suspicious that there may be something he was trying to hide, the colonel asked, "Why must he go so soon?"

"Our religion ... it requires that he be buried completely, no autopsy, and that we do it before sundown on the day of his death," the brother explained. "I must travel all the way back home. There is not much time."

"I understand now. We will have him ready for the journey in just a few minutes. We will help get him home in time for his burial," the colonel said, trying to be respectful of the brother's religious beliefs and grieving.

By eight o'clock in the morning, the country had awakened to the news and was reading the details of the assassination on the front page of the national newspaper for the first time. The newspaper had gone the extra measure to ensure that the people understood the man had died in the American hospital. Bracing for the worst, the camp leadership was stunned to learn that instead of being characterized as villains for the man's death, they were being hailed as heroes. Instead of being the political figure that he had been depicted to be, he was actually a bully and a thug in the small town. Having had enough of him, the town had banded together and conspired to carry out his murder. When the plot had failed and the man had survived, the people had become fearful of retaliation from his fellow ruffians. If he had died in their town's hospital, his friends' retribution against the hospital would have been severe. As it turned out, he'd died in the American hospital—a place where no one could reach and nothing could be done with regards to retaliation. Instead of riots, there was dancing and unconstrained celebrating in the streets throughout Kosovo.

Exhausted, the colonel took refuge on his office couch to catch a few minutes of sleep, but only a few minutes passed before the JAG entered and said, "Steve, sorry to bother you, but we need to talk.

Sitting up on the edge of his sofa, the colonel asked, "What's up?"

"You and the CG are about to be relieved of your commands. After that, who knows what the army will do with you. It's looking like it might be an article thirty-two hearing before a possible court-martial."

"Okay, you have my attention," the colonel said. "Didn't they look at any of the new evidence?"

"What evidence?" the JAG asked, somewhat frustrated. "Everything we have sent them has disappeared. There is nothing to support our case. I'm going to file an emergency appeal with the Fifth Circuit Court of Appeals in Germany, but without the evidence, well, it'll be a ..."

"Hail Mary?" the colonel finished.

"Yeah ... a real Hail Mary, and I'm not sure that they will even agree to hear the case. The odds of winning are clearly stacked against the two of you."

Standing up, the colonel walked across his office to the file cabinet. He pulled it open and pushed aside the hanging folders. Reaching deep to the bottom, he retrieved two brown-paper-wrapped packages from the drawer. "Do you think these could make a difference?" he asked.

"Files?" the JAG asked.

"Yeah … files," the colonel said with a devious smile.

"I thought you surrendered all of those to the ARMYCOM ."

"I did. They asked for all my files. But they didn't say anything about the copies."

It had been a long morning, and like the colonel, the general had dealt with enough issues surrounding the death of the man in the hospital OR earlier in the day. Back in his office, he took on the task of sorting through the myriad of reports from his battalion commanders reporting in, from the NATO commander's take on the assassination to the insurmountable case the army was building against him and his medical commander. Of all the stressors he faced, it was this latter one that bothered him most. Too much was at stake, and several outstanding careers were about to be sacrificed to protect a wanted criminal because of whatever he had on senior-ranking generals and congressional leaders back in DC. He was a mystery man. No one could confirm the fraudulent colonel's true identity, who he really worked for, or what his real purpose was. He was a conniving thief, liar, fraud, and a wanted man, yet someone was doing all that could be done to protect him.

Lifting the receiver on his phone, the general called the colonel and said, "Steve, this is the CG. I've got an idea. Colonel Weston claims to be a subject-matter expert on post-traumatic stress disorder. So I want him to give me and my key staff members a briefing on the subject in three days. We'll use your conference room." He returned the phone to its cradle.

Not certain of what the general's objective might be, the colonel pondered the pros and cons of the directive. On one hand, the idea was genius as it would expose the psychiatrist for the fraud he was. On the other hand, it could prove to be a total embarrassment to his command. Concluding the benefit outweighed the risk, the colonel proceeded to deliver the order.

★

It had been three days since the death of the man from the small town and the order issued by the general to the fraudulent Colonel to prepare a briefing for him and the command. Having billed the briefing as a big deal featuring the command's one and only expert on the topic, the conference room that doubled as a mini auditorium was overflowing with members of the command and medical staff. Standing at the podium, Colonel Weston felt a great sense of power and satisfaction. He was at last the most important officer in the room, and all eyes were on him, the way it should have been from the start. After all, he had not gone to them; instead they had come to him, asking him to share his knowledge and wisdom. That's exactly what he was about to do with the general, the chief, and the colonel, none of whom were worthy of this consideration or could possibly know or understand a tenth of his brilliance. He would teach them, and in turn they would hail him for being truly great ... the master. But why had they waited so long to recognize how truly smart he was? It was he who was at the podium, not the colonel whom he held in contempt, not the chief whom he equally hated, and not the general who was obviously not as deserving as him to wear the stars of a general. For now none of it mattered.

"Atten ... tion!" the orderly called out as the general entered the room.

"Take you seats please," the general replied as he made his way to the front of the room. Standing before the assembled group, the general said, "This morning, we are going to hear from Colonel Weston. I have asked him to brief us on PTSD, since this is a relatively new issue that is affecting our troops in combat. As a psychiatrist, he is an expert in this area." Turning to Colonel Weston, the general said, "The floor is yours." The general took his seat in the front row and settled back to hear what the colonel had to offer.

"Good morning, General," the psychiatrist said. "I am so glad that you have asked me to educate you and the others gathered here on this important topic. As you know, I *am* the expert in this area, and I'm here to tell you what this illness is and what you and your commanders must do to correct it." The doctor was clearly off to a bad start. "Here in Kosovo, we have mines and minefields. When soldiers are exposed to these, they experience PTSD. We can treat these soldiers with the drugs we have …" He droned on in a nonsensical manner.

Fighting against the urge to leap to his feet and shout loudly that the briefing was over, the colonel placed his face in his hands, realizing the idea had been nothing short of disastrous. The information was incoherent and incorrect, yet the doctor's self-importance and arrogance was blossoming. The colonel couldn't hold back any longer. He stood to take the podium, but the general waved him off, signaling him to let the psychiatrist continue. Another hour passed as the psychiatrist continued his nonsensical presentation. In the meantime, half of the staff resorted to other activities to occupy their time; some slept, even snored, and others engaged in small conversations on unrelated matters. They'd tuned out the colonel at the podium.

Leaning over to the colonel, the general whispered, "I think we've heard enough. Good luck!"

Following the general into the hallway outside of the conference room, the colonel asked the general, "Sir, can you help me understand what the meaning was to have an incompetent fraud brief the command on a topic of which he knows nothing about?"

"You see Steve, I needed to be able to document for our defense that Colonel Westin is indeed a fraud. All of the evidence we have to date has come from other commands or his peers.

I personally have not witnessed his incompetence until now," the general said.

Patting Colonel Franklin on the shoulder, the general said, "Thanks for the entertainment, Steve," and departed with the chief, and the JAG.

Returning to the conference room, the colonel returned to his seat. Without missing a beat, the psychiatrist continued his presentation.

Another fifteen minutes passed until the colonel could not take any more of the disjointed rambling. "Colonel," he said, "I believe we're out of time for the day. This briefing is over."

"Not yet!" the psychiatrist snapped back. "It's over when I say it's over! I have more information to present; you all must listen to it."

"Not today. We're done," the colonel said firmly.

The colonel was mortified as he returned to his office to sort out next steps in the nightmare that was now of epic proportion. Entering his office, he was surprised to see the chief nurse from the US embassy in Skopje.

"Hi!" he said, giving her a quick, friendly hug. "What brings you to our god forsaken camp?"

The nurse was beautiful, tall, slender, and shapely with long, dark hair. Her soft facial features and light olive skin were consistent with her Middle Eastern background. Her accent was intoxicating. Despite her beauty, she was confident and professional. "I have a problem at the embassy that I need your help with," she said. "The Marine soldiers stationed there need sometimes to see a doctor to treat their acute illnesses."

Somewhat perplexed, the colonel asked, "So what's the issue?"

"I've been told that they cannot come here but must find a clinic in Skopje. The ambassador's wife was turned away at the gate just last week. The ambassador is concerned and not sure that his wife or the soldiers will get the care they need going to a non-American facility. Why can they not come here? You are the closest American facility to us."

"That's ridiculous!" the colonel exclaimed. "They can come here as far as I know. We're all on the same team, aren't we? They're Americans serving in uniform just like us, or they're in government service through the State Department. I think someone along the line is a bit confused. Let me make a call while you're here. I think we can get this matter resolved pretty quickly." He lifted the phone receiver and dialed the MEDCOM headquarters.

"Bob, this is Steve. I need some clarity on a matter here in Kosovo. I'm being told that the ambassador, his wife, and the military personnel assigned to the embassy cannot access our medical facility. I find that hard to believe, since we're the only American medical facility down here."

"Your source is right," Bob replied quickly. "Embassy personnel are prohibited from using our facilities."

"That makes absolutely no sense here in the hinterlands," the colonel shot back.

"What you don't understand is that we are *not* on the same team. We are the Department of Defense. They are the Department of State. In other words, as far as we're concerned, they are the enemy, and we don't support them. They're on their own," Bob stated matter-of-factly.

"That's horseshit! How can that possibly be? We're on the same side working for the same country!" The colonel was stunned by the response. "That's the dumbest thing I've heard yet!" the colonel said passionately.

"Not my issue," Bob said calmly. "DOD policy. Have a good day."

Pushing the cancel button on his phone, the colonel ended the call with MEDCOM and dialed the general. Explaining the situation as it had been presented to the colonel, the general listened patiently.

"Steve, you're right ... it is a dumb policy. However, you're the medical commander here. Taking care of our soldiers—Marines, army, or whatever they happen to be—is part of our job. If we are required to take care of the contractors here on the base, there's no reason why we can't take care of our fellow Americans in the embassy. The ambassador is our nation's and our commander in chief's representative out here, so in the end I'm sure, as always, you'll do the right thing."

Hanging up the phone, the colonel turned to the nurse. "Matter resolved. We'll take care of the ambassador, his wife, and military personnel with a valid ID."

★ 33 ★

The silence was deadly as the general and colonel sat on either side of the speakerphone atop the end table in the general's office. The chief had taken up a position in the third chair opposite them, forming a triangle around the table. The only sound was the soft ticking of the electric clock that hung on the wall. On the opposite end of the line, the team of JAG officers representing the general and colonel had begun presenting their opening oral arguments before the justice of the United States Fifth Circuit Court of Appeals.

"Never in my wildest imagination did I ever think I'd find myself sitting here in this situation," the colonel said softly, looking down at the floor as if he were just speaking to himself.

"I know what you mean," the general replied empathetically. "Did you choose which noose you wanted?" he added jokingly.

The colonel didn't laugh.

"How do you think you'll look in handcuffs?" the chief added, hoping to add a bit of levity, but it too didn't work.

"Look, Steve … I won't give up. This isn't over until it's over," the general said, trying to reassure his commander. "We have to believe in the system we serve, despite the overwhelming odds … We have to keep the faith."

The pit in the colonel's stomach had grown to the size of a melon, and he was doing all that he could to keep from throwing up in front of his boss.

Listening carefully to the arguments being presented, the chief said, "We have done this by the book. I don't understand why those up the chain of command chose to cast it all aside. I hope I live long enough to know the answer someday."

"The charges against our clients are bogus!" the JAG argued. "These were fabricated in a vain attempt to cover up a larger conspiracy that our clients accidently uncovered in exercising their duties."

"Those claims are ridiculous!" the ARMYCOM legal counsel shot back in his opening remarks. "They don't have a shred of evidence to support their loony claim of a conspiracy or cover-up. This only underscores their incompetency and dereliction of duty as senior leaders in the army." The ARMYCOM JAG had played right into the defendant's legal counsel's hand. "ARMYCOM did all it could to investigate and collaborate these absurd claims but found absolutely nothing to substantiate the assertions. We consumed an inordinate amount of time working with their command, only to be ignored. We have repeatedly held out an olive branch, but the general and colonel tossed it aside each time, thumbing their noses at their superiors in an insubordinate and disrespectful manner. Therefore, the army has been left with no options other than to relieve them of their commands and try them on the charges that will be substantiated during the pending article thirty-two hearings. For the court to find otherwise would be almost impossible," the attorney argued.

The debate raged back and forth throughout the early afternoon like two teams battling for the Super Bowl championship. Each side presented what evidence they had or defended what they didn't have.

"Sir, the MPs are here," the general's aide announced as she stood in the doorway.

"Have them wait outside," the general ordered. "It isn't over till it's over," he added somberly.

By late afternoon each side had exhausted what proof they had to present before the judge. In turn, the judge had heard all of what he felt was necessary to render a decision.

"Gentlemen, I have listened carefully throughout the entire day as both sides have presented their arguments. Typically, it would take me about three weeks to render a judgment, but I am aware that time is of the essence and that a command and two officers in Kosovo are awaiting my verdict. As such, I am going to take a twenty-minute recess. When I return, I will render my decision. For now, this court will stand in recess." The judge banged his gavel once.

"How are you guys feeling?" the chief earnestly asked the general and colonel.

Glancing at the colonel, the general asked, "Steve, what are your thoughts?"

"Sir, this has been nothing short of a living nightmare. It's something that you read about in a news story about someone else, never thinking one day it could be you. I believe we did the right thing. Never in my wildest imagination did I ever think I'd be involved in something like this ... something so incredible and larger than life. I have always believed in what our country, our army, and our nation stands for. I will always believe in those institutions, though I know others do not hold to those same values. It's not the system that is failing the American people but those who are charged to uphold it. Unlike you or the chief, I don't have a good feeling." The colonel was more than simply emotional. He did all that he could to fight back the tears that were welling up in his eyes. Thinking about his family and the ones he loved, he could not imagine ever facing them again should he be convicted on false allegations. "Sir, we're simply a David in this god-awful mess. While we know what we have done was right, I'm not so sure the court is going to agree with us. For them, it will be far easier to maintain the status quo and go along with Goliath than to say we were right.

Personally, I'm feeling like I'm about to be sicker than I've ever been in my entire life." The colonel continued to fight back the tears that were now rolling down his cheeks. "Regardless of what happens in the next few minutes, it is important to me for you to know how forever grateful and indebted I am to you, the chief, and the JAG for sticking with me throughout this ordeal. When I felt abandoned by everyone close to me, you all never left. That is a bond that can never be broken, a debt that can never be fully repaid. Thank you."

"As I said from the beginning, we're all in this together," the general said.

"We're a team … now and always," the chief said.

The twenty minutes felt like a lifetime as the trio sat silently in the general's suite awaiting their fate. The slam of the gavel in the speakerphone suddenly jerked them back from their thoughts to the present situation. At the other end of the line, the judge announced, "The Fifth United States Courts of Appeal is hereby back in session. Gentlemen, I have had the opportunity to listen today to those representing the higher chain of command and those representing the commanding general and colonel currently stationed in Kosovo. I want each of you to know, for the record, that I have reviewed all the documents forwarded previously to the ARMYCOM pertaining to this case." In the court room, the ARMYCOM attorneys suddenly sat straight in their chairs, apparently surprised by this announcement. "The forefathers of this great nation founded our country on certain principles—freedoms, peace, and truths that are our nation's cornerstones. It is our duty to preserve these foundations. Our military is an instrument of power used to extend and impose the policies of our nation, ensuring the safety, security, and well-being of the people of the United States and promoting peace. Those who are placed in positions of power, leadership, and authority are given a sacred trust by the American people. It is their responsibility to ensure that this bond is protected and never broken. As senior leaders, you are charged always—not sometimes or when it is convenient but *always*—to do what is right, what is just, and what is truthful. This is an oath that every officer serving in the United States Army swears to. These men in Kosovo have been doing just that. Furthermore, all members of today's army are required to believe, live, and follow the fundamental values of honesty, integrity, and personal courage. I am dismayed and quite frankly surprised that the chain of command failed in such a major way to follow its own rules and ethics. If any of you had taken the time to review these documents, you would, or rather should, have concluded that there is beyond reasonable doubt overwhelming evidence to suggest culpability on the part of the senior leadership in the highest positions. If an investigation was to be had, the Department of Defense should have investigated the incompetency or negligence and potential guilt or innocence of those senior leaders higher in the chain of command, but that didn't happen. As such, the court admonishes the higher commands for their rush to judgment and for their catastrophic failure to do what was right when they had the opportunity to do so. As such, the court finds in favor of the command and its officers in Kosovo. The court hereby directs the army to do what it failed to do; that is to immediately relieve of his duties and take into custody one, Colonel William Weston. Upon his return to the continental United States, he is to be surrendered to the appropriate state legal authorities where warrants for his arrest have been duly issued. The court stands adjourned." The judge gaveled the court and departed the bench.

The colonel broke down in uncontrollable sobbing in response to the stunning verdict and the sudden release of pressure he had experienced throughout the day. Clapping, the chief added his satisfaction to the victory. "At last … there is true justice … those sons of bitches!"

Pulling himself together, the colonel, the general patted him on the shoulder, consoling him. "We won ... At last, we won ... thank God!" Drawing a deep breath and speaking softly, he said, "You started this case; it's only fitting you end it. The court has ruled, so I think you have a colonel to apprehend. There's a couple of MPs outside you can use."

colonel said, "I don't think we won; the American people won. Everyone needs and deserves something to believe in. Americans believe in our army; our soldiers believe in us. It's our duty to preserve that belief."

Intervening, the general said, "A minor addition to that, Steve: we too believe in our system."

Ensuring the process was done by the book, the colonel requested another colonel to accompany him to serve as a witness. Standing outside the psychiatrist's office door, the colonel reviewed his final plans. Knocking, he entered with the witness, leaving the two MPs stationed outside.

The colonel had never been in the doctor's office. For that matter, no one had ever set foot in the private sanctum, which in and of itself was odd as far as it went on military installations. The room was pristine, with a single row of neatly framed letters of recommendation spaced two inches apart, forming a ring around the room at the middle of the walls. Each one had a genuine signature, but each one was fraudulent. The physician had become a master at gathering signatures to place on his concocted letters, which he could use and enjoy in his inner sanctum. Beautiful hand-sewn Persian rugs accented the Italian leather sofa, armchair, cherry wood desk, and matching coffee table. His fine furnishings exceeded anything the general had in his suite. How he had managed to obtain such furnishings at the government's expense left both of the colonels baffled. Behind the desk, the doctor sat watching his visitors enter the room. He didn't speak.

"Good afternoon, Bill," the colonel said, still surprised by the layout of the office. "Where did you find such nice digs?"

"I'm a colonel of course," the doctor replied. "I am entitled to these furnishings. You should consider upgrading your office. It is paltry for a man of your stature and position. Perhaps *pathetic* is a better description. But then again, all of you are that. When will you learn that in order to have the respect of others, you must respect yourself? We colonels and the general should demand nothing but the finest from those who serve us. We do that by having the best, and then they will see and respect us." It was evident the doctor was suffering from severe delusions of grandeur.

"Bill, perhaps that's a conversation for another time, but now I need you to remove your weapon from your holster with your left hand and hand it to me please, pistol grip first." The colonel was being overly cautious before engaging in further conversation. Because of the Wild West–like conditions throughout Kosovo, all soldiers were authorized to carry loaded weapons at all times.

"I thought by now you and your colleagues would be in custody," the doctor said without moving. "Am I to assume I am in command now and you're trying desperately to take it back?"

"Not quite," the colonel replied calmly. "The court did not quite rule in that manner. Please … pass me your weapon."

Pushing back from his desk, the doctor stood and braced himself against the wall. Without speaking, he drew his M9 Beretta from its holster and released the safety. He then pulled firmly back on the slide, chambering a round in the barrel. Looking at the two colonels, he tapped the weapon's barrel in the palm of his opposite hand as he broke into a broad smile. Things had not gone according to the colonel's plan. Suddenly faced with a new set of unexpected circumstances, the colonel thought hastily about what his next move should be. *God, I need a plan and quick!* he thought.

"Bill, it's over," the colonel said calmly, hoping to buy a few moments of extra time. "I'm not sure what you're thinking, but whatever it is, it can't be good."

The doctor said nothing but continued smiling. Time was running out, and the colonel needed a plan. He could rush the doctor, but that might cause someone to get hurt or, worse yet, killed. He could summon the MPs, but that might escalate the delicate situation. Trying to reason with a delusional individual was also risky but worth the effort under the circumstances.

"I suppose if you're thinking of killing me, you might get lucky, but Colonel Martin will likely get the second shot off. Once the shooting begins, the MPs outside your door are going to come in here with their guns blazing. Either way, someone will take you out." Realizing that the delusional psychiatrist may not want to kill the colonel but instead himself, the colonel quickly changed tactics. "If you're thinking of hurting yourself, all that will do is create a mess and a lot of paperwork. I'll have to tell your family you died a coward, and they'll get none of your benefits. Is that the legacy you want to leave behind?" The colonel was building his plan on the fly, hoping it would work.

Still tapping his weapon, the doctor said, "I cannot leave here this way. The soldiers ... they believe me to be a great leader. I am, you know?"

"There's a side door that leads out of the building just outside your office. I will have the MPs escort you out that door, so no one will see you, and no one will get hurt. They won't handcuff you until you are out of sight from the soldiers," the colonel said.

"You are going to humiliate me, aren't you?" The doctor raised his voice.

"No," the colonel quickly answered. "You are a colonel in the United States Army, a leader ... a warrior." He was purposefully appealing to the doctor's narcissism. "I will not humiliate you in front of the soldiers."

Another minute passed in silence while the doctor pondered his options. Realizing he had no cards left to be played, he slowly handed over his weapon. The colonel called for the MPs, and the two soldiers entered the office. "Secure your prisoner and take him through the side door. Do not cuff him until you're out of sight of the soldiers," the colonel ordered.

"I am a great doctor, warrior, and colonel," the physician said as the MPs took firm hold of his arms.

"You're none of those things, you bastard!" the colonel replied firmly without remorse.

★ 34 ★

CAMP ATTERBURY, INDIANA

Staring at the document, the captain looked up at the colonel. "With all due respect, sir, I can't in good conscience sign off on this document."

"We have a deal, Captain, and I expect you to uphold your end of it," the colonel said tersely.

"But, sir, the stress ... that's off the chart! You're going to need some real help to process this stuff and decompress."

"That's horseshit, Captain!" the colonel said. Reflecting on his past experience during the Persian Gulf War, the colonel said, "Let me tell you about stress. Stress is sitting in a foxhole on some fuckin' god forsaken battlefield day after day engaging some asshole on the other side of that worthless piece of sand whose job is to kill you and you him. Stress is being in a firefight with that asshole and not knowing if you're going to clear that twenty-yard run in the open and having your legs feel like they're a hundred pounds each. Stress is operating behind the enemy lines and knowing if they catch your sweet little ass they're going to beat and torture the shit out of you before they kill you. That's stress! Believe, I've been there, done that, and now simply want to forget it and move on!"

"Colonel," the captain said softly, "you know this guy, his personality disorder. You know it is only a matter of time before he hunts you down ... and he *will* kill you. It's a part of his makeup. We need to mitigate that now."

"I can't live my life looking over my shoulder, Captain," the colonel said in a more relaxed tone of voice. "Yes, I know this guy, and I know what he may try to do, but I can't stop living because of it. I'll deal with it when the time comes. For now, it's simply time for me to go home."

Lifting the pen from his desk, the Captain signed the document. Taking his paperwork from the captain, the colonel stood up and looked at the document in his hand. He paused and repeated softly, "You do know, it's just time to go home." He turned away from the desk and left the room. For now the nightmare had ended. Torn between his love and passion for the army and his beloved Washington with his family and friends, the colonel longed to be home. "It's time to go home," he whispered a third time to himself.

ONE YEAR LATER

The two star commanding general sat at the cafeteria table sipping his coffee and awaiting the arrival of his new deputy commander. The general was thin and tall with a short cut neatly cropped military haircut. The mixed gray and brown hair along his temples, with the wire-rimmed glasses made him appear more like an academian than a warrior and one who preferred running to maintain his physique instead of weight lifting. Pulling up a chair, the new brigadier general took up a position opposite his new boss. While new to the position, both officers had history from years past when the new general had been a captain and the commanding general had been a lieutenant colonel.

"Welcome to Walter Reed Army Medical Center, Steve," the commanding general said with a big, welcoming grin. "Who would have thought we'd be working together again?"

"I have to admit, I never dreamed that I would be sitting here in this capacity having this conversation with you. A true once-in-a-lifetime dream come true," the new general replied.

"As the new commanding general of one of the medical regions in my command, you will have your work cut out for you. As my deputy, you're going to have an even bigger challenge, but I think you're up to it. Before we get started, I want to be certain we're both on the same page. Taking care of soldiers is job one."

"I agree," the new general said.

"Good, because I have a small problem," the commanding general said. "One of your officers is a patient here at the medical center. When you have an officer admitted, I want to know about it."

"Sir, with all due respect, I don't have any officers as patients here. If I did, I would know about it, and I would have notified you," the new general said, somewhat confused.

"You had a colonel in Kosovo who was wounded in action after he fell on a mine to save the lives of troops maneuvering through a field. I was more than just surprised to see that you failed to award him a Purple Heart or at least a Bronze Star for valor. He's been here a year awaiting surgery to remove shrapnel from his abdomen."

"Excuse me, sir; are you sure of what you're saying?"

"He also happens to be assigned to your present command."

"General," the new deputy said, "first, I never had a colonel wounded in Kosovo. Second, I don't have a colonel as a patient here, and third, who in the hell is this guy?"

"Colonel William Weston."

"Are you serious?" The new general was stunned. "Sir, with all due respect, are you nuts? This guy is a fraud ... a wanted criminal in eleven states. How in the hell did he get here? He was apprehended in Kosovo and was supposed to be out of the army and turned over to civilian authorities a year ago. This guy was never wounded. Has anyone actually examined him?"

"Not yet. Each time he's come up for surgery, he has graciously given up his spot to a more seriously wounded soldier from Iraq. I was taking him for some sort of a hero."

"A hero? Sir, he's a criminal who has been scamming the system hiding out here with full pay and allowances. How can it be that he has been here in the hospital for year and no one has questioned it? No one knows anything about this guy, but for some weird reason, someone higher up the food chain has been protecting him. I will bet a year of your salary against a year of mine this guy has no scars on his abdomen. Hell, he has no wounds!"

"Okay, General, let's see what's really happening." The commanding general used his cell phone to call the surgeon responsible for the case. "Good morning, this is the CG. I see you have a Colonel Weston scheduled for surgery on Thursday. Have you examined him personally yet?"

"No, sir," the major said at the other end.

"I'll hold. I want you to go and examine the colonel now and describe your findings to me," the general said.

A short five minutes later the major reported back. "Shit, sir! This is a benign abdomen. No scars … no shrapnel! I have no idea why I'd be operating on him or for what."

"Thanks," the general said, pushing the end button on his phone. The general dialed a second number.

"Yes, sir," answered the general's G-1, the chief of personnel.

"I have a fraud and wanted criminal in my hospital." The general was irritated to have been duped. "You have until the close of business to not only get his ass out my hospital but out of the army and turned over to the appropriate civilian authorities! Apparently, he was supposed to have been discharged and turned over to them a year ago, but he gave them the slip and took up refuge here. Now get it done right this time," the general ordered.

★

The newly promoted general's first day on the job had been long as he'd worked through the series of standard briefings with the staff orienting him to his new position. Leaving the medical command headquarters, he walked toward his awaiting staff car reflecting on the day and thinking about his beloved Washington. Standing at the opened car door, the general's aide smiled and gave a brisk salute as the general neared.

At three hundred yards the new general was no more than a silhouette to the naked eye. Taking a shallow breath, the man gently raised his rifle and pointed it in the general's direction. Bringing it methodically against his right cheek, he took careful aim, adjusting the sight on the Leupold VX-3 3.5-10x40 mm scope on his rifle. Sliding the safety switch to off, he held steady with the general's back clearly in the crosshairs of the scope. Slowing his breathing, he slowly tightened his finger on the trigger.

Made in the USA
Middletown, DE
26 February 2022

61858729R00179